'FLAG'

a novel

pat mcgauley

This is a work of fiction. Names, characters, places, and incidents either are the product of the author's imagination or are used fictitiously, and any resemblance to actual persons living or dead, events, or locales is entirely coincidental.

Copyright pending: Submitted, May 2006
Manufactured in the United States of America. PJM Publishing. A Shamrock Book production.

Library of Congress Control Number: 2006905441

Without limiting the rights under copyright, no part of this publication may be reproduced in whole or in part in any form without the prior written permission of both the copyright holder and the publisher of this book.

ISBN: 0-9724209-4-0
First Edition, August 2006.

Cover art illustration by David Wirkkula.
Technical manuscript formatting by Shawn Nevalainen
Author photo by the Hibbing Daily Tribune

Acknowledgements

The setting for this story could have been almost any place a confused teenage runaway from Hibbing, Minnesota might decide to go in order to get himself together. I discovered Flagstaff when visiting my friend Gail Nevalainen who had moved to 'Flag' in 2004. The city seemed pleasant and the NAU (Northern Arizona University) campus was a perfect fit for a story floating aimlessly in my thoughts.

As with all of my books, I have relied upon friends for story input and editorial insight. I want to acknowledge Ed Beckers, Rich Dinter, and Norma Grant. Their collective critiques have been most valuable. David Wirkkula created the striking artwork and Shawn Nevalainen formatted the eighty thousand words between Dave's covers.

Writing from Hibbing while setting my story two thousand miles away was a new challenge. A few research trips to Flagstaff helped me to get a 'feeling' for the place, but the people I met there were far more important in creating this 1975 story. I am most deeply indebted to Joe Meehan of the Northern Arizona Historical Society for all of his assistance. Joe enabled me to accurately timeframe the project.

Finally, and most importantly, I must thank each of you who are readers of my books. Your encouragement is the stuff that sustains my creative energies. When I completed *To Bless or To Blame* in 2002, I became committed to writing a chronicle of the Moran family of Hibbing through four generations of the Twentieth Century. If you enjoy 'FLAG', please look for my earlier stories at your local bookstore or on Amazon.

for Gail

PROLOGUE

July 1990

One memorable Friday night in mid-July, I was reminiscing over a drink with former classmates at Zimmy's Bar in downtown Hibbing. At nine, our group would be heading out to the Mesaba Country Club for the Class of '75's fifteenth reunion. Later, as we had often done as high schoolers, our group would probably finish the evening with a Sammy's pizza in the popular restaurant down the street.

"I can remember as if it were only yesterday...feeling like I had the world by the tail as I stepped off the stage with my diploma," Pudge Arneson recalled. "Damned if I didn't have that wrong. Totally wrong!"

We all laughed along with Pudge's admission. Pudge and Owen Norgard, sitting across from me in the booth, had been friends of mine back then. Both had turned out to be more successful than most of our contemporaries might have expected. Like many of our classmates, the two of them now lived in the Twin Cities suburbs. Pudge was a dentist in Eden Prairie and Owen was an engineer with Honeywell Corporation, living in Eagan.

None of us had seen each other in more than ten years. "I'm damn proud of you, Owen." I lifted my gin and tonic in toast. "I never would have guessed that you'd finish college, much less get a graduate degree."

Pudge clinked his glass with ours and gave Owen a clap on the back, "Ditto here! If I remember correctly, you were pretty strung out back in those days."

"Strung out? Hell, I was half blitzed during my senior year. My first two years at St. Thomas only made things worse. Had to try it all, you know...but coke put me on the bottom of the world, man," Owen grimaced at the sobering memory. "I think I had one foot in the grave when the sun finally came out."

I nodded knowingly at Owen's bald disclosure and could have added that his problems were even worse than mine during our last year in high school. I chose not to. All of that was behind him—behind each of us.

"You both went to St.Thomas, didn't you?" Pudge inquired. "When I went off to East Lansing, I lost touch with all you guys."

Owen laughed, gulped at his unadulterated Seven-up. "That was the *plan,* Pudge. But, Mr. Pissed-off-at-the-world here..." he pointed his finger in my direction, "well—our friend Amos had ideas of his own. He was going to show his parents a thing or two. Right, Amos?"

Pudge's eyebrows lifted, "What's that all about, Amos?"

I gave my wife's hand a squeeze under the table. She was probably the only one in the world who knew the entire story. "Owen's right about that. To say that I was angry is an understatement: I was obsessed! My parents were separated at the time and I was hell-bent on getting away from here—far away."

At Owen's insistence, I shared my 1975 'runaway' story.

Twenty minutes later, a man I hadn't noticed sitting in the booth directly behind us stood and turned toward our table. "Excuse me, you might not remember me, but—"

I had to think quickly—then it came to me: "Mr. M?"

Our former teacher smiled widely at the recognition. His was dressed casually in jeans and sweatshirt and his hair had grayed, "It's been a long time...let me see: Paul, or Pudge wasn't it? And Owen...and Amos Moran, of course. How did I do with the names?"

We all offered a congratulatory handshake to the old man, "Well done," we applauded in unison. Then each of us introduced our wives.

"You're retired now, aren't you, sir?" Owen inquired.

Before Mr. M could answer, Pudge interrupted: "You've written some books, haven't you?"

The teacher nodded affirmative to both questions, "Some historical fiction— stories about the early days here on the Range." Then he looked directly at me, "Amos you might be interested to know that your great-grandfather, Peter Moran, was one of the characters in my first book. Maybe you've read—?"

Then a stroke of recall made me feel embarrassed. Yes, I should have remembered that, but I hadn't read any of his books. If I lied I would probably make an ass of myself. "I'm sorry," I apologized, "I've always meant to...but, you know...I never seem to catch up with all the *required* reading at the office." My excuse was lame and I knew it.

"I understand." The old man smiled forgivingly, his deep-set, Greene eyes seemed to have riveted on me. "I couldn't help but overhear some of your post-graduation story, Amos. I probably should apologize for eavesdropping a bit—a bad habit I've gotten into over the years— but I found it quite fascinating."

I didn't know whether to feel complimented or offended. I had probably been talking louder than I realized in order to over-speak the pulsating din of jukebox music and other conversations enveloping the room around us. "No apology necessary. We're all just catching up on these past fifteen years. Would you like to join us, sir?"

He shook his head, but seemed to keep me in his focus, almost as if the others at our table weren't there—or mattered little to him. "I'm sure you all have lots to talk about tonight, I just wanted to say hello."

I had the strange feeling, however, that he wasn't quite ready to leave. An uncomfortable feeling. "No...please...won't you have a drink? Meet our wives?" At the invitation, we all scrunched more deeply into the booth to allow some sitting room.

He placed a hand on my shoulder, smiled, " Thanks...but, perhaps another time," he said amiably. Then, half turning away from us, he paused: "Amos, could the two of us get together for coffee one of these days? I'm visiting some old Hibbing friends through next week and have lots of idle time to fill."

I wanted to ask, "What about?" but swallowed the question. My calendar for next week was plugged with litigations, party political activities, and Chamber business. Yet, Mr. M had been a favorite teacher of mine back then. "It would be my pleasure, sir...any time that fits your schedule." With one sentence, I had just placed all of my appointments on the back burner without really intending to do so.

"I'll call you one day next week," he said. Then he wished us all well and walked away.

"What was that all about?" Owen puzzled.

"Maybe he's got a legal problem," Pudge offered.

I shrugged, "I really don't have a clue."

My curiosity lingered for days after our get-together on that July evening in Zimmy's Bar. He called on the following Wednesday morning and we met for lunch at the Old Howard.

As it turned out, we met several evenings that week and the next. The end result of those hours of conversation we shared was the story you are about to read. To me, it's a very special story...mostly because it is *my story*.

Amos Gerald Moran

August 1975

Flagstaff police officials report that the approximate time of death was between eleven P.M. and one A.M. The victim has not been identified and both his age and address remain unknown. The apparent cause of death was a stab wound. Captain Rudy DeJarlais, the first officer at the murder scene, refused to elaborate on details or speculate on motive. A source close to the investigation, however, has conjectured the crime was "a drug deal gone bad" but would not rule out robbery. Two males, whose names were being withheld, told police that the victim was from Los Angeles and had been residing in Flagstaff since June.

1/ AMOS

Second thoughts were like regrets and he held few of them. Although a part of him wanted to call home and apologize to his parents, the better part knew that was not going to happen. To do so would be to admit that he had made a mistake.

Amos Moran stared absently from the second floor window at the unfamiliar street below—a single capillary in the circulation system of an unfamiliar city. Behind him was his dimly lighted, squalid, and equally unfamiliar apartment. Surrounding him, in the larger scene, was a pine-shrouded landscape with a backdrop of majestic cone-shaped mountains. This place was as unique as the surface of the moon.

Why was he here?

For the past ten days, and for over two thousand miles of distancing himself from the past, he had wrestled with that essential question—why? For the first time in his life, Amos was completely alone. Yet, this was exactly what his escape was supposed to be all about—shedding a painful past and beginning a new life in some distant place. Toward that end he found a modicum of satisfaction in a mission accomplished. And, to the best of his knowledge, nobody knew where he was. Despite putting a past tense on everything left behind, his smug attitude of achievement had already become a hallow shadow of what he imagined it might be. Perhaps reality was as simple and as profound as the traveler's lament in a Kristofferson song lyric he'd heard on the KAFF radio station on his way into town, *'...freedom's just another word for nothing left to lose'*.

'FLAG'

As they had a million times, Amos' thoughts meandered like a river...

    To his father...
    To his mother...
    To his friends...
    To his home town...
    To his senior year in high school when his plan began to take form and substance...

Strangely, indulging those memories had become a chosen form of masochism—an ongoing exhuming of 'what-ifs' that Amos seemed to covet, embrace, even crave. When he searched his depths for understanding or perspective he became even more deeply preoccupied with attaching blame than with finding truth. To him, truth was as sharp as a razor-honed knife: everybody was in this *game* for themselves. That Amos was no exception seemed disturbing at first, then comforting. He might argue convincingly that what he was doing was no different than what *they* had done. *They* being his mother and his father. A certain essential rationale escaped the carefully taped box in which he had conveniently packaged the past—would he be here if they were still together?

Obviously and admittedly, Amos Gerald Moran struggled mightily with punishing the two people he loved the most, with finding some sense of self-justification, and with trying to better understand the one common denominator of everything that had happened over the past year. With that acknowledgement, Amos had forced himself to do a serious examination of who he was. If he was going to begin a new life...he had better have a much firmer grip on the person who had to live through it.

Outside, beyond his smudgy window, the garish neon pulsations from the Orpheum Theater splashed over his face. A face much too chiseled for only eighteen years. His deep-set Greene eyes closed tightly against the throb piercing across his temples. "Dear God, don't let me cry!" Amos chose the prayerful petition over a command to "Be a man for God's sake!" Sometimes he would acknowledge that he wasn't a man...not yet, anyhow.

The headache and the grip of anger in his stomach were as familiar as they were dreaded. Usually a few deep breaths would quell the symptoms that had been an almost daily occurrence over the past months. Stress stuff.

"Damn!" his curse stabbed into the stale air of his sparsely furnished apartment. For a long moment he slipped into his mantra of deep breathing and positive thought. "You've got the power, Amos... You've got the power..." He counted his credo of renewal between hard breaths, five times, six times, seven...

Thrusting his hands deeply into the pockets of his jeans, he turned away from the window and paced the creaky hardwood floor.

Friday night: bored, alone, confused, and more angry than at peace with himself. It was Labor Day weekend in Flagstaff. His college classes would begin on Tuesday of the following week. As he wandered across the small living room, Amos forced a smile. "Not much, young man," he said to himself. "But everything you need for now," his self answered. The apartment was above McMahan's 'new and used' furniture store. "I wouldn't give you thirty bucks for everything in this dive" he said to Jacob Levitt, the landlord who wasn't in the room to argue the point with him.

Sparsely furnished: a well-worn floral sofa, a cigarette burned table with a dim aluminum lamp, an oak desk and chair beside the single window, a kitchen with functional appliances and a formica-topped table with two torn vinyl chairs. Off the hallway on the left was a small bathroom with an uncurtained shower stall, to the right the single bedroom offering a sizable chest of drawers, a sagging double bed, and side table. A forty-watt bulb illuminated the dingy space.

The headache wasn't going away. At the kitchen sink he drew a glass of water and popped three Bufferin. Like everything else, the water tasted strange. Like everything else he would have to get used to it. "Killing time," he mumbled to himself. "People kill time and time kills people." Amos remembered the quote from his high school history teacher. A crooked smile creased his face—all of his memories had their roots two thousand miles away.

"What to do?" Back at the window he peered across Aspen Street. On the corner of Leroux stood the historic and formerly elegant Weatherford Hotel, down the street was the blinking Orpheum offering a Steve McQueen movie. Near an alleyway niche a congregation of several men loitered in the growing shadows. He watched them. A few were Native Americans, others Mexicans, but most of the transients were Anglos. All of them were down-and-outers, winos, denizens of the downtown Flagstaff streets. He'd seen them the night before, too, and earlier that morning. During the daytime they dispersed to other parts of town only to return at nightfall. Amos wondered if he might see similar beaten-down men if he were peering from an apartment window overlooking Howard Street back in Hibbing. Again the waves of nostalgia drifted across his thoughts as he remembered home. But home was behind him now— home was history.

It was eight-thirty. At ten Amos was planning to meet a kid from Prescott whom he'd met while registering for classes on campus the day before. Billy Greene had told him that the Latin Quarter, or 'L.Q'. as Greene called the bar, was where most of the college crowd hung out on weekends. While wandering the streets that afternoon, Amos had located the bar on the corner of Butler and San Francisco, an easy walk of six blocks to the south. He checked his wallet for the false ID he'd bought last year. Minnesota's drinking age was eighteen, in Arizona it was twenty-one. That might be a problem. He was resolved not to use the phony under any circumstances.

Time dragged slowly. He turned away from his window perch and contemplated how to carve out a chunk from his idle waiting. Amos pondered going for another walk in the mild early evening. But he would be walking down to 'L.Q.' in another hour or so. He regarded the Greene-covered Spiral notebook resting on the desktop. He had purchased textbooks and supplies at the N.A.U. bookstore after registration on Thursday. He considered doing some simple budgeting from his past several days of travel. A sizable portion of the nine hundred eighty dollars in his wallet when he left Hibbing was already spent. He had not used the Visa card his father had given him since St. Paul. In order to cover his trail, Amos spent cash for all the gas, meals, and motels between Hibbing and Phoenix.

Along the way to Arizona, he had registered at every motel as Larry Quiggin and used a 4708 Julien Street address in Denver. Quiggin was an old Hibbing buddy, and a student at Regis University in Denver. Amos always parked his Minnesota-plated El Camino a distance away from, or behind, the places where he stayed overnight. At some point in time, Amos was certain, his 'totally-cop' father would be tracking the Visa card as well as checking motel registries.

Amos had deferred half of the tuition for the first semester; his outstanding balance would be deducted from his work-study earnings at the campus cafeteria kitchen. His deposit and one month's rent totaled ninety dollars. Amos had two hundred and forty-three dollars in cash remaining. His checking account balance from the First National Bank in Hibbing was another hundred and eighty-two dollars. But he would not write any checks for quite a while.

Recounting the past eleven days between Hibbing and Flagstaff, Amos could not escape the feeling of a fugitive felon. *"...Freedom's just another word for nothing left to lose..."*

2/ PACK MORAN

Hunched over the telephone on his kitchen table, face pinched between his large hands, Pack Moran cried. He was not a weak man by anyone's measure but had become vulnerable to emotional upheavals in his life. Over the past few years there had been more than a few. On this Friday afternoon, he felt as if his world had become unstitched at the seams. Amos—his only child and the very essence of his being—was missing.

"Foolish kid...stupid Dad," he admonished hoarsely through a deep sob. "What in God's name have you gone and done, Amos?"

Rubbing at the throb in his temples, he regarded the phone as he might stare down an adversary. For too long the telephone had been the delivery mode of stressful news. He was contemplating a call to Maddie. His estranged wife would take the news much harder than he had and, more likely than not, get into the blaming game they had been playing for the past several months. "It's our fault!" she would say in no uncertain terms. And Pack would be at a loss to argue the point.

Pack replayed the past ten days. Amos had left for St. Thomas College in St. Paul on the eighteenth of August. More than two weeks before classes were slated to begin. "Dry-land training for the hockey program" Amos had lied. "Don't call for a couple of weeks," he had pleaded with both parents. "Just let me find my way without my mom and dad checking up on everything." Both had promised to give their son the space he wanted. Pack thanked God that he had broken that promise.

He had just gotten off the phone with Father Devon O'Malley at St. Thomas. "I'm sorry, Mr. Moran, but your son is not registered here." He and the priest conversed briefly about the apparent confusion. "We did send him an acceptance letter last spring—in April—and we have his transcript on file...but, we haven't heard anything from Amos yet," O'Malley said. The college registrar also confirmed that the hockey 'Tommies' did not have any fall training programs.

Pack made arrangements to visit the campus the following morning.

A quick call to Jim Kaim at the First National Bank confirmed another of Pack's suspicions. "Yes, he did, Pack. On the sixteenth. Amos closed out his savings account—seven hundred and eighty dollars."

Pack pondered, he had given Amos two hundred before his son left for school. So, his son had nearly a thousand dollars in cash to go along with a Visa credit card. The new card was to be used for tuition, dorm, books, and other college expenses.

Pack had to call Maddie. Before dialing, he said a quick prayer that they wouldn't argue or rehash past issues. He also prayed that the man his wife had been seen with of late was not at her place on this Friday afternoon. *That man* was Clayton Conroy, a community college teacher—and, a 'nice guy' according to those who knew him. To Pack's knowledge, Clay and Maddie had coffee together at the college a couple of times and sat next to each other at a community concert in late July.

"Thank God," Pack said under his breath. His tight-throated "Hello Maddie, is this a good time for us to talk?" was followed with an almost cheerful "Yes...it has been quite a while."

"I'm afraid I'm calling with some bad news..." he almost said sweetheart, but caught himself in time. He went on to explain. "I know I promised Amos that I wouldn't call for a couple of weeks— well I did.

Actually, I've called a couple of times since Wednesday. Anyhow, his jerk of a roommate, Owen Norgard, kept feeding me some pretty lame excuses. 'He's at the library', 'He's at the gym', 'He's out with the guys'... Just a few minutes ago I found out he's none of the above, Maddie. Amos has not even registered at St. Thomas. Our son's been gone ten days and I have no idea where he is."

A painfully long silence passed between them. Pack could feel Maddie's concern from two miles away. Ruefully, he wished that he could hold her, comfort her, share the heartache they both were feeling.

"Pack... Owen told me that Amos was 'out with the guys' when I called about six last night. Owen promised that he would have Amos call me back. I've been waiting all day."

She began to cry.

"Don't get overwrought, hon— Maddie. Please." Pack tried awkwardly to console, swallowing hard on the empathy that welled in his chest. "Let's not think the worst..." Yet, in the back of his mind a 'worse case scenario' always played with his psyche. He went on to explain that he was going down to St. Paul in the morning. "He's probably hanging out with the wrong kind of kids down there, sowing those wild oats he's stuffed inside all these years. Please try to relax over this...say a prayer." He paused over his last words, "I'm not coming back until I've got something tangible."

Pack chose not to mention the thousand dollars Amos had in his pocket. It would only cause her some unnecessary worry right now. With that kind of money a person could go almost anywhere and inciting Maddie's anxieties would have her biting her nails all weekend.

Maddie considered offering to make the St. Paul trip with him, then thought better of the idea. Too much time together would invite too much tension.

The two of them had not been communicating very well during their yearlong separation.

They left the ten-minute conversation on a relatively good note—no arguments or unpleasantries—and Pack's promise to call when he learned something: Anything!

Maddie swallowed a temptation to take blame for whatever was going on with Amos. She knew well enough that Pack suffered the same guilt. Neither could shirk acknowledging how seriously their behavior was hurting their son.

Pack Moran was a cop with the Hibbing Police Force. For nearly thirteen years he had been the Department's Chief, then he had resigned to drop back into the ranks of 'just plain cop'. That unexpected decision had been a big story in the local news back in 1970. Most would readily acknowledge, however, that Pack Moran could be expected to do the unexpected. He was tenacious and stubborn in near equal measure, and often didn't play by the rules. The current Chief, Oscar Sundval, considered him to be a rogue officer and had twice cited Pack for subordination on petty ethics code violations—a politically correct way of saying that Moran had used 'unnecessary force' or threatening language in the line of duty.

The fact that Pack held a passionate abhorrence for drug-pushers and wife-beaters could not justify the physical and emotional abuse he gave to those who committed such crimes. One citation resulted in a five-day suspension. In an alleyway behind Fifth East, Pack gave Stewart Abernathy a taste of what the brutish man had just given his wife. Abernathy was hospitalized that night and needed extensive dental work later.

When giving the son of a prominent Hibbing citizen his rights (Pack had arrested Mark Webb for selling 'speed' from his car in front of the Lincoln Junior High) Pack had told the suspect "And you've got the right to have your rich fucking dad hire a sleazy lawyer to beat this rap". His later apologies to Chamber of Commerce President Willard Webb did little to alleviate the negative reactions of the Hibbing business community. Pack despised the Miranda ruling as 'cops having to cuff themselves'! Episodes like these, however, had moderated Pack's diligence to duty.

The disappearance of a local woman the year before he quit his job as Chief had frustrated Pack to the point of absolute disrespect for the criminal justice bureaucracy. He was positive that the girl had been murdered, and equally positive that the murderer was her allegedly amnesic boyfriend. But a snarled complex of jurisdictional issues complicated by the lack of a corpse, had thwarted his every effort to initiate prosecution.

Pack stared at a bottle of Bushmills which was sending waves of temptation from the countertop only ten feet away. Six months without a drink had been a tough test of his willpower. How easy it would be to have 'just one' right now. Thank God there was a pot of coffee simmering on the range. He got up, poured himself a cup, and looked out his kitchen window. Only an arms length away was his bird feeder and the black-capped chickadees were flittering from trees to feeder, and back again, like frenzied sprites who wanted to eat one seed at a time—a thousand times a day. Pack loved the variety of birds, wild creatures, and butterflies that his flower gardens attracted. The darting and diving chickadees amused him the most.

But this afternoon he was too distracted to appreciate their antics.

He though of Amos and tried to get into his son's thoughts. Pack's police training, which included some heavy doses of psychology, had always served him well with the adaptive thinking process of relating theory to actual events. There had been a marked change in the boy when he and Maddie separated nearly a year ago. Actually, it would be *exactly* one year on this coming Sunday. Labor Day weekend was somehow cursed. It was on that holiday that he had been involved in a nearly fatal accident with a motorcyclist two years before. Ironically, that collision seemed a harbinger of bad things to come and, even more ironically, to occur in perfect, one-year increments.

Pack mused over the past twelve months, focusing on specific episodes, or behaviors, that were triggers he had somehow missed, or failed to take proper note of. Amos' friendships changed. They had talked at some length about that. Amos had decided not to go out for hockey in his senior year—but he did play baseball with many of his former chums. Amos, he was almost certain, had experimented with cigarette smoking (in violation of the athletic code) and, probably had done some drinking as well. But there had never been even the slightest indication of drug use despite the casual popularity of marijuana with kids his age. What else? To his credit, Amos had kept his grades at honor roll status. Pack had talked with his son's guidance counselor in periodic conferences throughout the year—there had been no school-related issues, or behavioral concerns from any teachers. To his surprise, Amos had even taken a bit role in the spring play.

The week before Amos left for college, Pack and his son spent a weekend fishing, canoeing, and camping at Sturgeon Lake. They had talked about lots of things, but as he recollected now, easy things— mostly sports related. The reality that both he and his son were avid Twins fans apparently resulted in too many hours of wasted dialogue. Sports had always been a conversational 'safety zone' for the two men. In every discernable aspect, however, Amos seemed in good spirits, anxiously anticipating his freshman year at St. Thomas, and even excited about being on his own for the first time. They talked about classes for pre-law, prospects of making the hockey team, Brady Hall—the dorm he would be housed in- and college life in general.

Over the weekend there had been no mention of his mother, nor of the painful separation. Obviously, his son was mature and clever enough not to raise any flags.

Now, Pack had some uncovering to do. Like an ill wind stirring in the back of his thoughts was the frightening possibility of an abduction. The Morans had had a tragic history in that regard. Pack's mother had been abducted in a nationally famous case nearly forty years ago, and nearly twenty years ago his childhood friend had been kidnapped in Hibbing. That pal, Jerry Zench, had been murdered!

A shrill ring shattered his reverie. Tensing inside, he waited on a second, then a third ring: The pessimist inside expecting bad news...

3/ THE LATIN QUARTER

Amos pushed the notebook with all of his scribbled budget-balancing numbers aside. Money was not a serious issue at this time. Although his headache had abated, his conscience stirred in a familiar circle behind his eyes. How much of his running away was pure and unadulterated anger? How much was simply a deeply felt disappointment? How much was his desire to abandon them as they had abandoned him? Despite his every effort, Amos had not properly reconciled the whole experience, nor had he come to grips with how events he had been unable to change had, in fact, changed him dramatically. And, because of his persistent uncertainty, he would continue to justify his rebellion as his way of proving that he didn't need them anymore. Amos was fully cognizant that he lied to himself as much as he had lied to others. "Damn!" he cursed, snapping the yellow pencil in half. "Why am I here?"

Resting toward the back of his narrow desktop were framed, and deliberately separated, photographs of his mother and father. Mom was posed with a wide smile, her long blond hair swept back and tied with a Greene bow, and her delicate hands folded in her lap as she sat on the living room carpet beside the Nativity scene arranged under the family Christmas tree. His lovely mom. She was the freshest-smelling, most completely feminine, and loving woman he had ever known. The Greene sweater she wore was a Christmas gift that he had given her the year before. He choked on the memory and looked away. "Sorry, Mom..." he mumbled to himself.

On the other side of the desk was a black and white photo of his father, looking serious and professional in his police uniform while leaning against the squad car with 'Chief of Police' emblazoned in black letters on the white door panel. That had been when— five years ago already? Dad was the definition of masculinity in every regard: six-feet tall, athletically trim, barrel-chested. Amos smiled at a transient thought, his father was emotionally inhibited, too. For better or worse, Amos was the proverbial 'chip-off-the-block' in more ways than not.

A photograph of the two of them together was stuffed among assorted mementos in the bottom drawer. Memories of his former 'family life' were memories unworthy of display. Also in the drawer was a stack of three hockey pucks glued together from his hat-trick against Eveleth in his junior year, a baseball from his two-hit shutout of Duluth Denfeld last spring, and a class ring that he never wore. Amos was traveling light. A trunk of clothes, toiletries, and some sports equipment. Not much more.

He checked his wristwatch. Nine-thirty. Where had the past two hours gone? He decided to walk the several blocks to the 'L.Q.' and leave his car parked off-street behind the furniture building. Amos had resolved to drive his '69 El Camino with its conspicuous Minnesota license plates as little as possible.

That was going to be a hardship. His deep blue colored, V-8, three-speed floor shifted beauty with polished mag wheels, and leather bucket seats was a head-turner. His pride and joy had taken him from Minnesota to Arizona without a problem.

The evening held a pleasant breeze sweeping down from the mountains and displayed a plethora of sparkling stars across wide, clear skies. Amos wore a pinstriped Gant shirt, faded jeans, and boat shoes on his bare feet. He was comfortable and the walk felt refreshing after being cooped up for hours. Hustling through the busy traffic on famous 'Route 66', he narrowly beat a train rumbling through town on the noisy Santa Fe Line. The city of some thirty thousand was a bustling place. What had first attracted him to Flagstaff was its familiar and richly pine-scented air. The smell brought him back to the family cabin on pristine Sturgeon Lake outside of Hibbing.

Amos' original plan had been to hookup with his friend, Mike Rapovich, in Phoenix. Rap was a Chisholm native and a sophomore at Arizona State University. But Phoenix in late August had proven more suffocatingly hot than he had imagined. Amos realized almost immediately that this was not where he wanted to be. Overheating in the sweltering sun, he spent about three hours touring the sprawling campus. He had his high school transcripts and application forms tucked in the back pocket of his khaki shorts, but couldn't bring himself to enter the registration building. Sun-baked and sprawling ASU was not for him. Although Rap was expecting him, Amos didn't bother to call the number he had stuffed in his wallet.

  Maybe, Amos considered at the time...just maybe, college wasn't going to be in the cards for him. Maybe he would find some place where he could find a job and simply hang out for a few months while he made up his mind on what he wanted to do with his life. Maybe he would make his way back to Denver. Amos was enchanted with the mountains he had driven through on his way to Phoenix. And his old buddy Quiggin was a student at Regis in Denver. Maybe?

Amos hummed the melody of an Elton John song as he walked south on San Francisco at a leisurely pace. Several college-aged kids were out on this lovely Friday night. In the inky black sky above the stars glittered as he had never seen them sparkle before. Wondering if the different latitude here would change perspectives, he stopped to locate Orion.

As his eyes focused on the constellation, a pair of eyes from across the street were focused on Amos. Sadie Kearney had first seen him the day before. He was ahead of her in a class registration waiting line. He seemed confused, but smiled through the hassle of getting his classes approved. After getting his registry forms signed, he located a bench off to the side of the wide room and opened a student handbook. She could see that he was trying to figure out the campus layout. Good looking, nice smile: he carried himself with an unspoken confidence. He wore wrinkled, olive-colored khaki shorts, a black T-shirt, and expensive Eastland shoes. Sadie always noticed shoes.

When it came to boys, Sadie had always been old-fashioned, inhibited. It was her staunch conviction that the guy should always take the initiative. Although she had been on her share of dates, the boys she was most interested in meeting never seemed to call. A strange impulse welled inside. She knew, somehow, that she wanted to meet this stranger who was starring at the stars from across the street. What to do? She laughed to herself as the dilemma played in her thoughts. What's the worst-case scenario? You scare the poor guy away? He thinks you're some kind of weirdo? "Well," she took a deep breath before crossing the street, "Go for it Sadie Kearney—nothing ventured, nothing gained."

Finding a pocket in the traffic flow, Sadie hustled across the avenue. "What'cha up to, goodlookin'?"

The perky question caught Amos quite by surprise and almost caused him to stumble on the curb. A pretty coed had sidled up to his elbow without his notice.

"You look like you're lost in thought, young man" the girl said. Her voice reminded Amos of Carol Lawrence, a neighbor and classmate from home. He continued to connect everything *here* in Flagstaff with everything back *there* in Hibbing.

"Guess I was at that. I mean, lost in thought," Amos smiled easily.

"You new in town? Here for college?" She recognized him from registration the previous day but chose not to mention the incident.

"I'm both. Planning to hookup with a guy I met yesterday on campus. He told me the 'L.Q.' was the local hangout."

"He gave you good advice. That's where I'm headed myself. I'll lead you there if you'll promise to buy me a drink. I hate to go into a bar by myself...and my friend Sally, who was supposed to meet me here— well, I can't seem to find her anywhere."

"You've got yourself a deal," Amos offered his hand to the strikingly attractive girl at his side. "So, with whom will I be drinking this lovely starlit evening?"

Sadie frowned, "Kinda waxing poetic, aren't you? You asking me for my name or commenting on the weather?"

Amos enjoyed the easy lilt of her voice and the expressive pout she flashed in his direction. He grinned, "It is a nice evening, but I guess I was asking for your name."

"Well, my name's Sadie. Sadie Kearney." She was flirting she knew, but it was fun. It wasn't often that she allowed her inhibitions to melt so easily. Maybe it was the lovely evening, at that? Smiling, she continued with a rush: I'm an Irish lassie, a NAU soph, education major so far. My whole life's been here in Flag, and I'm unattached at the moment!" Sadie's laugh revealed even, white teeth. "That's an abbreviated biography, my new friend. Your turn now, but try to keep it as simple as possible. I didn't really dig the poetry stuff too much."

Amos amused over Sadie's banter and the staccato introduction she had given in one swift sentence. He would reciprocate in kind, but carefully. When first meeting Billy Greene the previous day, Amos had used his middle name. He planned to do that with everybody he met. "Name's Jerry Moran, an Irish lad with family lines back to the 'Ole Sod' as some like to call the Emerald Isle...here in Flagstaff from Denver. Sorry to admit, but I'm just a lowly freshman, Miss Sadie Kearney."

"Just Flag," she interrupted. "If you want to blend in with the locals."

"Got it. I've been here in Flag for three days now. Not a bad experience so far, I guess. And, I'm going to do something pre-law."

Sadie gave him another wide smile. "Well then, Irish Jerry, we very well could be related, you know. We Kearney's go back to Donnegal, and my mother, an O'Brien, was born in Denver— my Grammy still lives out there. Where abouts did you live in Mile High?"

Amos swallowed hard, fabricating the familiar address he'd been using the past several days. "Over near Regis College. Julien Street." He used his friend Larry Quiggin's address for yet another time.

"Don't really know that area. Grammy's place is in Mountain View. Regis neighborhood, huh?...sounds kinda fancy; your folks rich Jerry?"

Amos breathed a sigh of relief. "Inherited money."

"Nothing wrong with that. We've got some, too." Sadie laughed at her fabrication. The Kearney's had seen better times than these.

Amos nodded his approval without reply.

"You a Catholic, Jerry Moran?" Regis was a Catholic college and Sadie imagined the neighborhood to be likewise.

"Born and raised...but a little out of practice these days."

"That's O.K.—my folks like it when my boyfriends are Catholic. While I, on the other hand, don't much care."

Amos laughed at her candor.

"Boyfriends? That's plural. I can only imagine you have several." He much preferred talking about religion or dating or anything else to questions about Denver.

"Only one at a time, Jerry."

"And...is there one now?"

"Not at the moment." She wrapped an arm about his elbow and gave him the brightest smile. "But the night is young."

After a non-conversant half-block, Sadie broke the lull. "Here we are, my friend. As usual, the place is hopping."

At the door, Sadie flashed her Arizona Driver's License.

Amos had a sinking feeling as he reached for his wallet. This was going to be risky. If the bouncer questioned his ID or made any comment about Minnesota, his string of falsehoods would sink like a handful of rocks. He held his breath...but the bulky doorman simply gave him a nudge inside. "Whew," he whispered to Sadie, "You almost lost the free drink I promised you. Do you think I look twenty-one?"

She laughed, gave him a serious appraisal. "Not really. We'll have to get you fixed up with an ID for next time. All of us have one."

Amos laughed, too. But beneath the laugh were traces of worry and fatalism. When would his incredible string of luck run out? Surely, he was bound to get tripped up by something he said or did. Another false identification was all he needed in this deepening charade.

4/ SLOW DANCES

Waylon Jennings' throaty 'Amanda' wafted in the air of the crowded, fuggy bar. Clouds of cigarette smoke hugged the ceiling and the smell of spilt beer emanated from the scuffed hardwood floors. Sadie took Amos' elbow, leaned up to his ear to be heard over the din of blurred voices and music, "I'll grab that table over there," she gestured, "while you try to find your friend. What can I order for you?"

"Whatever you're drinking is fine." Amos hoped it wasn't anything with vodka. Vodka had proven to be his nemesis on past occasions. "Catch up with you in a few minutes." He gave her shoulder a light squeeze, craned his neck to look about the smoke-filled space.

Billy Greene was tall, lanky, and redheaded. He was wearing an unbuttoned lumberjack plaid wool shirt over an NAU T-shirt. "Hey, Bronco!" Greene had spotted Amos in the crowd. "C'mon over, join us for a beer." Greene was sitting on a bar stool with a group of other young men. Amos joined them.

"Guys, this here's Jerry Moran. New in Flag, comes from Denver. Jerry, this is Freddy Forlan, Johnny—we call him Unitas—Uhlander, our highly touted quarterback this fall, and Mike Avery. Mike's my dorm roomie at Bury, doesn't play football but stay away from any pool table where he's hustlin' a game—he'll clean your wallet."

Amos shook hands all around. Small talk with guys, especially athletes, had always been easy for him. "You play ball, Jerry?" Uhlander made a quick physical appraisal of the kid from Colorado.

"Baseball," Amos answered.

"What dorm you in?" from Mike Avery.

'FLAG'

Amos had slipped through the cracks at registration. Most freshmen had dorm assignments. "I'm off campus," was all he said. Amos passed on the offer of a Coors, "Billy... Mike, I met a girl on the way over here. She's got a table and I promised her a drink. Why don't you guys join us when you get a minute." He reshook all the hands, and excusing himself, stepped away from the bar.

On the table in front of Sadie Kearney were two Bloody Marys.

By eleven-thirty, Amos was feeling the vodka. A crowd of Sadie's friends had joined their table along with Billy Greene and Mike Avery. Sadie remained flirtatiously fun throughout the evening, enjoying the new 'Bronco' moniker that Amos seemed to be stuck with. "Don't you just love Jerry's beard?" Sadie asked her blond friend, Sally James.

Amos hadn't shaved since leaving Minnesota nearly two weeks ago—part of his 'in cognito' look. "The intellectual look," Amos said in the spirit of the good time and teasing banter. He was thoroughly enjoying himself, the people he'd met, and the wide variety of music. And, Sadie, far more than anything else.

Sadie Kearney was petite and shapely, a brunette with full mouth and sparkling Greene eyes. And, always breathlessly animated! She spoke with her hands, sang along with Abba and Elton without inhibition, and teased incessantly. Sadie was just about the easiest girl to hang out with that Amos had ever met. Good times with fun people always seemed to fly by much too quickly he realized.

The combination of vodka and sensory overload, however, were draining Amos' energy. He hadn't sleep well in weeks. He tried to excuse himself but couldn't get away without one more drink—from Bill Greene this time.

"We haven't danced yet, Jerry. I want to feel swept off of me feet tonight." Sadie's smile was as infectious as her comment was unusual. The Hollies song, *The Air That I Breathe*, was wafting an allure above the crowd noise.

"Swept off your feet? That's a challenge. I'm no Gene Kelly, but let's give it a whirl, Sadie." Amos took her hand in his and led her to the edge of the cluster of slow dancers. She nestled close and felt good.

"Love these lyrics, Jerry." Her eyes and his were Green on Green as they glided in easy unison. She hummed the melody. "You're not too bad when you lead...and you smell really great, Jerry. Canoe?"

Amos laughed at her recognition. "You know your scents." The Hollies finished; Jim Croce's *Time in a Bottle* was next.

"Another one of my favorites, and it's slow, too. Let's do two in a row. I've got to have a lasting whiff of Jerry Moran before I let him drift off into the Flagstaff night."

"Flag," he corrected. Amos whispered her name into the lament of the lyrics *"...if I could make days last forever..."* as his lips softly brushed against her ear.

Sadie gave him a puzzled look, "If you could, what would you do?," was all she said. She rested her face on his chest. The dance was over.

Amos swallowed the last of his drink and got up to leave. Sadie bent over, gave him a peck on the cheek. "Oh...that beard tickles," she giggled; blushing slightly for the first time.

"I think you could get used to it, Sadie." Sally winked while sharing a laugh with her girlfriend.

"Same time, same place tomorrow night, Jerry." Sadie's smile was a glow that outshone the brightest stars in the Flagstaff sky. "Labor Day weekend is our last big fling before classes next week."

Amos shook off the ribbing that he'd had too much to drink; mostly from Bill Greene and Sally James, and promised to join them all on Saturday night.

Walking back to his apartment, Amos smiled to himself. Tonight he had truly felt like a different person. Maybe this was where he, Jerry 'Bronco' Moran, really belonged. Yet, he was troubled. How long would he keep this *Jerry* charade going? Was it really necessary? His driver's license read Amos Moran; so did the college records on file—both identified Hibbing as his permanent address. So what if he was from Minnesota? Lies and deceptions were contrary to his nature... "Drop it, Amos," he chided himself. "Just go with the flow—for now. Don't analyze everything to death—have some fun with being Jerry." Anyway, once he had a better grip on things he could begin cleaning them up.

Letting go of his troubled thoughts, Amos remembered that last dance. Sadie Kearney was incredible! There had been *something* almost magical between the two of them all evening. He remembered her scent, the feel of her body next to his, her bright eyes and full mouth, her laugh, and her quick and teasing wit. Everything about Sadie had been almost mesmerizing. He had never been in love before, but he surely felt something quite exciting with her. He had never made love before, either. Maybe...maybe Sadie Kearney was going to be something special in his new life. The thought was a pleasant one.

~

It was just after midnight when Amos plopped in bed. Either Amos was too tired to sleep, or his thoughts were too full of Sadie. He got up to walk around the apartment . The garish neon flash from the Orpheum down the street was aggravating. Tomorrow he would locate a hardware store and purchase a shade for the window and a shower curtain for his bathroom. Maybe he should make a list. This place was almost depressing. He lit a Marlboro, only his third of the day, then wandered into the kitchen for a glass of milk. His stomach was queasy.

He walked to the window...

.

Everything happened so suddenly. One of the three darted across the street, kicked the derelict in the shin and caught the man's weight as he began to teeter forward. Then he saw what looked like a short, quick but forceful jab to the victim's stomach. The assailant, his back to Amos' window, allowed the older man to topple into a heap at his feet on the sidewalk. Gripping a shoulder, the younger man rolled the vagabond to his side, went inside his shirt, and pulled out something. A package? Just as quickly as he had crossed the street, the assailant hastened to join his colleagues in the shadow of the building below the window. The three of them raced down Aspen Avenue and out of sight. Everything had happened in the brief space of a minute.

A mugging. None of his business. One punch should not have done much damage, even to an old man—probably knocked the wind out of him. The vagrant couldn't have had much money on his person anyhow. Maybe it was drugs. So much of that these days. The incident hadn't even awakened the two other drunks who lay passed out only a few feet away. None of his business.

Amos rinsed the glass, put out his cigarette, and went to bed. When he finally fell asleep, a nightmare caused him to toss and turn...a dream in which the details were never quite clear enough to piece together in any coherent pattern. In the dream he was bloody and in enough danger to fear for his life. A similar dream would hauntingly recur for weeks to come.

5/ MADDIE MORAN

Whenever Pack called it was like picking the scab off an old wound.

Maddie Moran sat rigidly on the straight-backed wooden chair beside the small telephone table off the foyer of her too large, and too empty, Victorian home. Her wealthy, and often too generous, in-laws had helped her and Pack with the substantial down payment for their Michigan Street home years before. Maddie had decorated the spacious house in comfortable, even cheerful, simplicity. Recent events, however, had washed away the cheer of home and hearth that once resided here. Memories and old photographs were hardly the stuff of fulfillment.

With Amos off to college and trying his new wings the empty nest syndrome was more than an emotional void. She had felt physically depleted for nearly two weeks: tired and despondent, even nauseous. Her son not only centered her life, Amos had always given her a sense of purpose and self-worth. For Maddie, he was her source of strength, and she now realized, the wellspring of her weakness. If anything ever happened to Amos—

Maddie could read the concern in Pack's voice. Whatever he might have lacked as a devoted husband, he more than compensated for as an involved and supportive father to their son. Again: the husband and father quandary. Was she really being fair? Pack had far more virtues than shortcomings and was probably a far better husband than most.

Whenever Maddie revisited their marital issues, she got down on herself. Tonight, there were more important matters to resolve. She knew that Pack was as worried about Amos as she was. And if anybody in the world could find their son, Pack could do it. Pack would do it! Maddie had to brace herself with that confidence. Whatever Amos was up to, or wherever he had gone or hidden—if he was hiding somewhere— his father would find him. Pack could locate tracks on a sheet of ice. Thank God for that.

His voice. Whenever she heard Pack's voice she could feel the tiny hairs on the back of her neck tingle. It had always been that way, but even more so since their separation. They didn't talk often and when they did their words, like their emotions, became strained, sharp-edged, wounding. Not a day went by when Maddie didn't reflect on that traumatic Labor Day one year ago. The quarrel was followed by Pack's stomping out of the house, only to return the following day to pick up a few belongings. Much of his wardrobe still remained in their bedroom closet. Maddie would never throw them away and, from time to time, she would rediscover his scent in them. When she did that, there was pleasure and pain in equal measure.

Perhaps Maddie had seen that crucial day coming for months, maybe years. From early in their eighteen-year marriage there had been signals—subtle at times, glaring at others—that underlined the incompatibilities that most couples either reconcile or learn to live with. A miscarriage in their third year, and another seven years ago, had left her feeling unfulfilled, estranged. The support she seemed to need so desperately in those hurting times simply wasn't there. So, she went inward to that place of loneliness one creates in order to cope with feelings that soon become exclusive and isolating. Admittedly, she was building walls—and praying that Pack would knock them down. Maddie lived behind those walls for hours every day, but never fully escaped them. Through countless sleepless nights she dreamed of and mourned Meghan and Michael, her unborn children. Those dreams, often photographic and always profound, were never shared.

Neatly folded inside her Bible was an anonymous verse that she read as often as she did John's Gospel. It was something she had picked up in a college psychology class and saved. The lengthy verse was titled 'Please hear what I'm not saying'...

'FLAG'

Don't be fooled by me.
Don't be fooled by the face I wear.
For I wear a mask. I wear a thousand masks.
Masks that I'm afraid to take off,
And none of them are me...
I give you the impression that I'm secure,
And that I need no one.
But don't believe me. Please...
Beneath dwells the real me in confusion, in fear, in aloneness.
But I hide this...
That's why I frantically create a mask to hide behind...
To shield me from the glance that knows.
But such a glance is precisely my salvation; my only salvation,
And I know it...
It's the only thing that will assure me of what I can't assure myself,
That I'm really worth something.
But I don't tell you this. I don't dare. I'm afraid to...
So I play my game, my desperate pretending game...
You alone can break down the walls behind which I tremble.
I fight against the very thing that I cry out for.
But I'm told that love is stronger than strong walls
And in this is my hope.
Please try to beat down those walls with firm hands.
But with gentle hands.
For a soul is very sensitive.
Who am I? I am someone you know very well.
For I am every man... I am every woman.
Please hear what I'm not saying.

Dabbing at her tears, Maddie replayed the conversation she had had with Pack. Amos was not at St. Thomas. He had lied to both of them. That hurt her as much as the news that he was missing. Regardless of circumstance, and there had only been a few over the years, Amos never lied to either of them. Never! Was the discernable edge in Pack's voice fear? From the subtle conjectures of Pack's explanation of what was happening; she understood him to believe that Amos was probably sowing some oats, hoping to find some fresh air in this newly discovered freedom from hearth and home.

"Damn!" Maddie rarely cursed. "How self-absorbed can I be?" She realized that she had failed to wish Pack good luck on his trip to Saint Paul. Part of her wished she was going with him…but— She would have to call him back later and apologize.

Restless and at odds with herself, Maddie eyed the book that Pack's sister Maribec had dropped off weeks ago. Mary Rebecca Moran had been Maddie's best friend for years and her only confidante through the painful separation. "Maybe this will give you some insights," Maribec said of Gail Sheehy's acclaimed *Passages*, a best seller about women's crises. But the book only frustrated Maddie. Pack did not fit the mold of any of the men Sheehy had depicted; nor did she see herself in any of the *searching* women. At best, *Passages* seemed to give ammunition and justification to those who wanted to begin new lives without their spouses. She had quit the book somewhere near the middle.

Maybe something Maribec had said years ago made the most sense. "He's a Moran, honey. Never forget that we Morans are loners at heart." Maribec had never married.

Maddie needed to get a better grip on her broken composure. Lifting herself from the chair she walked absently into the nearby living room. Her knees felt rubbery and her lower back ached with stress. "Get a grip, girl," she reproached herself with less muster than she wanted, Amos' framed graduation picture hanging between shuttered windows on the south wall smiled out across the space of the room. "How could you lie to your mom, Amos? You've broken my heart." Maddie lost her fragile grip on her emotions of the moment, dropped to the sofa and wept unabashedly. She could not remember ever feeling so abandoned and so desperately alone. Within minutes she was sleeping fitfully.

~

Pack reluctantly picked up the phone.

"Maddie...what's wrong? You sound terrible." He often wondered if she thought of him when she was depressed. If she somehow needed him—even half as much as he needed her. Why couldn't they *really* communicate with each other? What was the block? Pride? Admitting to mistakes made? Honesty? Probably all of that, probably more than that. Far more often than he would admit to her or anybody else, Pack had thought about Maddie's insistence that they get counseling. "When you can't do something by yourself—you get help!" Maddie's appeals, however, fell like futile blows on his armor of pride. Whatever, he was uplifted by the sound of her voice—however emotion-choked it was. "I'm sorry I said that. What I mean...you don't sound terrible at all... I can tell you've been crying."

"To put it mildly, Pack. I'm sitting here looking at Amos' picture and going to pieces. He's run away—I can feel it. And we are—"

Pack could finish the sentence for her. "Yes, we are to blame. We hurt that kid more than we know."

A long pause crept between them. This was difficult territory for both.

Maddie broke the uncomfortable silence. "I can't talk about that right now, Pack. It's all too hard. But, after you called, I realized that I hadn't...well, I should have wished you well on your trip. You know I'll be praying."

Pack didn't reply.

"I hope you know that I want to be involved. I need to help in any way that I can. But, I don't think I can be of any help going with you tomorrow."

"You got a date tomorrow, Maddie?" As soon as he said it he bit his tongue. Maddie's having been seen with a college teacher gnawed in the pit of his stomach. Even when people were discreet, cops knew everything going on in Hibbing. Clayton Conroy was a decent guy, but—

Maddie considered hanging up. Clayton taught a literature class she had taken that summer. Their relationship was strictly platonic.

"Sorry again, Maddie. That was uncalled for; a cheap shot. I didn't mean to..."

Rather than engage this issue, Maddie swallowed her anger. "Please do call when you get back. As I said, I want to help in any way I can—you know that, Pack. I'm just worried sick...and, I'm angry, too. Our son lied to us. And lies are the stuff of a deeper trouble."

6/ SATURDAY MORNING IN FLAGSTAFF

Amos thought he had heard sirens sometime around four in the morning but slept through the distraction. This new place was full of new sounds. In Flagstaff the rumble and roar and bugle horn blare of freight trains splitting through the city at all hours of the day and night would be the hardest to get used to. When he finally awoke, the alarm clock on the bedside table read six-twenty. He was hungry and there was nothing in the apartment to eat. The taste in his mouth was terrible, but his eyes focused clearly and he didn't feel the drag of a hangover. Grocery shopping would be on his Saturday agenda. And a window shade; he'd make a hardware store list. Before getting out of bed, he replayed the previous night in his thoughts. Sadie Kearney. He smiled at the lingering memory: "Same time, same place," he recalled her saying when he left the Latin Quarter. Today was going to be a great day!

From his window, he saw the commotion on the street below. Two squad cars blocked both entries to Aspen Avenue, an ambulance idled off to the side, and yellow crime scene tape was strung around the space adjacent to the open alleyway. A blanket-covered corpse lay on the sidewalk. Amos found his Levi's slung over the kitchen chair, pulled a Willie Nelson T-shirt over his head, slipped into his moccasins, and headed toward the stairway.

On the street were several onlookers; ten or twelve people including several apparent vagabonds. At the edge of the mingling throng, Amos spotted his landlord. Jake Levitt looked as if it was the end of the day rather than the beginning. His baggy gray suit was wrinkly, tie loosened at the white-gone- to-yellow collar, face stubbled.

"Good morning, Mr. Levitt. What's going on?"

"Nothin' good about it. Some bum got stabbed over there last night."

Amos gestured toward the blanket, "Murdered?"

Jake Levitt gave him a look deserving of a stupid question, nodded.

Amos could feel the blood draining from his face. He had seriously misjudged what happened the night before. And worse, he had simply turned his back on the man and gone to bed. Did that make him an accomplice to a homicide—by negligence?

"Ya din't see nothin' from up there, di'ja?" Levitt lifted his eyes toward the apartment window.

"I...ah, I wasn't here last night." His words were tight.

Levitt offered a strange look.

"Went down to the 'L.Q.' with some guys. Stayed late and might have had too much to drink. I really crashed when I did get in." Amos forced a laugh. Be careful he told himself. You've said enough.

"Cuz, if'n ya saw anythin' ya otta tell that guy over there. DeJarlais." Levitt waved a purple-veined hand toward the uniformed officer hovering near the body.

"Like I said, I didn't see anything."

"Ya, nobody saw nothin'. That's what I heard 'em say. Even them drunks cross the street, none of 'em knows a damn thing 'bout what happened. Strange. Strange as hell if'n ya ask me."

Amos edged away. It was uncomfortable being among the curiously milling street people but he was reluctant to make an abrupt or conspicuous departure. Captain Rudy DeJarlais, looking frazzled and red-eyed, was walking in his direction. Amos felt a chill. He didn't want to begin a new set of lies to complicate those already in place.

"DeJarlais." Levitt intercepted the officer. "Wha'cha findin' out? Still nobody know nothin'?"

Amos backed toward the corner of the McMahan's furniture store. When he was certain that DeJarlais wasn't looking his way, he slipped into the doorway, and raced back up the stairs to his apartment.

What to do now? Amos was tormented. He, the son of a cop, afraid to get involved? His father would never forgive him. But, Amos did not want any part of a murder investigation. Not here, not now, no way! It was no business of his. He didn't really know anybody in Flagstaff. And those few he had met knew him as Jerry, from Denver. He did not dare to risk becoming Amos Moran from Hibbing, Minnesota. Everything was too complicated. Even what he saw from the window after midnight the night before. Even that was a blur. What had he actually seen? Amos sat at his desk, closed his eyes, probed his memory.

Three men walking east on the north side of Aspen.

Younger men. College age he guessed—but couldn't be certain.

One of the men, tallish he thought, ran across the street.

There was a kick...then a stomach punch. No, it must have been a knife. Good God, it had to have been a knife! Jake Levitt said the guy was stabbed.

The perpetrator? About Amos' size, around six-feet. That was a guess. What was he wearing? Amos squinted hard to force it out of his memory. A long coat, a trench coat. Dark-colored. And...yes, the cap! That was it. That was the one clear memory from the startling assault that seemed vivid in his memory. A tossle-like cap. Strange for the mild evening. The cap had a light colored ball at the top.

The other two guys. They were directly under his window—he couldn't remember much of anything about them. Probably the same age as the assailant. One of them seemed large, broad-shouldered. But he couldn't be certain. All of them could run pretty fast.

What else? When the old man went down, Tossle-cap did a quick frisk under the victim's shirt. Took something...a package of some sort.

Then, the three men raced east on Aspen.

That was it.

Amos could feel another headache coming on. His stomach growled in a protest of neglect. At the kitchen sink, Amos splashed cold water over his face. What was going to have been a great day had really started out on the wrong foot.

~

By nine that morning, the body had been removed and the street below cleared of activity. The yellow tape, flapping in the wind, was all that remained of the horror that had occurred. Amos was famished. After showering and putting on his last clean shirt, he headed over to a café on Birch where he had eaten dinner the day before. The late morning was gorgeous—sunny and cloudless. After pancakes and sausages he decided to walk off the heavy feeling of overindulging. Wheeler Park was only a couple of blocks away.

From a park bench he peered toward the purple bulk of Humphries Peak which dominated the northern landscape. Flagstaff was situated on a high plateau below the San Francisco Peaks: the brochure he had scanned said the city's altitude was 7,000 feet. The cone top of Humphries rose another five thousand feet and the Snow Bowl near its acme was a winter skiing mecca. Although dramatically different from back home, he was beginning to feel comfortable here.

So much had happened in the past several days that his head was still spinning from a combination of sensory overload and lingering guilt. After leaving Phoenix and spending a couple of days in the awesome canyons of Sedona, Amos was thinking of heading back to the Denver area. But all that changed when he drove the switchback highway from Sedona to Flagstaff.

Leaving the panoramic red rock wonders, and gaining altitude every mile, Amos pulled off the narrow roadway just ten miles south of Flagstaff. The majestic Douglas firs and Ponderosa pines scented the air with a familiar northern Minnesota richness. It was almost like being in McCarthy Beach State Park outside of Hibbing—without the lake. Later, after driving around Flagstaff, he discovered the NAU campus.

'FLAG'

Not an hour went by, however, when Amos' thoughts did not slip back into the past. He would readily admit to being homesick. And, when he allowed himself to be honest, there was a tinge of apprehension—with a dash of regret. He remembered the fishing trip that he and his dad had taken shortly before Amos headed for St. Thomas on the first leg of his deception. "You'll get homesick at times, everybody does." His father went on to say that 'Home is where the heart is...' and offered an interesting theory to the timeworn cliché. "Those of us that are born in Hibbing", he said, "have a *Hibbing Heart*. Nothing will ever change that. It's like the earth here is magnetic and always pulls at you."

If that alleged magnetism was working on him now, it was his sense of guilt that troubled him the most. He had hurt those he loved the most. His mom and dad would probably know he was 'missing' by now. Especially his dad. Nothing ever slipped by Pack Moran, Hibbing's 'super sleuth'. Amos chuckled to himself. "Have you got everything figured out yet, Dad?"

Thoughts of his father were always balanced with thoughts of his mother. Her love had been the most sustaining element of his life. Her easy charm, engaging laugh, her feminine touch to everything in his otherwise masculine world. Her good and thoughtful advise on everything. Maddie was an insightful former teacher with wisdom beyond her years. Amos remembered her telling him to always listen. *Try to hear what people are not saying.*

And he mused about his questionable friends—his trusted co-conspirators. Were they still covering up for him? Owen Norberg was a jerk and a loner and a druggie, but he could be counted on to keep their secret. Owen had agreed to lie about being Amos' roommate at St. Thomas. Jeff Serrano, also living in St. Paul, was solid, unshakable. Amos was certain that his father would connect with both of them at some point. Larry Quiggin at Regis College in Denver was no more than a red herring. A clever subterfuge for when Dad got into his investigation mode. Mike Rapovich—Mike would be confused. Amos had planned to join him in Phoenix. There wasn't much that Rap could tell anyone except that Amos never showed up. So, that would be a dead end for anyone in his pursuit. Amos had covered his tracks pretty well. Jerry Moran would be hard to find.

He thought about Sadie Kearney and the good time at the 'L.Q.' the night before. Pretty...fun...teasing...provocative...delightful... Sadie. He wondered if he would see her at the bar that night. Would he ask her home? Might they kiss? Make out? It would be great if he had his car. No. How would he explain the Minnesota plates? Amos resolved to get some new plates—even if he had to steal them from some old, abandoned, heap in some junkyard. He would keep his eyes open for such an opportunity. He laughed to himself—was he beginning a life of crime?

Back at the apartment, Amos put away two bags of groceries, installed a new blind on the living room window, and hung the vinyl shower curtain. The street below remained quiet. Yellow tape still flapping in the afternoon breeze. Amos remembered the name DeJarlais, the cop from the crime scene. What had the policeman learned about the murder? Who had he questioned? Would he, or some other cop, be knocking on his door? What had Jake Levitt and DeJarlais talked about earlier that morning? *WHAT WAS AMOS GOING TO DO?*

7/ *THE CLASS OF '75*

On Sunday, September First, 1974, the young life of Amos Moran took a sharp turn off of the road he had been traveling for more than seventeen years. He would never forget that day. The last Sunday of summer vacation

'FLAG'

was a gorgeous northern Minnesota day: A bright and cloudless blue day—yet, at the same time, the darkest day he had ever lived. It was the day before Labor Day...but more deeply etched in Amos' memory, it was the day when his father left home. Oddly, there had not been any precipitating events—his parents had not been drinking and there had not been any conspicuous quarrels between them. No...the parting of Pack and Maddie Moran after eighteen years of marriage was more of a quiet agreement, or mutual understanding, than anything else.

"Your father and I can't live together right now," was Amos' mother's description of what had happened. "We still love each other very much."

"I just can't get through to her, Amos. She doesn't understand me...I've tried, but we just don't seem to be able to communicate." His father told him the following week.

Both had promised him that they would "work things out" in time.

To Amos, none of what had happened made any sense at all. Mom remained miserable most of the time, and Dad was no better off than she while living by himself in his little cottage south of town. During the first weeks of their *separation* it became apparent that neither of them were doing anything to 'work things out'. Yet, when asked how things were going between them, both would tell Amos that they needed 'time' and 'space' while assuring him that they still loved each other—and him, more than anything. Of course, they assuaged any concern that *he* might have had anything to do with *their* problems.

For the most part, Amos' senior year at Hibbing High School was a blurry experience. Not so much that it passed by so quickly, or that Amos experienced any fog of oblivion...mostly, it was more like a vague period of searching— trying to figure out who he really was. In that regard, Amos would readily admit, that during that time he became his own best friend and his own worst enemy. Decisions that had been as automatic as brushing his teeth or washing his hands before eating now became calculated acts. His changed circumstance at home required thoughtful changes in how he perceived and acted in every other area of his life.

And decisions made at age seventeen, without the benefit of a parent's wisdom, experience and insight, are often faulty or counterproductive. But Amos would rationalize everything he did with one simple criterion: *they* were the ones who screwed up...so who really cared if he did, too?

In September, Amos resolved to keep his grades at National Honor Society standards. Realizing this objective was not a major challenge for him. He was bright and he knew it. And giving his studies a high priority was something that he would be doing for himself and no one else.

In October, Amos made his first critical decision—a very difficult decision with calculated consequences. He visited with Coach Perpich and told his respected hockey mentor that he would not be playing hockey his senior year. Perpich was a gentle giant of a man, and the kind of person who did not pry and did not push. In his gruff voice, he simply said: "We will miss you, Amos," and wished him the best of luck. Amos had been a third-line wing on Hibbing's lauded state championship team of two years before.

Two things resulted from his decision to quit playing hockey. First, and most importantly, he had greatly disappointed his father. Pack Moran had been an almost legendary athlete at Hibbing High School in the fifties, and remained very active in the city's youth hockey program. Hurting his father was, however, a deliberate statement—a reciprocal punishment!

Secondly, Amos' circle of friends changed dramatically. This was expected and presented no big surprise to him. High schools are a network of cliques. In H.H.S., as in most public high schools, there are several discernible groups within the student body. The 'jocks' were the self-anointed and primary aggregation— others were the arts kids (drama, chorus, band, etc), the brains of math and science club notoriety, the shop kids who were usually car fanatics as well, and the druggies and drinkers who dressed and behaved in conspicuous rebellion. Some boys managed to keep themselves at the fringes of these identifiable cliques without any clear affiliation—but not too many.

In most social respects, Amos kept mostly to himself while endeavoring to get along with, and be accepted by almost everybody. In doing so, he matured in ways which otherwise might not have happened. He learned a great deal about people's differences and gained a more realistic perspective about life in the middle lane. Jocks were not really that much different from the brains or the thespians or the woodworkers from shop classes. All of them wanted to be cool in their own way and get along more than almost anything else. Sometimes the jocks, the foolish and popularity-driven ones, were even among the drinkers and potheads. Anything to garner student body votes for Homecoming King.

Amos became a regular spectator at the weekend sporting events, 'one of the guys' at Armory dances, a late-night 'chip in for pizza' hang-outer at Sammy's, and occasionally...one of the seniors at a kegger party in the boondocks of Six Mile Lake or Biker's Field. Once, he tried something called 'Acapulco Gold' with a different crowd who did their thing at the Greenehouse in Bennett Park.

Amos earned a spot on Mr. Hysjulien's math team, earned the NHS gold pin for academic achievement, placed third in the VFW essay contest, participated in the Spring Play (*Jesus Christ Superstar*), and led the baseball team in batting average and pitching victories. All in all, Amos was able to straddle the cliques and have a fulfilling senior year. School was the *only* center of his life.

~

In March, Amos turned eighteen—the legal drinking age in Minnesota at the time. The hockey season was over and baseball practices hadn't begun. So, he and some friends got drunk together.

Owen Norgard was a fringe kid who did drugs, was a whiz at calculus and worked on designing props for the stage crew. Owen was a loner who was as bright as he was chemically screwed up. Yet, Amos and Owen were the best of friends. Pudge Arneson was an affable jock and the captain of both the football and hockey teams. Carol Lawrence was a basketball cheerleader, NHS president, and member of the debate team. Jeff Serrano played shortstop on the baseball team, tinkered with cars for hours on end at Matt's Garage, and was a huge Bob Dylan fan. Krissy Bizal was the lead singer in a local rock group called 'Hematite' and played Mary Magdalene in the spring play. Mike Rapovich was an old friend from the Moran's lake home, and a jock from Chisholm. He was currently dating Krissy.

The six of them were celebrating Amos' birthday and his letter of acceptance from St. Thomas at Owen Norgard's house on Pill Hill. "I'm planning do something kinda crazy after graduation," Amos confided to the group lounging and playing music in the spacious basement rec room. It was late in the evening and he had been drinking cans of Coor's beer for nearly three hours.

Among them, only Owen knew what Amos' crazy plan was all about. Owen smiled, but said nothing at the time. It was their secret. He shot his friend a quick frown of disapproval.

Amos, waving off Owen's apparent warning and badly slurring his words, raised his glass: "Heeere's tooo St. Thomas!"

Owen added, "Heeere's to getting the hell outta Hibbing next fall."

They all laughed and toasted.

"Just like our own Bobby Zimmerman," Serrano had to mention his icon and Hibbing's most famous exile. Having said that he went to the stereo and put on a Dylan album. He found the selection he wanted and began singing along with the lyrics of *'The times they are a'changin.'"* Krissy Bizal's beautiful voice raised above the others as they sang in harmony with Bob's soulful lament.

The Dylan music was a perfect diversion. Amos, not yet completely inebriated, chose not to elaborate any further on his plan. By midnight, Pudge and Carol along with Rap and Krissy had left the party, leaving Amos with Owen and Jeff. "You gonna tell Serrano?" Owen asked.

"What do you think?"

Owen and Amos had considered including another conspirator to the plan for some time. "I'm for it, Amos," Owen said. So far only he and Mike Rapovich were involved. He turned his gaze on Serrano. "Okay...remember that what Amos said earlier about doing something crazy, Jeff? Well, here's what's going on—" In more lucid speech than Amos could have managed by this time, Owen went on to explain that Amos was going to sneak off to Arizona next August.

"Arrizzonna...sunnn and funnn." If too much beer had slurred Amos' speech, it had relaxed his inhibitions as well. "They really, really fucked me over, Jeff," he said of his parents. "Yessiree, they really did a number on your ole buddeee, Amos. August's gonna be pay back time for Patrick and Madeline..."

Jeff Serrano, who had to drive home later, had been nursing his beers throughout the evening. He grimaced as his friend's anger and frustration surfaced. Like everybody else in this small town, Jeff knew about the Morans' separation. But he had always had the impression that Amos was handling the misfortune well. Obviously, he was wrong. Amos' pain was both razor sharp at some times and as blunt as a sledgehammer at others.

Amos' eyes teared as he rambled almost incoherently through a realm of self-pity. "Don'tya see, Jeff...they don't really give a shit about me—it's all about themselves. It's bullshit...that's what it is—Bullshit! And I'm gonna show 'em that Amos can take care of himself."

Amos had little memory of that night. His first hangover was a doozie—his head throbbed, his stomach raged, and his throat burned from vomiting. He wondered if the fun had been worth the suffering.

Owen had to tell him about everything the next day. "Our plan has added a partner, Amos," he explained. "Not only were you bombed...you were really pissed-off last night."

Amos tried to find any detail of memory from the void that was his birthday party. After the Dylan songs, everything else had been erased.

Owen said, "I almost felt sorry for Jeff...you sure let it all out, Amos. After you passed out, Jeff had to literally carry you out to his car."

Amos had a pang of shame. "I'll have to apologize to Jeff," was all he could say about what had happened.

In June, Amos graduated eighth in his HHS class of more than 400. The opulent high school auditorium was filled to capacity to hear Vice President Walter Mondale deliver the Commencement Address. Both Maddie and Pack attended the ceremony but sat in different sections of the huge room.

That summer, Amos worked for a contractor on the Hibbing Taconite Plant project, purchased his beloved El Camino, and spent as much time as he could at his grandparent's cabin on Sturgeon Lake. His 'plan' had

'FLAG'

evolved from something he needed to do to something of an obsession. Amos was emotionally distancing himself from Hibbing and from his parents with every passing day. While at the lake he played hoops with Mike Rapovich, when in town he hung out with Owen Norgard. His parents' efforts at reconciling their issues—whatever they might have been, Amos still remained in the dark—were somewhere between nil and nothing.

As Amos' anger festered like a storm gathering momentum, so did his impatient resolve. In his dreams, he began to see himself in different places: Trekking through lush, Greene, tropical jungles; strolling along the white sands of endless ocean shores; climbing purple mountains toward floating cotton-ball clouds. The recurring dream patterns were vivid—especially the mountains.

One night in June his mother went to a string quartet concert at the high school with a college teacher named Clayton something. Without Maddie's notice, Amos slipped into a back row to watch them. At the intermission he spotted his father in the crowd. 'Pack the cop' was doing his own surveillance.

The experience that night made him sick to his stomach.

By mid-August, Amos was ready. He had spent a weekend at home with his mother, allowing nothing to interfere with their time together. They baked cookies, played Yatzee, snacked on junk foods endlessly, and even polished off a bottle of wine. They talked about St. Thomas, his plans to come home every third weekend, and all the other things a boy and his mom can reasonably talk about. Through it all, there had been very little mention of Amos' father. "When I think of him (Pack) I get all bound up inside," Maddie confessed.

He went on a weekend fishing and camping excursion with his father. They packed a football, wiffle balls and plastic bats, lawn darts, and a case of Budwieser, along with their tackle boxes. The two men talked Twins, Vikings, Gophers and St. Thomas from Friday afternoon until late Sunday night. Again, the missing parent did not enter into the conversations. "If one of us could only the break the ice... I think we could start getting things back together," said his father.

Amos understood where both his 'Humpty-Dumpty' parents were coming from, and held faint hope that they would be able to put the pieces of their broken marriage together again. Their love, it appeared to him, had shriveled like a prune.

Most importantly, as far as Amos was concerned, each of his parents had swallowed his every deception. His planning of every detail had been as thorough as a teacher's lesson plan. And all three of his co-conspirators were as committed as he was to pulling off his escape without a hitch.

To both Maddie and Pack, Amos had been as clear and as convincing as he could possibly be: "Please, leave me alone for a few weeks. This is *my* thing...let me have it!"

If Pack could understand his son's need for space, Maddie struggled with the concept. "Two weeks at the most," she insisted. "In two weeks I want a call from you, Amos." A reluctant compromise was struck.

Before leaving Hibbing in mid-August Amos visited his high school. He wanted to pick up some extra transcripts, but even more than that, he simply needed to walk the corridors of that palatial building one last time. More than any place other than his home, it was here where Amos Moran had been shaped. As he wandered through the historic hallways and soaked up the familiar smells, he remembered how huge this place had seemed to him as a freshman. Four years had shrunk the school, made it both familiar and comfortable. His times here were like a treasure trove that he could carry along with him wherever he might go. The school was like an art museum with its hand-painted murals in the marbled entry foyer and in the spacious library. Amos walked past the main hallway's inset trophy cases, up the polished brass-railed staircase to the math wing's walk of fame, looked into Room 200 where he had his seventh period study hall.

More than any other feature of the two-block long landmark; the opulent auditorium was easily Hibbing's greatest source of pride. Hanging from the ornately frescoed ceilings were cut glass chandeliers that could grace the ballroom of an European castle.

Every classroom was a small chunk of gold for his memory chest. Despite the awesome architecture and the manifold artistic embellishments, it was the human element that struck Amos more than anything else. He remembered his teachers and coaches—those fonts of knowledge and molders of the clay that had become his unique personality.

After nearly an hour of sublime contemplation, Amos returned to his freshly polished El Camino waiting outside, drove to the bank to make a cash withdrawl, and headed south on Highway 73. He had said his goodbyes to his parents and grandparents and made unspoken farewells to Hibbing. By one in the afternoon it was off to St. Paul and the College of St. Thomas where he had no intention of enrolling for the fall semester. The Twin Cities, however, were only a brief first step toward whatever was beyond. Probably—but not yet certainly—Arizona.

8/ ST. THOMAS

Where was Amos?

During the four-hour drive to St. Paul, Pack Moran cursed himself for failing to recognize the deception woven by his eighteen-year-old son. Maybe he deserved it. Both he and Maddie had hurt the lad more than either of them wanted to admit. But admitting to their mistakes required better communication than they seemed capable of. Painfully, he remembered his conversation with Maddie the night before. Why couldn't he find the words to break the ice? Or worse, why couldn't he just *say* them? It wasn't really a matter of not knowing his feelings—it was more about some stupid masculine pride. ' I'm sorry' and ''I love you' would go a long way in melting the ice.

The Labor Day weekend was oppressively hot and Saturday traffic a challenge. Pack had no love for the Twin Cities and rarely made the nearly 200-mile trip. A couple of Twins games in the summer and the Vikings-Packers game in the fall was more than enough.

The dashboard clock read 10:45 as he turned off I-94 and headed south on Cretin. "Clever kid...dumb Dad," he chided himself for the umpteenth time. "Had to try out his wings, I guess." After several blocks he spotted brick-faced O'Shaughnessy Stadium where he would meet young mister Owen Norgard. Owen was a sophomore at St. Thomas and his son's roommate. Or so, Pack had been led to believe. Supposedly, the two friends had been assigned a dormitory room together at Brady Hall.

Specific details of the past week played in his thoughts. His first call to the Brady Residence Hall on Wednesday morning was answered by Owen with a stuttered: "He's at the library, sir." Owen had promised Pack that Amos would call back later. The second call, later that day, also got Owen: "Sorry, you've missed him again. Hasn't he called you back, sir?" On Thursday, he talked with the dorm's floor resident. "Mr. Norgard's roommate is Gary Riley, Mr. Moran. We don't have an Amos Moran here at Brady." The revelation from his next call, to the college registrar, Father Devon O'Malley, came as no surprise. Amos wasn't registered.

Two calls to Owen were unanswered. Pack called O'Malley again.

"I'd like to ask a favor of you, Father," Pack said. My son is missing. I'm going to drive down to St. Paul tomorrow morning. Please get a message to a student named Owen Norgard, he's a friend of my son's, and have Owen meet me about eleven...outside the stadium on Cretin. I'll be looking for him tomorrow."

On Friday afternoon, Pack visited the high school and found Amos' counselor, Elmer Salvog, in the guidance office. His son had indeed been accepted at St. Thomas and Elmer was surprised to learn that Amos was not already registered. "I talked to him a couple of weeks ago. Everything seemed set to go." Salvog mentioned that Amos had picked up three additional high school transcripts for his personal files. "Kinda unusual, I'll admit, but nothing to raise my eyebrows." Pack did not tell Elmer that his son was missing.

The call to Jim Kaim at the bank was another piece to a puzzle that Pack was determined to put together.

As Pack pulled to the curb at storied O'Shaughnessy Stadium, he saw the lanky figure of Owen Norgard leaning against the brick wall. "Let's take a walk, Owen, my legs are stiff from the drive." Pack could never picture this young man and his son as friends. Norgard was bright enough, came from a respected family, but was never involved in much of anything while in high school. Stage crew for a spring production was his only credit in the yearbook that Pack had checked the night before. One of the 'fringe' kids that Amos had befriended during his senior year.

"I think you have a pretty good idea why I'm here, Owen."

"Yes, sir."

The morning sun baked the wide concrete sidewalk bordering Cretin and the air was saturated with traffic exhaust, but it felt good to have his feet on the ground after being cramped for hours. It was much too hot to beat around the bush with this acne-scarred, longhaired punk. "Okay, tell me...where's Amos?"

The young man's eyes remained downcast, as if he was counting his large footsteps one after the other. He was slow to answer—as if he hadn't heard the question. A weak smile crossed his face. "What do you know, Mr. Moran?"

Although Owen had not slept well the night before, and was still stressed by O'Malley's stern mandate: "You will meet Mr. Moran tomorrow morning!" Owen had smoked a joint and felt reasonably relaxed. He had known all along that his pledge to Amos was going to get him in some hot water. But the loyalty to his friend was inviolable.

Pack let the smug answer to his question pass for the moment. This kid would be easy meat. "What do I know? I know that Amos is not here. I know that you are a part of the lie he gave me. I know that you are a loser. I know that you've smoked a joint recently—you reek of it. I know that I could get you expelled from college. And, I know that I'm not leaving here until I've got a straight story from you. So, don't play any foolish games with me. Where is my son, Owen?"

Owen was visibly shaken. Like every kid in Hibbing, he knew that Pack Moran was nobody to mess with. Amos had warned him more than once when they were discussing the plan. "My dad will lean on you" Amos said. "But he'll be more bark than bite. If you're respectful to him he won't lay a hand on you." Owen would try his best to follow Amos' advice despite the intimidation and the threats.

"I don't know, sir. That's the truth. I last saw him...I think it was a couple of weeks ago, maybe less. Anyhow, he told me that you and his mom would probably be calling the dorm at some point, sir." Owen would punctuate his sentences with a respectful *sir*. "He asked me to give you both some kind of runaround, that's the word he used, 'runaround'. Make up some kind of excuse. Said he needed a week or so...said he wasn't going to register here. Wasn't going to hang around the Cities, sir."

Pack gripped the young man's elbow to slow his pace, then steered him toward an elm tree shading the corner. "You have trouble with eye contact, Owen? Is the sun too bright for you? Now, look at me and tell me what he was planning to do. I want to see your eyes, Owen. Got that?"

At six-three, Owen was a few inches taller than Pack, but much slighter of frame. The grip on his arm sent a sharp twinge of pain toward his shoulder. "Don't bully me. You can't just grab me like that," he protested, wondering if what Amos had told him about 'bark and bite' was really true.

Pack smiled, "You know your rights, don't you Owen? You're a smart kid, right? This is some kind of police brutality and you're going to tell your lawyer about it—isn't that how it goes, Owen?"

"No, sir. I mean, I'm no dummy. But—"

"But what? Look, young man, we both know I'm a cop. What you don't seem to understand is that I'm a father—first and foremost. My son is missing. You're involved in that. An accessory. Are you getting this picture?"

"Yes, sir." A cold apprehension moved down his neck. But he owed Amos—big time! His friend had covered for him last winter when he stole money from his parents. "I don't know what to tell you, sir. I'm sorry about Amos and I'm sorry for lying to you. I probably should'a told you I didn't know where he was when you first called. I don't want any trouble, sir. Really, I don't."

Pack could see fear in the beady eyes of Owen Norgard; he was lying, and Pack would press his inquiry. "Sorry doesn't cut it with me. I'm just not buying your story. I cannot believe that Amos would tell you to give me and his mom a 'runaround' and just leave it at that. You're not stupid,

Owen. You asked him what's going on, right? You two guys are old buddies. He told you something. Now, lets quit talking in circles."

"I'm telling the truth, sir. When he said he wasn't going to hang around at St. Thomas, he said he needed...well, he said he needed to get away for a while. I asked him what that meant and he just blew me off. 'Let you know later' is all he said. I probably should'a pushed him about that, ya know, but I didn't."

The diesel engine of an eighteen-wheeler, a squeaky-braked city bus, and a steady stream of traffic along the avenue drowned out their conversation for a moment. The air was as thick with city noise as it was with city fumes and smells. Being in the city always made Pack long for the quiet streets back home. How did people live with this every day?

Waiting for the traffic to abate, Pack tried picturing the exchange between the two friends. His hard eyes still riveted on Owen. A skilled interrogator, he knew the buttons and when to push them. A gut feeling told him that there was more to this story and that others were involved. He considered the fragments Owen had provided. Not much—not enough to build even a weak theory. He would push the lighten-up button.

Owen's long forehead beaded in nervous perspiration. There was one item of diversionary information that he hadn't divulged. Something he and Amos had talked about—if a situation like this should arise. He would wait to see how this confrontation played out.

"Who else knows, Owen? You're part of this cover-up: tell me who else was Amos in contact with."

Owen pulled out his handkerchief, dabbed at his brow. He and Jeff Serrano had gone over their story the night before. There were three of them tangled in Amos' conspiracy. Owen, Jeff, and Mike. Only Jeff was living in St. Paul and he had been warned to expect a visit from Pack Moran later this morning. Owen prayed that none of them would melt. He cleared his throat,

"You know Larry Quiggin, Mr. Moran?" Quiggin was a red herring in the boy's cleverly contrived scheme.

Pack nodded. Quiggin was someone Amos had gone to Assumption School with, a classmate in high school, and teammate on the baseball team. Something was coming.

"Well, Larry is out at Regis—a private college out in Denver. Last time we talked, Amos mentioned Larry. He said that you and his mom had some good memories of Colorado. Didn't say what they might be...but he told me he'd like to see the mountains out there some day, maybe look up Larry if he ever got out there. I don't know if that's of any help. I mean, he did say he wasn't going to hang around here."

Pack swallowed hard on his Colorado memories. He was both surprised and pleased that Amos had remembered them, shared them with his friend. He and Maddie had put the boy through a lot of pain these past few months. Pain that was at the bottom of what Amos was doing now...pain that was being paid back to his parents. He tucked the Quiggin information in the back of his mind, then probed. "Who else from Hibbing is here at St. Thomas? Kids he might have been in touch with while he was down here?"

Owen expected that question to come up. There were several names he could throw out, but this was where Jeff Serrano came into the picture. Serrano was going to play dumb and his roommate Eddie Maras didn't know anything about what was going on. "After he left me, he said he was going to hang out with Serrano and Maras. They've got an apartment off campus—down on Grand. They might know something I don't, Mr. Moran." His spirits brightened. "I can show you where they live, it's only ten minutes from here."

Pack knew the two young men, both Hibbing graduates. "Let's go."

9/ COLORADO OR ARIZONA?

Jeff Serrano was just getting out of bed, his long hair was tousled, and he looked seriously hung over. Serrano claimed he hadn't seen Amos in months but said that he remembered his roommate, Eddie Maras, telling him that Amos had crashed at their place one night a couple of weeks before. "I was over at Susie Brandt's that night. Amos hung out here with Eddie while I was gone. Sorry I can't help you, Mr. Moran. Eddie might know something. I'll give him a call if you'd like. He's working at Ruminators this morning."

Ruminators was a bookstore on Grand, just off Snelling Avenue and only a few blocks from where they were.

"You haven't seen Amos in months?" Pack was surprised. Jeff would be one of the first people Amos would be in contact with down here. He and Jeff had always been a lot tighter than Amos and Owen Norgard.

"Nope... I missed him when he was down. Like I told ya, I was at Susie's that night. She will tell ya that. So will Eddie."

Pack noticed a furtive glance between the two boys. Jeff was going overboard with alibis and his hangover seemed to have cleared up quite suddenly. He smelled something foul. "You can bet your last dollar that I'll check on that, Jeff."

Serrano said nothing. Amos' father was a cop, and a damn good one—this wasn't going to be easy, and if Pack Moran found out— he was going to be in big trouble. But, like the others, he'd promised Amos. And he wasn't going to be the one to mess it up. If Owen could keep his mouth shut, he could too.

"One of your Hibbing buddies comes down to the Cities and you didn't even make an effort to see him, Jeff? Just blow it off. I have a problem believing that."

Serrano shrugged, "I had to patch up some things with my girl, you know. Amos said he understood that."

Pack caught the slip of tongue, but said nothing.

"You could talk with Eddie, Mr. Moran."

"I'll do that." He glared at young Serrano. "We'll be talking again later. Count on it!" He let that cloud hang in the air.

Jeff Serrano gritted his teeth; wishing now that he hadn't been at Amos' birthday party back in March. If he had stayed home that night, none of this would be happening. Now, he would have to sweat over the next time Pack Moran stopped by to visit. He cursed under his breath.

"C'mon, Owen, another stop to make." Without another word, and with Owen still in tow, the two of them headed east on Grand toward Ruminators. Big Eddie Maras was an affable former football lineman who carried two-eighty on a solid frame. He recognized Pack immediately and offered a crunching handshake. "Well. I'll be...looking for a good mystery or crime story, Mr. Moran?" he laughed easily.

Pack smiled for the first time that morning. "Not right now, Eddie, but I am trying to unravel a mystery of sorts. Hope you can help me out."

"Happy to." He looked over his shoulder at the clock behind the cashier's desk, "Say, I've got a lunch break in about ten minutes. I'd be happy to show you a place down the street and let you buy me a burger."

"You've got it."

The hamburger joint on Snelling reeked of pungent greases—French fries and hamburgers were the standard fare. The three men shared a window booth looking out upon the lunch hour pedestrian and automobile traffic.

Even on this holiday weekend, everybody was in a hurry to get somewhere. The sights and sounds and smells of the city could be distracting to Pack if he allowed them to get into his small town psyche. But he blocked them out, focusing all his attention on the matter at hand.

Careful to keep his emotions in check, Pack summarized Amos' disappearance and apparent efforts at covering his tracks. "So, I'm down here to try and find a thread, Eddie. Owen here claims he doesn't know much of anything, and your roommate, Serrano..." Pack scratched the back of his neck. "Your roommate said you might be able to help." He would be careful not to conjecture on Serrano with Owen Norgard present. Anything said here would get back to Amos and tangle his efforts more than necessary.

"Sorry to hear about Amos, Mr. Moran. Yeah, he stayed at my place last...lemme see, I was off...would have been Sunday or Monday...ten days or so ago. I'm pretty sure of that. And, I remember, he wasn't quite himself. Kinda down I thought. You know, like he was kinda into his own thing. We had a couple of beers, some Virginia girls stopped over."

"You and Jeff and Amos...and the Virginia girls?"

"I don't know where Jeff was."

Owen's eyes darted from his ketchup dripping French fry to Pack. Pack pretended not to notice. "Did Amos tell you anything about what was going on with him? About not going to college, not hanging around the Cities, about needing to get away?—that's what he told Owen. Anything you can remember might be helpful."

Eddie Maras rubbed his bearded chin with the back of a sizable hand. "Tryin' to think. We didn't talk about college—I've taken this semester off, ya know, gonna put away some money—but...jeeze, I can't think of anything."

"Did he say anything about Quiggin out in Denver? Or anybody else you both knew? Anybody out of town?"

Maras squinted, "No...nothing about Quiggin...but come to think of it, he asked me about Mike Rapovich, that basketball player from Chisholm. Remember, two years ago?"

Pack nodded.

"Anyhow, Rap's out at ASU in Phoenix. Amos said he'd talked with Rap a couple of times. This summer. Said something like, 'It must be nice out there' or, 'Wouldn't mind being out there'...You know, something like that."

Owen squirmed in his seat. Without being aware of it, Maras was screwing things up. He would have to do some repair work.

Pack lit a cigarette. The Rapovich's had a cabin on Sturgeon Lake not far from the Kevin Moran place. Amos and Rap spent time shooting hoops whenever the Morans visited the lake. "You say that Amos and Rapovich have been in touch with each other over the summer?"

"I got that impression."

10/ RUDY DEJARLAIS

Usually the preliminary legwork on a capital case was assigned to a senior department sergeant. Rudy DeJarlais was handling the Flagstaff murder investigation for two reasons: One a quirk of circumstance and the other a directive from his Chief. On that early Saturday morning, a bartender at Bozo's named Bob Gibbs had noticed the pool of blood surrounding the corpse on Aspen Street on his walk home from work. Gibbs raced to police headquarters only a block away to report what he had seen. The desk officer, realizing that Sergeant Kraft was out of town for the weekend, called Rudy at home. Rudy was the first police official on the scene. Chief Roth, who was nearing retirement, wanted his best man (he often used the baseball term "closer'") to handle the capital case.

"Damndest thing!" DeJarlais told his partner, Arlen Begay. "We can't even ID the guy." The Flagstaff P.D. Captain sipped his Styrofoam cup of tepid coffee. The two cops had clipboards on their laps and were finishing reports while sitting in their squad car at the curb in front of the police station on Birch Street.

DeJarlais said, "Those alley vagabonds over by the Orpheum called him 'Donuts'—seems when he arrived here, from LA we think, he had a box of donuts in the paper bag with his belongings. Passed them out to all the Aspen creeps."

"Just 'Donuts'? From LA? Lots of luck, Captain." Begay was a full head taller than DeJarlais, a broad-shouldered Navajo, and the best partner Rudy could ever hope to have.

"Sometimes luck—"

"...Is a lot better than skill."

DeJarlais shrugged, handed Begay his clipboard with a knowing smile. The two of them had been together for eight years. Over time, they developed a bonded rapport far deeper than simple familiarity and companionship: Rudy and Arlen had shared so many conversations that each could finish the other's sentences.

"No witnesses, no motives...what we got to work with?" Begay shook his big head of long, black hair. "Where are we going to look for our stroke of luck?"

""Who's on the top of your list, Arlen?"

"' Heebie?"

"Mine, too. For openers, we're gonna have to find our Mr. Henton somewhere. See what he knows."

Harry Henton had been a denizen of Flagstaff's streets for as long as either man could remember. Over the years, DeJarlais had befriended the little drunk, and a twenty-dollar bill had given him more leads than he could count. Harry 'Heebie-Jebbies' Henton was DeJarlais's snitch—Joe's Place or the Club '66 were notorious bars on opposite corners of Santa Fe and San Francisco were his favorite hungouts most of the time.

Begay read his partner's mind. "Let's check out Joe's."

It was only ten-thirty in the morning but the long bar at Joe's was already half-filled with it's sad cast of regulars. Harry was among those getting their 'eye-openers'. The small man with large protruding ears, and strands of hair that could be counted, had a nervous condition that caused his head and shoulders to shake almost uncontrollably. The spasms, Heebie contended, could only be controlled with serious doses of Jim Beam.

DeJarlais and Begay had a system. They would never call out Heebie when he was with others. Begay would go to the door, and in loud voice, bellow an Irish name: "...Any you guys seen McCarthy?" McCarthy was fiction of course, and so were O'Brien and O'Malley, McNulty and McMullen and a long string of fabricated Irishmen. Their simple code has always worked well. Within half an hour, Heebie would meet the cops at Dee Dee's Diner, a few blocks away on Beaver Street. Heebie always had apple pie alamode and a vanilla milkshake, and usually left the café with a few bucks in his pocket.

The pie and milkshake were waiting on the back booth countertop when Heebie arrived forty minutes later.

"Wha'cha lookin' for, Cap'n?" Heebie's fork sliced into the pie and the pie into his mouth within ten seconds of his sitting down, back to the door, as always. "The stabbin' last night?" He was stuffing his second bite without looking up. "Heard 'bout that. 'Donuts' it was, right? Over on Aspen."

DeJarlais nodded without reply.

"A drifter. S'pose ya know that. Been 'round Flag a few months. Likable guy, I guess." Heebie looked up for the first time. "He did drugs, Cap'n. Always had some Greene in his jeans—know what I mean?"

"Tell me about it, Heebie."

"Well...I ain't fer sure. Grass and speed, I heared said."

DeJarlais puzzled. Donuts was a drifter and a drunk, didn't fit a cop's profile of a dealer. "What makes you think so?"

"Like I tol ya, he's got some Greene. Now, Cap'n, you can figger that out. Where's he gonna get money?"

"I'm listening."

"O.K. Here's the pitchur. Guy comes in from LA. Nobody's never seen'm before. Ever few weeks some strangers show up—nice car, lots of jewelry types, ya know. They been seen talkin'—Donuts and them Nigroo guys."

DeJarlais would check this out later. Drugs pissed him off more than anything, and Flagstaff had a problem. He nodded without reply.

"Every now an then, ya see some college kids hangin' out over round the Orpheum—at night, ya see. Donuts knew somuvum."

DeJarlais hadn't found money or drugs on the corpse. If what Heebie was saying checked out, there was a motive.

The three men talked about the drug matter for a few minutes. Begay got them back on track. "We've gotta find out who did it, Heebie. Help us out."

The little man slurped the last of his shake, wiped his narrow lips with the back of his hand, flashed a knowing smile. "You guys gonna give me a few bucks to get thru dis weekend?"

"Depends," said Begay.

Harry Heebie-Jeebies Henton knew more about the streets and bars of Flagstaff than the entire police force combined. And, when DeJarlais and Begay left the café half an hour later, they had a name—a legitimate suspect in the murder of the man known only as Donuts.

Sometime after midnight that early morning, Sam Yazzie made a conspicuous appearance at Joe's Place. Yazzie had a wad of money, and to the delight of all present, was spending it freely. Yazzie was one of maybe thirty street riffraff that DeJarlais kept tabs on. A tribal clan relative of Begay, Yazzie had a violent streak and had been jailed several times for battery episodes. Further, Sam Yazzie didn't have 'a pot to piss in' as the saying went. According to Heebie, Yazzie was dropping fifty-dollar bills on the bar, and did so until the wee hours.

Sam Yazzie's squalid apartment was off an alleyway only a block from Joe's Place. When the two cops entered through the half-opened doorway the squat Navajo was passed out on a bare mattress in the corner of the room. When awakened he became obnoxious and had to be cuffed. His answers to questions matched his bloated blood-alcohol content. Booked on a preliminary 'drunk and disorderly' they took the angry Indian downtown. Yazzie would be allowed to sleep it all off in the Flagstaff jail—pending more serious charges that might provide a new address for a long, long time.

Rudy DeJarlais was forty-eight, a veteran of twenty-two years in the department, and had investigated more than a dozen homicides over the years. Experience had taught him to never jump to conclusions. Sam Yazzie had a record and was capable of violence. But that was not enough. The apartment was being sealed pending whatever forensics might come up with—namely a murder weapon. Rudy had other matters to check out. He needed an ID on Donuts, and a lot more information on the drug activity in the Orpheum neighborhood.

From the station he called Wesley Walters. Walters was a Coconino County social worker who knew more about the street people than probably anybody else in Flagstaff. He was their 'guardian angel' of sorts, kept tabs on who was homeless, hungry, sick, or in need of any special attention.

"Got a few minutes this afternoon, Wes?" DeJarlais didn't need to identify himself, both had been on a first name basis for years. "One of your down-and-outers was murdered last night—or this morning. All we know is that the deceased was known as Donuts. Smitty's (the County Coroner) at the morgue right now."

Walters cleared his throat. "Donuts?"

"That's our best guess." DeJarlais would not say where he got the name.

"Jesus, yeah, I know him, Rudy. What happened—beat up, shot?"

"A knife, Wes. Bled to death on the street. Over on Aspen."

"Strange guy, that one, Rudy. Been here for a couple of months, always kept to himself...always had money. Fact, he's got a room at the Weatherford I think. Unusual for a street guy. He wasn't a wino like most of the others, I never even saw him drunk. Nobody messed with him."

"Drugs?"

"Wouldn't be surprised. I've seen him on campus a few times. Went to the library there."

DeJarlais played it straight with those he trusted. He trusted Wes Walters. "We brought in Sam Yazzie this morning. Somehow he came into a lot of money. What's your read on that, Wes?"

Walters didn't respond immediately. He knew Sam Yazzie well. "I don't know, Rudy. A lot of money? That's hard to figure. I wouldn't put it past Sam to rob a guy, but knifing someone...I really don't think so."

"Maybe you're right. Anyhow, I gotta run, Wes. Who is this Donuts?"

"Name's Axel Evering according to my file. Came from the Los Angeles area back in May or June. I could give you a positive." Walters promised to get down to the morgue that afternoon.

DeJarlais called the Weatherford. Axel Evering had had a room at the hotel since June Third.

11/ SORTING OUT THE STORY: ST. PAUL

After dropping off an unsettled Owen Norgard and thanking Father O'Malley, Pack was back on the road to Hibbing by mid-afternoon. He was leaving St. Paul with a few leads to follow, some deep suspicions, a dose of anger, and a heavy heart. Kids! Pack was not naïve regarding youth these days. He realized there was a unspoken but impenetrable code among kids in trouble. He would contact the Quiggins and Rapoviches later that night. Owen Norgard and Jeff Serrano would be on his back burner until...

He would call Maddie, too. That would be the hardest matter on his agenda.

The drive home was punctuated with stops at Toby's in Hinckley for coffee and gas, and the Moose Lake roadside DQ for a milkshake.

At the counter in Toby's Pack stared at his wallet-encased graduation picture of Amos. He smiled over Maddie's features in the brown eyes of his son. Amos had his mother's nose and full mouth, too. Pack also saw himself. The square line of his jaw, auburn hair, and—he had to admit—solid masculine features. Absently, Pack's finger touched the hockey scar on his chin; one of three noticeable scars from a life lived on the edges of danger.

Above his right eye was the knife wound from a barracks fight in Korea, and on his neck a bullet lesion from another cop in a '56 murder apprehension.

At forty-three, however, Pack Moran still carried his high school weight on a solid six-foot frame. Women still looked twice when he was in the room.

During the forty miles of pine, aspen and birch between Floodwood and Hibbing, Pack's thoughts drifted back to something Owen Norgard had mentioned earlier. Amos had shared his and Maddie's good memories of Colorado with Owen. Pack smiled easily. It had been back in 1956, he and Maddie were traveling to Sacramento to find her estranged father. They were in love when they left Hibbing and had become engaged while sitting at a patio table outside a motel north of Denver. Pack's arm warmed her shoulders as the sun dropped beyond the majestic mountains... "You really blew it, Patrick!" He was talking to himself for the hundredth time that afternoon. "Maddie is the best thing that ever happened to you—" he choked back a surge of emotion, "And you let her get away. Stupid, stupid..."

How many times had he wondered why things happened as they did? Maybe a million, maybe more. Although 'separated' for nearly three years already, neither had taken steps for a divorce. His few dates had convinced him that he was probably still too much in love to make any kind of relationship with another woman even remotely plausible. Would that ever change?

∼

"Maddie." Back in Hibbing, Pack had several phone calls to make. His wife was first.

"Just fine, thanks. A little road weary, I guess." He went on to tell hear about his St. Paul experience. "So, we've got our work cut out for us.

Obviously, Amos has disappeared somewhere. Maybe he's still in the Cities, but I doubt it. My guess is that he has taken a road trip—likely west."

After her 'How are you?' and 'What did you find out?' Maddie listened without question or interruption for ten minutes as her husband related his story. She cried.

"Maddie, it's still early enough for me to make a few calls and get down to headquarters. I've got to get an APB on the wires and do some map work while I'm at it. A couple of hours. If it's not too late I'll call you again later."

"I'll wait up. Is there anything I can do?"

"Nothing I can think of right now...but, I'm not going to try to be a Lone Ranger. We're in this together—" He wanted to end that sentence with sweetheart, but couldn't.

After assuring Helen Rapovich, Michael's mother, that nothing was wrong, Pack got her son's phone number in Phoenix. "I talked with Michael this afternoon, Mr. Moran. He didn't say anything about Amos."

Dick Quiggin from Chisholm had played softball with Pack years ago. "Yeah, Larry's doing just swell at Regis. Would you believe he's a junior already. It's costing Elsie and me a fortune...but what we don't do for our kids, right Pack?"

Pack called Larry Quiggin in Denver from his police office phone. The young man was well mannered, respectful. "I can't believe what you're telling me, sir. Where in the world did Owen Norberg ever get the idea that Amos might be heading out to see me? I've got to tell you, Mr. Moran, Owen is bad news. Just the idea of Amos hanging out with him gives me the creeps. Between us, Owen's a pothead. Don't know how he ever got into St. Thomas."

Fifteen minutes with Larry Quiggin convinced Pack that Owen had jerked him off. Quiggin promised to let Pack know if he heard anything at all about Amos. "I can't believe that he would do something like that. Amos is one of the straightest kids I know, sir."

There was no answer at Mike Rapovich's address in Phoenix. Pack looked at the short list of calls he needed to make. Months before he had worked on a credit card 'identity theft' case. An official with Visa's Minneapolis office had been very helpful. He found John Larson's home phone number in the old files. He hated to call the man at home, especially on a holiday weekend, but John's help would be essential. "John, Pack Moran from up in Hibbing." The two men rehashed the old case for a few minutes before Pack made his request. "My son's missing." Pack explained the circumstances and promised to do all the necessary paperwork to get a credit card trace going. John Larson was great. The Visa account manager would initiate a trace on Tuesday morning when the office opened.

"I may be on the road by then, John. My instincts tell me that Amos is out of state. I'll check in with you on Tuesday."

Mike Rapovich was expecting the call. Owen Norberg had phoned him from St. Paul that afternoon. "Mr. Moran, I don't want to be involved in this shit—excuse me—any more. It seemed like a pretty good idea at first, but I don't know what happened." Rapovich explained that Amos had, indeed, planned to come to Phoenix and enroll at ASU for the fall term. "He called me from a pay phone outside of Des Moines more than a week ago. Said he was on the highway, said he'd probably be here in three days...but that he was going to take his sweet time." Rapovich's voice was contrite: "Honest to God, Mr. Moran, I ain't seen Amos since last summer."

Mike explained the plan as he understood it. "I should not have done what I did, Mr. Moran. I knew it was wrong, I told Amos that, too. And I knew that one of these days you would catch on to what was going on." Amos and he had made arrangements to share a room for a while: Until Amos found a place of his own. "But I ain't seen him...at least not yet. That's the truth, sir. I don't have a clue where he might have gone, but it's not here in Phoenix."

Back at his little house south of town, Pack chose more coffee over the tempting bottle of Bushmills. His Rand McNally atlas was spread across his tabletop. He called Maddie again. Pack explained that he had started the APB and called the State Highway Patrols in both Colorado and Arizona, had talked to the Visa people, and both Larry Quiggin and Mike Rapovich.

The last anyone had heard from Amos was on the afternoon of August twentieth near Des Moines. "I have to believe the kids, especially Rapovich, Maddie. Amos was planning to go to Phoenix. Maybe he did...my gut feeling is that he headed west on I-80. It's a stab in the dark, I know. But before heading off toward Des Moines or anywhere else I'd like to be more certain."

This time, Maddie was composed and focused. "I have to agree. So, what's next, Pack?"

Pack had been considering an outlandish strategy in the hope of determining which direction Amos might have taken from Des Moines. His idea was to call police departments in cities that had exit ramps on I-80 across the nearly four hundred miles of Nebraska between Omaha and Ogallala. The local cops would do anything they could for one of their own, especially in a missing child matter. From them he could get phone numbers of major truck stops and make calls to as many of them as possible. Amos' El Camino was distinctive enough to be remembered by a gas station attendant or cashier watching the outside pumps. The odds that he might find any affirmation of his theory that Amos was headed west from Des Moines, however, were too prohibitive.

It was nine o'clock. Pack had done everything he could think of from here in Hibbing. He wouldn't sleep tonight...nor would Maddie. Both he and his wife shared a passion for making things happen. Staying and waiting would be like spinning his wheels in a snow bank.

Pack swallowed hard, "Maddie, I've got to do some packing. I'll call the Chief and tell him I need some time off— maybe a lot of time."

Maddie's heart pounded. "Listen to me, Pack, an hour ago you promised that you wouldn't try any Lone Ranger bullshit: Your words, not mine. Either I'm going with you or driving myself! And this is not negotiable."

12/ SUNDAY IN FLAGSTAFF

The *Arizona Daily Sun*, Flagstaff's newspaper, headlined 'TRANSIENT MURDERED"

> *The body of an unidentified male believed to be in his fifties was discovered by Flagstaff police at approximately 3:30 A.M. on Aspen Street near the Weatherford Hotel. According to Captain Rudolph DeJarlais, the victim was stabbed and robbed by an unknown assailant. DeJarlais said that a suspect was in custody but would not release the name to the Daily Sun. The investigation is ongoing. Anybody with any*

'FLAG'

information is asked to contact the Flagstaff police department.

The Sun has learned from a source inside the department that the victim was about fifty and from the Los Angeles area. Although unconfirmed when this issue went to press, it is believed that Flagstaff police are holding local resident Samuel Yazzie in connection with the crime.

The so-called Los Angles drifter's *real* story, however, would never see print in the *Arizona Daily Sun*. Perhaps it was better that way. Axel Evering had been a drifter for years. And, he was a dealer. His life had been a collection of tragedies and mistakes. There was only one ray of sun that touched his shadowed life, indeed, only one reason for living. Axel Evering had a daughter from a failed marriage back in the early fifties. Missy Moore was her name. Every Wednesday night, precisely at seven, he called her from the public phone at the Weatherford Hotel. Every Thursday morning he sent her money to live on. Missy's life, like that of her father, was lived at the edges of misfortune and fatality.

On Wednesday when Axel made his call, the phone was answered by Diego, the man Missy was currently living with. "She's gone, Mr. Evering. Missy's gone!" Axel could tell that the young man was high on something; Missy never missed his weekly call. "I don't understand," he said. The man explained. Missy had 'O.D.'d' on cocaine earlier in the week.

Axel Evering did not cry that night, but he did make a decision. The poison that killed his daughter was the poison he had been selling to young people on the streets of Flagstaff. "Never again!" he vowed to himself. But, he knew that his *business* was not something that one could simply walk away from. He knew too much. The LA goons would never allow him to call it quits. Axel Evering began making plans to move on to another place. A place where he might try to start over again. He would leave for Phoenix or Vegas on Monday, then—?

Amos was showered and dressed early. After breakfast he would go to Mass. From his window he peered at the quiet and shadowed street below. The morning sun was making its way down deserted Aspen Street. The transients must have found another place to spend the night. A well-dressed couple were talking on the sidewalk beside the brick-faced Weatherford Hotel. Hotels had always been a part of his family's life. Grampa Kevin had owned the landmark Androy Hotel in Hibbing for many years and Amos had been a busboy there while in junior high school. He remembered reading about the Weatherford in his Flagstaff brochure. It must have been quite the place years ago; but, over time, the building seemed to have settled ungracefully into old age. Despite her age, she presented—like the beloved Androy which also dominated a prominent commercial corner—a façade of charm, fortitude, and integrity. Teddy Roosevelt had been a guest there, as had the noted Tombstone sheriff, Wyatt Earp. Western author, Zane Gray had written a book, *Call of the Canyon*, while residing in the historic structure. Adding significantly to the Weatherford's colorful past were rumors of ghosts (a honeymooning couple who were murdered there in the 1930's) haunting Room 54. Amos held an interest in history and was determined to learn more about the past of this intriguing hotel and the city as well. He made a mental note to visit one day with Mr. Henry Taylor, the new owner of the hotel dominating the opposite side of Aspen Street.

Turning away from the window, Amos located his wallet and wristwatch on the desk. Whatever happened today, Sadie Kearney was going to play an important part. He couldn't wait to see her again, hear her laughter, relax in her comfortable companionship. The thought of Sadie brought an easy smile to his face. The thought of the murder scene beyond his window erased the smile. Amos could not shake the lethargy of torment. What was he going to do?

Amos sipped coffee in the Weatherford Hotel's lobby while reading the Sunday morning edition of the *Daily Sun*: *Transient Murdered* headlined the front page in bold black. The beginnings of a headache throbbed at his temples. He wished he could get a look at this man, Yazzie, who was being held. Somehow, that might ease his troubled conscience. If the man's appearance fit what he had seen from the window, it would be a closed case to his way of thinking. One way or another, Amos had to find out.

Sitting on a sofa across from him, Amos eyed a nattily dressed gray-haired man. The elderly gentleman was smoking an expensive meerschaum pipe while reading the *Sun*. Amos would try to engage him in some small talk. "Excuse me sir," Amos said across the space. He withdrew a Marlboro from his package, "Do you happen to have a lighter or a match?"

The man slipped his glasses up his nose, gave Amos the look of disdain that often passed between generations. He pulled his lighter from the watch pocket of his vest and held it out without a word.

"Happened right out there, I guess." Amos gestured toward the window facing Aspen. "The murder in the paper," he clarified as he lit his cigarette.

The old man nodded his head, "Damn drunken Indian done it. Paper says they got Sam Yazzie in jail."

Amos puzzled—an Indian? "You know him? This Yazzie fellow?"

The man looked down at the paper with an expression of disdain, "Seen 'em around. One of them no good bums who likes to hang around and make decent folks feel uncomfortable all the time. Flagstaff's got too many of them types. Didn't use to be that way, son. No siree. Used to be they'd run those kind right out of town. Shame."

"Yeah," Amos agreed. "Courts give folks too many rights these days." He sat down on the other end of the wide leather sofa. "They sure do make people feel uncomfortable—even me. This Yazzie a big guy?"

The old man laughed. "Big guy? Not at all. But he's mean enough. And he's a drunk besides."

"Just can't place him. I thought Yazzie was the tall one. Tall and slender. Wore a tossel cap all the time."

"Tall and slender? Jeeze, you ain't describing Sam Yazzie. He's built like a bullet—short, stocky, with a long, black ponytail. Indians like that ponytail look for some reason. Make's them look like women if'n you ask me."

Amos did not reply. The Indian community here probably got more than their share of bad-mouthing and discrimination. Like everywhere else he imagined. Troubled by what the man had told him, Amos got up to leave.

"It just isn't safe around here any more," the old man said. "Did you see the story buried on page five?"

Amos had not. He opened the paper and found what the man was probably referring to. He scanned the story. Gertrude Brown was a seventy-two year old woman who had had her purse snatched on the sidewalk in front of her home on Friday afternoon. She claimed to have lost more than two hundred dollars in cash. "The Brown story?" Amos asked.

"An old girlfriend of mine," the gentleman smiled more to himself than to Amos. "Years ago, of course. What's this place coming to?" he mumbled to himself.

Amos crossed the street feeling the weight of the world on his shoulders. If the old man's description was correct, Sam Yazzie was not the murderer. The assailant was not short and stocky. And, Amos would have probably noticed a ponytail—even under that unusual wool cap.

Amos walked up Leroux in the growing morning sunshine into a stiff northerly wind. Another headache was coming. At Cherry Avenue he turned left toward Wheeler Park. Several pedestrians were on the sidewalks heading in the same direction as he was. On the corner of Cherry and Beaver he spotted the edifice of an attractive stone-faced, and gargoyle adorned, Gothic church—the Nativity of the Blessed Virgin Mary.

Amos knew where he needed to be right now. Inside the large church, he found a pew near the vigil lights to the right side of the ornate altar with its magnificent mural backdrop. Two angels stood at the sides of the inspired painting. He knelt before the statue of Saint Anne with Mary, crossed himself, and began to pray. Tears formed in his eyes as he beseeched God's forgiveness for all that he had done. His litany of lies and deceptions had been a long one. Minutes later, he got up and lit a candle below the statue. Again he prayed from deep within his heart... "Mary, Mother of God, pray for me. Help me to do the right thing, as hard as that will be. I know an innocent man is in trouble and that I may be able to help." Amos closed his eyes, "And, somehow give me the strength to make things right with my mom and dad, too. I have hurt them terribly..."

During Mass, Amos felt like a Catholic again. How many months had it been since he last worshipped? Everything around him seeped into that deep hole inside, filling his void with a warm swell of spiritual ardor. His thoughts drifted back to the Blessed Sacrament Church in Hibbing, to being an altar boy, daily mass while attending Assumption School. Good memories. He thought of his mom and dad, and of having what his father called a *Hibbing Heart*...and the surge of homesickness that connected to memories.

And, he thought of Samuel Yazzie in the Flagstaff jail—for a crime he didn't commit. Despite his deep feelings of guilt, he went to Holy Communion that morning, promising his God that he would get to confession in the next week. He offered his Communion for the strength to do the right thing.

Mass uplifted Amos' sagging spirits. He would take his promises seriously, but not right now. He remembered the name from the crime scene, the name in the morning paper—Rudy DeJarlais.

13/ SAM YAZZIE

On the Friday afternoon of the murder, Gertrude Brown entered the Valley National Bank to make a cash withdrawl. Next week she would be taking her '70 Buick back to the garage for some repairs. Her trusted mechanic at Teddie's Tune-ups and Tows had always serviced her cars. This time it was another muffler and tail pipe, radiator flush, points and plugs, tire rotations, and the routine oil and filter change maintenance. The cost estimate was $188.00. Without conscience, Teddy Dahl had bilked the old woman of a small fortune over the years.

Behind Gertie in the bank teller line was a stocky Navajo man. Sam Yazzie had a personal check from his sister in Winslow to cash. The $15.00 check was his birthday gift. His sister was the only person in the world who remembered or cared. Sam waited patiently as the old woman in front of him carefully counted out three fifties, two twenties, and two fives. She tucked the small envelope with two hundred dollars into her brown leather handbag where he noticed other loose cash among the assorted women's stuff inside. Sam had not seen that much money in a very long time.

'FLAG'

Gertrude did not notice the man following her home. Apparently, nobody else did either. At her front gate, she felt the tug at her elbow—then a fleshy hand over her mouth. She tried to turn around but the assailant gave her a sudden push forward. Her glasses fell to the sidewalk as she stumbled. When Gertrude caught her balance and turned, all that she saw was a shadowy figure running down the street. She screamed to no avail.

Shaken and confused, she unlocked her front door and picked up the phone. "I've just been robbed" she cried in a voice shrill with anger. "Right in front of my house!"

Rookie Officer Roland Loshe filled out Gertrude's report while sitting at her small kitchen table. "Can you describe the man who took your purse, Miz Brown?"

"You haven't touched the nut bread, Officer." Gertie's tone was indignant.

Loshe obliged. Widow Brown had made a social occasion out of his visit. Her table was set with fine china plates and shiny silverware.

"Elmore could eat a whole loaf all by himself," she smiled at the memory of her late husband. "He was a mill worker, you know. Forty years at the plant. When he retired in '67, June it was..." Gertrude went on for about five minutes.

Loshe checked his watch, "We should finish this report, ma'am. Now let's get back to the man who stole your purse this afternoon. Can you describe him?"

"I certainly can, officer," she said. "He was mean and stinky!"

Loshe swallowed a laugh. "Uhm...that's good, I'm writing it all down, ma'am. Anything else; like—was the man tall?"

"I'd guess he was a giant. That's what I'd say. A hand about the size of that—" she pointed to a large globe on a living room table.

"Do you remember what he was wearing?"

"Clothes that smelled of cigarette smoke and body odor, too."

"Yes...can you tell me what kind of clothing?"

"How could I ever hope to do that, officer? My glasses were knocked to the sidewalk. I told you that already—didn't I?"

Loshe thanked Gertrude for her excellent report and promised to get right on the case.

"Just so long as I've got my money back by Monday morning. I've got to get my car into the garage again."

Loshe would do his best, "Well, Miz Brown, these things do take a little time, you know." He wouldn't tell her that her chances of ever getting that money back were slim to none.

"Here, take some along with you," Gertrude wrapped two thick slabs of her nut bread in a napkin.

~

Sam Yazzie had never robbed an old woman before. He felt badly about what he had just done. How far he had sunk over the years. When things turned around for him, when he sobered up and got on his feet—he would remember the old woman. He would pay her back every last cent, and even a little more. He made himself a promise.

At a liquor store on Santa Fe, he bought a bottle of Canadian Club instead of his usual cheap Ripple wine. Top-shelf liquor—how long had it been since he had indulged himself with the best? His late afternoon drunk would be a royal treat. Later that night, he would wander over to Joe's Place and buy a few rounds for the guys.

By seven-thirty on Friday night, however, Sam Yazzie was passed out on the bed in his apartment. He would not awaken until nearly midnight.

14/ SADIE KEARNEY

There were three Kearneys in the Flagstaff phone directory. Amos remembered Sadie telling him that her family lived about a ten block's walk from the NAU campus. He dialed Edward Kearney on Verde Street. Mr. Kearney answered, called to his daughter "...Sadie, for you. I think its Brian Lofley."

"Hey, Brian, what's up?"

Amos froze on his end of the line.

"Er...Brian? No, it's me." Amos was confused, his mouth dried instantly. Who was Brian? She probably had a boyfriend and hadn't told him. "No..." he repeated. "I'm sorry, Sadie. This is Jerry Moran—we met Friday night?"

A long pause. Sadie had been disappointed over Jerry's absence the night before and had hoped that she might hear from him today. "Oh... Pinocchio," she said. "Is your nose beginning to swell? You told me a big lie the other night."

Amos' mouth went dry. How could she possibly know? He felt as if his world was sinking deeper into a hole. What could he say? "What do you mean, Pinocchio?" squeaked out of his tight throat. "I don't—?" Amos was tempted to hang up the phone...and run.

"So, where were you last night? You said you'd meet me, and that was a lie. And your audacity to call me after standing me up, for ruining my evening entirely. I fear that I may never, ever be able to forgive you." Sadie slipped easily into her tease mode. "Whatever relationship potential we had has gone down the drain. Swooosh!"

Was she serious—or just being the Sadie he remembered? His confusion jumped up a notch. Before he could utter a word of defense, Sadie laughed. "Just kidding, Jerry. If you give me a proper apology, and promise never, never, to tell me another lie, I'll erase your name from my black list."

Amos sighed audibly, told another lie. The night before he had considered going back to 'L.Q.' but decided to stay at the apartment instead. As it turned out he did little more than mope about in his pool of self-pity. He could be moody, sometimes morose. The murder weighed heavily on his conscience. "I had some bad Chinese food...my stomach was in absolute protest all night." He would try to pick up some lost ground, "But I thought of you—even dreamed about you." That was honest. For the past many hours, Sadie had been on his mind more than any girl he could remember.

Sadie warmed inside. He had dreamed of her—how nice! She was about to ask Jerry if it was a wet dream but swallowed the notion: That might be pushing her glibness a bit too far. But she so much enjoyed teasing the new kid in the neighborhood. "Was I fully dressed...in that dream, I mean? Or...? Men have such potent libidos, you know."

Libidos? What were libidos? He felt naïve, but wouldn't risk asking. "You were like I remembered, I guess. I can't say exactly what you were wearing."

Sadie could sense that her comment had gone over his head. That was just fine with her. She would get him off the hook. "I'm glad to hear that you were thinking of me, Jerry. How are you feeling today? Is the bad stomach business over?"

"Oh yeah... I'm fine now."

"I suppose you're simply dying to see me again. Am I right?"

"Absolutely. That's why I called."

"What did you have in mind for a Sunday afternoon? A seduction?" Sadie wished she hadn't said that. If she wasn't more careful she might scare him off. Why was she being so pert, so audaciously forward? It was fun to be this way, but—?

"Just an abduction," he countered. "At least for now...who knows what follows that?" Amos was surprised at how easy it was to find rejoinders to Sadie's teasing banter. It was great fun to be able to laugh along with her risqué innuendos. So, how might he follow up on her apparent interest in seeing him again?

Remembering what they had talked about on Friday night, Sadie asked, "Did you get to Mass this morning, Jerry?"

"As a matter of fact, I did. It's been a while."

"Ten 'parent points' for you, Jerry. You're absolutely sweeping me off my little feet."

"I can be dangerously charming, you know. Especially on sunny Sunday afternoons."

Sadie liked the answer. "Well, let's not tarry, Jerry," she laughed in thorough amusement at her witty little poem. "What's on your mind and where can I meet you?"

Amos wanted to stroll around the campus. He had his class schedule in his pocket and hoped to get a feeling for the layout and learn the location of various buildings. "For a three-star, guided campus tour, with a knowledgeable NAU sophomore, I'd be willing to compensate the effort with an ice cream cone of m'lady's choice."

"My tours are strictly five-star, young man. And my price is more like a burger and fries. Even a freshman from Colorado must know that you pay for experience."

"How about my walking over to your place in an hour or so?" Amos considered that her Verde address was only several blocks east from his apartment.

Sadie dismissed the idea. "I'll meet you at the Student Center." She was not ready to have Jerry meet her parents. Not yet.

They agreed to meet in two hours outside of Prochnow Auditorium on the north edge of the campus.

∼

Sadie Kathleen Kearney was neither as blithely flip nor as fancifully glib as she might seem to those who only knew her superficially. Beneath that taunting-tease and fun-loving exterior was buried a trove of serious stuff. Sadie carried some heavy weight on those slender shoulders of hers. Her older brother, Michael, had been killed in Viet Nam—March 19 or 20, 1971—more than four years earlier. He was only nineteen and Sadie fifteen at the time. The two of them were closer than sibling opposites might ever hope to be. He was her *big brother*, and her protector, and her role model for every boy she might meet.

Mikey was one of 215 casualties of what was called 'Operation Lam Son 719, a South Vietnamese ground offensive inside Laos. American troops were providing artillery support, air strikes, and helicopter lifts. By most definitions, the operation was a failure. Mikey, serving with B Battery, 1st Battalion, 39th Artillery, was killed by enemy 82mm mortar fire near a place called Lao Boa. Sadie knew all this, and more, because she researched the battle for a high school history project. She received an A. She learned about how Mikey died from a stranger who had shown up at the Kearney's front door a year later.

Jimmy Forrest, a handsome young man from a place called Carlton in Minnesota, had been Mikey's buddy with the artillery outfit. He had made the trip to Flagstaff so that he could meet his friend's family and assure them that Mikey Kearney was a hero—smiling on all of them from heaven. Jimmy had been with her brother when he died.

'FLAG'

Jimmy cried a lot that afternoon. Everybody did. Before leaving the Kearney's living room, Jimmy told Sadie something that she would never forget. "Your brother was the finest man I ever knew. I still see those smiling Greene eyes of his a hundred times a day."

Later, Sadie checked her atlas and located the little town of Carlton. It was a small dot, west of Duluth, and tucked next to a place called Cloquet.

Sadie's older sister, Maggie, died tragically the following year. Maggie was a tomboy, loved hiking and mountain climbing. Maggie was careless, too. While scaling a ledge in Walnut Canyon, outside of Flagstaff, Maggie lunged for a rope being dangled by a friend further up the steep canyon wall. She missed, and fell more than two hundred feet. Maggie was only seventeen teen when she died.

These two tragedies had made Sadie an only child for the first time in her life. A life complicated by her father's decline into alcoholism, and her mother's clinical depression. Sadie assumed responsibility for managing nearly all of the family affairs. She did so with love and devotion and without ever uttering so much as the mildest complaint. Yet, the series of tragedies indelibly shaped her—gave her a simple, but sustaining, philosophy of life. Live every day as if it were your last!

Sadie thought of her brother Mikey as she strolled through the blighted southside neighborhood fringing the eastern edge of the campus. Like other areas in Flagstaff, the Ellery Avenue environs had lapsed into a degenerated state of disrepair. As a little girl, Sadie had been forbidden to cross Butler into the 'Southside'. One day, when she was ten or eleven, Mikey walked her across the street into the sinister neighborhood. With the tour came advice she would never forget... "Never be afraid of people, Sis...and respect those who have so little." To this day, however, her parents would disapprove of the shortcut she was taking through these decrepit streets on her way to the auditorium. And, to this day, Sadie remained confident and comfortable wherever her footsteps took her.

With thoughts of Mikey came thoughts of Amos. It was strange how that was happening to her. She knew that she had been a flirt on Friday night. Jerry's easy innocence was enabling, opening a side of her personality that was fun for her to play with. She realized that he was new to Flag when she first saw him at registration and later, when she watched him walking down San Francisco Avenue. Jerry had been looking in every direction as if for the first time. Walking slowly, almost tentatively, almost as if his mind was carefully processing a street map. Then he stopped to contemplate the stars...everything after that moment was a high that still had her floating.

It wasn't until later that evening that she really noticed Jerry's eyes. They were Mikey's Greene eyes. And they were pools of the same innocence. That realization triggered an attraction that she had not felt before. A happy and a sad sensation that she felt challenged to better understand.

Passing the football practice field, Sadie saw several of the guys she grew up with playing a pick-up game of touch football.

"Hey, Sadie, we need a center." Brian Lofley hollered in her direction.

Sadie saw Sally James and Niki Johnson waving. "C'mon, Sadie—we're kicking butt," chided Sally.

"Maybe later. I'm meeting someone," she yelled across the space and over the howl of the afternoon wind.

"You can play on *my* team," Troy Tomlinson called in his typically egotistic manner, with emphasis on the 'my'. "I'll even let ya go out for a few passes."

"Wow, that's making me *really* excited, Troy. Really—you'd *really* consider throwing me a pass?" her emphasis on 'really' underlined how privileged she ought to feel. "I'm *really* sorry...but I can't right now."

"You're no fun, Kearney," Troy turned away and called for a huddle of his team.

15/ CAMPUS TOUR

As he watched her approaching from nearly a block away, Amos felt the slightest flutter in his chest. A gust of wind fanned her long hair, billowed the loose pale blue blouse she wore— she waved, called ahead: "Don't just sit there, Moran...rescue me from the clutches of this monstrous hurricane."

Smiling widely, Amos was quickly on his feet and walking toward the damsel in distress. When he reached her he spread his arms for an embrace.

"Aha...the promised abduction!" Sadie gasped melodramatically.

Amos broke out laughing as she snuggled into his arms. Her dark hair had the familiar smell of strawberry. Intoxicating. He squeezed her then withdrew, placing his hands on her shoulders, met her eyes. "Sadie, I didn't intend to do this...I mean, to hug you. I just..." He stumbled over his words. "I mean, I just did it."

It was Sadie's turn to laugh heartily. Then she paused, lost for a moment in his eyes... "If you hadn't given me that little hug I would have punched you good—right in the stomach."

For a brief moment, that nightmarish stomach punch of Friday night flashed across his thoughts: he dismissed it as quickly as it had arisen. "I done good then," he said.

"Not too bad for a freshman. I'm sure you'll get better in time...with the proper instruction."

They kidded back and forth for a few minutes: Amos matching wits with Sadie quite admirably. When she mentioned her five-star campus tour, Amos handed her his class schedule. Sadie ran her finger down the Tuesday classes and locations, frowned, and shook her head. "Jerry, I'm afraid you might need a tutor for some of these; who helped you with this schedule?"

"Doctor Waverly, in political science I think."

"Did you do something to make him mad at you?"

Amos puzzled, "I hope not. Why?"

"Well, maybe you registered late; because two of these classes are the toughest ones here—English Comp. 101 with Ruth Darby, and Statistics with Doctor Death—Mr. Sand. . I took Sand's class myself last year. Research papers, book critiques, stand-up-and-talk-in-front-of -everybody stuff."

They toured the campus at a leisurely pace, Sadie expounding on architecture, university history, timesaving shortcuts, and everything else imaginable. She explained the significance of the Riordon Mansion bordering the western edge of the sprawling hodgepodge of old red stone buildings and new construction. The Riordon family fortune had much to do with NAU's rapid expansion. From the Gammage Building where he had registered last week, they looped from one building to the next, ending at the Liberal Arts Building where Amos had a second period Western Civ. class.

"You must see the Skydome on South Campus, Jerry. It's the pride and joy of Flag."

The new athletic building was truly an impressive sight. "Gosh this place is huge," Amos understated his impression. Why was it that, until only a few days ago, he had never even heard of Northern Arizona University? An hour had already flown by when they found themselves on a return loop which brought them along the side of the football practice field. The pick-up game was still in progress.

"Sadie, we need you!" Sally yelled from amidst a cluster of guys. "We're not kickin' butt anymore."

Amos froze.

"Can't do, Sal. This rich kid from Denver's taking me out for steaks," Sadie shouted back.

"Work up an appetite, then," a taunt from Brian Lofley.

Sadie shook her head, looked at Amos. "What's wrong, Jerry?" His face had drained of color. "You got that Chinese food sickness again?"

Amos shook his head without reply. His eyes squinting at the team Sally James was playing with.

"Jerry? Planet Earth to Jerry Moran."

"I'm sorry...I just..." He didn't know how to complete his thought without inviting trouble.

"You don't look so good," Sadie said.

"No, I'm fine. I just thought I saw someone I knew from Hibbing," he lied. His slip of the tongue was lost in the moment. "That tall kid over there. The one with the tossle-cap." Amos was positive that he was looking at the young man from Friday night. The one who killed the transient on Aspen.

"Troy? Troy Tomlinson? I went to high school with Troy. Or, as he would say, 'Sadie Kearney was in *my* class'—everything with Troy is ego-centered. God's gift to women and all creatures great and small. Once you can accept that, he's okay I guess. And, he's rich."

"Troy Tomlinson. Reminds me of a kid named Murphy. Anyhow, he's rich, huh?" Amos would try to soft-peddle his identity issue and regain his lost composure. "How so?"

"His folks, his step-father mostly, own a big chunk of Flag, the rest belongs to the Babbitt's."

"Babbitts? Who—?"

Sadie laughed, "That question, my friend, would tell anybody that you don't have clue number one about this town." She explained that Flagstaff was Babbitt country—politically, economically, and in most every way imaginable.

"Do you know what attracts me to you, Jerry?"

Every time Sadie called him Jerry, and that was often, he felt a twinge deep inside. A hurting twinge. A guilty twinge. He was Amos, and he didn't have the courage to tell her or anybody else. How could he continue to live with his lying? Sadie deserved an honesty he just couldn't give her. At least, not now.

"Are you interested?"

"What? Sorry."

"I just asked you to guess why I'm mildly, *just mildly*, attracted to you, Jerry Moran?"

"My charm. My sense of humor. My intelligence. My good looks. My athleticism, which I haven't told you about, yet. I can go on, but it's probably my modesty more than any of the above."

"You hide 'all of the above' quite well, Mr. Moran. Seriously, there are two things... First, you have the most alluring eyes. I see an honesty, and an innocence, I think. And something else. Eyes that, when you're not looking directly at me, are troubled about something. There is a mystery about them."

"Wow! That analysis almost makes me feel naked." Amos tried to laugh but failed miserably. "Troubled?"

"Somehow I think that I'll get a better read on that later. I think you're going to open up, gradually."

"I haven't opened up?"

"No. I'm sure of that. We're in the early stages of...of whatever? Being cute and clever and careful, you know. That's okay. It's supposed to be that way."

Amos could not respond to that. Sadie was a woman of alluring depth, a perception beyond her years. He had no doubt that she would 'open him up' and deeply afraid that she would not like what she saw. "Okay, my mesmerizing eyes. What else, Miss Kearney? You said *two* things..."

"I didn't say mesmerizing. But...the second thing attracts me, and frightens me, both at the same time. Jerry, I like that you are not from Flagstaff. That you don't know anything about what's gone on here before—what, less than a week ago? And that means you have no idea about the star-crossed Kearneys. Yet, it scares me that one of these days you will."

Amos frowned in puzzlement.

"That's all for now. Let's get my hamburger and fries. I'll take a rain check on the steaks you promised."

"What steaks?"

Sadie only winked.

CHAPTER 16/ HALF-TRUTHS

The Beaver Street restaurant's rustic decor wasn't fancy but the place wasn't crowded either. They found a table in a corner near a window. The red-and-white checkered oilcloth table covering was stained from years of candle drippings and the wooden floors were well worn.

Conversation between them had been almost non-stop, yet Amos believed he was doing most of the talking. Sadie had asked him why he came here—to Flagstaff. He was honest. Without getting too choked up, he explained the trauma of his parents' splitting up. "I was really messed up when I got here," he admitted. "But...with everything so different—especially the mountains—I realized that this might be a place where I could really start over."

Sadie puzzled over what Jerry had just said but kept her question inside. Jerry came from mountains! Why would they be anything *different*?

"Anyhow, I really got into blaming everything that wasn't right with me on them. Convenient, wouldn't you say?" Amos didn't wait for any response as he continued purging his soul. Telling another person helped him get a more realistic perspective. "They never *really* explained what happened between them. So, that left me to figure things out for myself. That's always bothered me more than they could ever know."

"What did you figure out for yourself, Jerry?"

Amos fingered his bearded chin almost nervously. "I really got negative about it all. The one thing that struck me most was probably... probably their selfishness more than anything. They both were more into themselves than each other—the 'I' replaced the 'we', or something like that. Dad was spending more time away from the house and Mom was getting more into her shell. They weren't talking like they used to. So, I began a separation of my own. My rebellion, I guess." He explained how he gradually withdrew during his senior year: different friends, going to beer parties (he called 'keggers'), dropping hockey his senior year. "...But I kept my grades up through it all."

Sadie nodded, reading the pain in Jerry's recollections. A logical trailer to the topic of parents would be *her turn* to divulge family secrets of her own; something she did not yet want to do. She shifted the gist, "...Was your senior year a bummer, Jerry?"

"Not really, some of it was actually fun. I had a small role in the spring play—we did *Jesus Christ Superstar*—and that was a blast." He laughed at the memory, "So, among all my many, many talents...I'm also an accomplished tenor."

"Did you have a solo?"

"No. And, truth be told, I only had five lines." Amos winced at what he had just said. *Truth be told!* How honest was he prepared to be? There had been some obvious gaps in his explanation of the parent issues he'd explained moments before. And Sadie was a perceptive young woman.

An awkward silence passed between them—their first all day. Amos could almost see the wheels of thought turning in Sadie's mind.

Sipping her Coke, Sadie tried to put Jerry's confusing story into a readable pattern. She hated to put him on the defensive, but there were gray areas nagging at her curiosity. "What did your parents think about all this? I mean, taking off to Flag like you did?"

The dreaded question was finally staring Amos in the face. *Truth be told*, he reminded himself. Yet, he did not want to paint himself into a corner from where it would require another network of lies to get him out. A *half-truth* was the best he could do. "I didn't tell them where I was going. I guess I kinda just took off." He would not go into his elaborately contrived scheme. Not yet.

"You ran away? Without telling them? Why, Jerry?" Sadie's questions had an icy coating to them.

"What can I say? I don't have a good answer; and believe me; I struggle with that question every day. So much so that I've been giving myself headaches over it." Amos was being honest and, in doing so, only feeding Sadie's growing confusion. "Maybe I'm a coward when it comes to my parents—especially my dad. Maybe I should have been up-front and just told them 'I'm taking off on my own for a while'...but I couldn't do it that way. They probably would have talked me out of what I really *had* to do. I didn't want to have to explain myself."

Amos remembered when his friend, Buddy Novak, had learned that his girlfriend had been cheating on him. Buddy didn't confront her at all. He simply dropped out of high school and enlisted in the Marines. Bold and audacious: case closed! Amos didn't have the guts to do anything so dramatic. "I just did what I thought I had to do," he shrugged.

"You didn't want to hurt them?" Sadie met his eyes. "Is that it, Jerry?"

"I'm sure that's part of it. Jeeze, I honestly don't really know. Sometimes I think that I didn't want to hurt them by laying my feelings out on the table and at other times I believe that hurting them was the biggest part of my running away. Does that make any sense at all?"

Sadie nodded in half-belief. She would let him off the hook for now. "I really hope you figure it all out, Jerry. For everybody's sake." Sadie resolved to let the matter rest until Jerry brought it up again. If he had issues—*everybody* had issues!

"I hope so, too." Amos reached over the table and found Sadie's hands, smiled weakly. "Now it's your turn. Tell me about your family and your high school stuff."

The pizza they had ordered was delivered and their pitcher of Coke refilled. Sadie talked about Flag High. She had been a cheerleader as a sophomore, she quit that in her junior year, "rah-rah Eagle cuties is what we really were" and our teams usually lost. She had lettered in gymnastics, was on the yearbook staff, and participated on the speech team. "Which explains why I am so eloquent and articulate, Jerry." She went to the Senior Prom with Brian Lofley, and Sally James had been her best friend for years.

Amos listened intently. "If you could describe yourself in one word, Sadie...what might that be?"

Sadie considered the question, stroked her lower lip as she mused for a long minute. "I think I would say *uncomplicated*. Yes. I keep my life on an even keel for the most part. Ups and downs are upsetting to me."

Amos liked her answer. Everything about what he had shared concerning himself had given an opposite impression. His life at the moment was just about as complicated as a jigsaw puzzle. He smiled, "My life's going to find an 'even keel' one of these days. I'm an optimist at heart."

Amos plucked a slice of pepperoni from an uneaten wedge of pizza. "Tell me more about Sadie Kearney."

She laughed at the recall of their first meeting. "You must have thought that I was some kind of wacky extrovert. I mean the way I approached you on the street the other night. What was it I said, 'What'cha up to, good-lookin'?" Then she giggled almost uncontrollably and blushed as she did so. "I've never done anything like that before in my life. That's the honest truth, Jerry. I don't know what came over me."

Amos joined her mirth of the moment and confessed that he nearly stumbled on the curb when she first sidled up next to him. He explained that he was, like her, an inhibited person by nature and would probably have spent the night hanging out with the guys at the bar if she hadn't taken the risk of introducing herself. They talked about social conventions and personal hang-ups and the difficulty of meeting people you wanted to meet and the awkwardness of dating and how foolish it was to get too uptight over 'what other people might think'.

Sadie relaxed in the comfort of Jerry's conversation and even more in his easy presence. Big parts of his life might be in turmoil right now but his sense of humor and mature perspective would somehow get him through the issues he wanted to resolve. He knew how to laugh, smiled often, and was getting a clear grip on who he really was. She had a feeling that she might become a part of the healing process that Jerry needed. She hoped she could be.

Her contentment was bolstered by the reality that, in their two hours together, Sadie had successfully kept her family in the closet.

17/ PACK AND MADDIE

"This really feels weird," Maddie said. "I haven't seen you in weeks and now we're planning to take off for 'who knows where?' together. I'm scared, too." Her laugh rang hollow. Maddie hadn't slept all night. "Did you call Mom and Dad?"

"We talked until after midnight last night."

Mom and Dad were Angela and Kevin Moran. To Maddie, her in-laws were more like parents than her estranged biological ones: Her mother Maureen lived in the Cities and her remarried father Shaun in Sacramento. Maddie seldom spoke with either of her parents and saw them less. In marrying Patrick (Pack's given first name) she became a part of one of Hibbing's most prominent families. The Morans had been movers and shakers in the community since it's earliest days.

"What did they have to say?" Maddie asked as Pack loaded her suitcase into the trunk.

"It was kinda strange, Maddie. Dad got really choked-up, had to pass the phone to Angie. Mom was cool, almost analytical. They both blame us, of course, but wouldn't say as much."

Maddie nodded knowingly.

Conversation between them was tight and constrained for the first two hours— from Hibbing to Hinckley. So much so that Pack turned on the radio south of Floodwood. When they did talk; they talked about Amos. Hidden below the surface, however, were feelings that each of them had been unprepared to deal with for much too long. If, at some point in this trip, they could finally shed their stifling and prideful inhibitions, maybe an honest dialogue could surface between them. Hopefully, this was both opportunity and destiny.

More than anything, Pack wanted to heal the hurt in Maddie's heart and assure her that his love had never faltered despite the painful separation.

And, for her part, Maddie wanted Pack to know about her *walls*: how she needed his hands to break them down. But to do so...gently, patiently, lovingly.

As they pulled into Tobies in Hinckley, Maddie began to cry. "Do you realize that most of what we've said about our son has been past tense? Amos *was* this or that... Pack, it's almost as if we're thinking he's gone for good. I feel terrible."

Pack tried to reassure, "He's fine. I don't have a doubt in the world about it. But, maybe you're right; we've been talking like a pair of pessimists. No more of that, okay?"

"And no more crying—I promise, Pack," Maddie dabbed her tears. After fixing her mascara and applying fresh lipstick, she smiled. "No more crying," she repeated with a resolute smile.

They had lunch south of the Cities where Pack called Chief Sundval at Hibbing police headquarters. He briefly explained what was going on. The Chief told him to "take as much time as you need" and asked that he call in every day or so. After BLT's and coffee, Maddie suggested that she drive the next stretch of highway: "A couple of hours so you can take a break," she offered.

The next miles were a quiet time, but a comfortable time nevertheless. Pack reclined his seat and relaxed as the agrarian countryside passed by. His thoughts followed his eyes as he watched Maddie at the wheel. Her long hair, slender arms, delicate hands. A glint of sun caught her diamond wedding ring. A smile of reality crossed his tired features; *she's still my wife*...despite everything, she's still my wife. And, there were sexual thoughts as well. How long had it been? More than a year. He visualized her naked and felt a stirring. The smile was lost in regrets. Somehow, he was more determined at this moment than he could ever remember...somehow, he was going to win her back. Pride was his bane and he knew it. To admit 'I was wrong' had always been much too hard for him. No more! Pack realized he could not have a meaningful life without love, and he knew the love he needed was sitting only inches away.

Maddie surrendered the wheel to Pack after a coffee and restroom stop north of Des Moines. It was approaching nightfall and both were tired. "How much further are we going to push?" Maddie asked.

Heading west, they would be facing the last hour of sun: "You know me well enough, Maddie. I'll drive all night if you don't tell me when to stop."

She laughed, "Caffeine and adrenalin will only take us so far; let's just not overdo it, Pack. We've got a long trip ahead."

On West I-80, there were more trucks than cars. Pack set the Old's cruise control at seventy-five and stayed in the left lane. Miles were quickly swallowed.

Maddie slipped back into the contemplative mood she had enjoyed during her driving time. She liked the fact that Pack was comfortable in the absence of conversation between them. It would have been difficult for each of them to try to manufacture superficial dialogue. Strangely, her thoughts of the past hour were more focused on Pack than on Amos. She smiled inwardly: He still wore his wedding ring. As difficult as the past year had been for her, the thought of divorce had seldom crossed her mind. Maybe...maybe that would be the critical foreshadowing: If either of them were to remove their rings—?

With her eyes on his strong hands came memories. It had been a long time but she could still remember those hands caressing her. Pack had always been a sensitive lover, a patient lover—concerned with her satisfaction. There was a nostalgic heat to her thoughts as she wondered what might happen between them over the next days. She swallowed the tormenting 'what ifs'—it would have to be a perfect situation. Maddie hoped that her husband had not lost that creative touch of making *things* happen.

Pack reached over for her left hand to give her an assurance that he was still doing fine. He missed her hand; touched her thigh instead. An awkward moment for both. "Sorry..." Pack said. Embarrassed, he fumbled for the radio volume button on the radio

Maddie smiled, said nothing. If only he had been reading her thoughts. Then, maybe he had. Maybe his thoughts and hers were on the same wavelength.

"Let's try to get just beyond Omaha," Pack said. "Then call it a day."

Maddie wondered, 'then what?'. She bit unconsciously at her lip. Then what? She guessed that Omaha was still another hour away. "That's fine with me, Pack. It's you I'm worried about. Don't overdo it for my sake."

Pack smiled at her concern, "I'm doing fine." In the back of his thoughts, however, he realized that time on the highway only prolonged the inevitable overnight stop. How awkward was that going to be? Would it be separate beds or separate rooms?

The deejay on an Omaha station said, "I used to be indecisive, but now I'm not sure." Maddie laughed. Pack laughed, too. It was like ice breaking between them. "Where does a forest ranger go to 'get away from it all'?" he continued. Maddie threw her head back and laughed even heartier. She loved to laugh—needed to laugh. "Give a man a fish and he will eat for a day. Teach him *how* to fish, and he will sit in a boat and drink beer all day." For two minutes they both laughed. Maddie turned off the radio, "I wish I could thank that guy. He really gave me something I've needed all day."

"Both of us, Maddie."

It was dark and quiet on I-80. Maddie began to doze. Her head fell onto Pack's shoulder. Just like old times, Pack thought. The best times of his life. Only the two of them going somewhere together. Anywhere. How deeply he loved this woman. Could he possibly tell her that?

Pack's eyes were heavy when he spotted the exit ramp at York, Nebraska. It was nearly eleven and they had traveled well over seven hundred miles that day. Maddie stirred as Pack braked the Oldsmobile in front of the flashing neon motel sign. Pack went inside and returned in five minutes.

Maddie was nervous, "Where are we, Pack? I've been half-sleeping."

"A little town called York." Pack explained that he was too tired to go any farther. "How are you feeling?"

"Pretty wiped out." Maddie forced a smile. "You've got us a room?"

Pack took her hand and helped her out of the car. "Believe me, this is pretty awkward, Maddie. But I think I know what we should do." He held out his hand, "Take your pick." Pack had two separate room keys.

"Thanks, sweetheart," she gave him a kiss on the cheek.

'FLAG'

By eight the following morning—Labor Day— the two well-rested travelers were heading west from York, Nebraska toward Denver.

18/ *LABOR DAY*

Amos slept late on Labor Day morning. As he lay in bed he remembered the day before. Was it possible to be so much in love— so fast? He met Sadie on Friday night, spent most of Sunday with her, and now, less than sixty hours later, he was totally smitten with Sadie Kearney. He thought of their plans for that afternoon. Sadie wanted to take him hiking on Mount Elden, a peak in the San Francisco Range to the east of town. A trail the locals called ''Fat Man's Loop' she told him. She would borrow her father's car and pick him up about one o'clock by McMahan's Furniture store on the corner of Aspen and Leroux.

Questions passed through his thoughts. Would he show her his grungy apartment at some point that day? Would they make out? He had kissed her for the first time when they said 'good night' the night before. A brief kiss, but so wonderfully remembered this morning. How did she feel about him? Really? He was certain that she liked him a lot—but?

How long would he keep up this charade? When would he feel safe enough here in Flagstaff, and with her? She had told him that she saw 'trouble' in his eyes. And, honesty, too. How many lies had he told Sadie already? Hundreds? When would *Jerry* slip up? Or better, when would *Amos* confess? Last night he had come dangerously close to tripping over some of his lies. And every time she called him *Jerry* he felt a pang of guilt.

As troubled as he was about a relationship based upon his deceptions, something else was bothering him even more. He had witnessed a murder. He was almost positive who had killed the man across the street.

Troy Tomlinson. An old friend of Sadie's. A rich kid from a prominent Flagstaff family. Who would ever believe it? He thought of the cop, DeJarlais. And a man named Sam Yazzie, sitting in jail right now. What was Amos going to do about all that?

Amos decided to do something he had often done before when he was deeply troubled. When his dog had been run over by a car. When a favorite teacher had died unexpectedly from an aneurysm. When his mother had told him about the *issues* that she and his dad had to work out. When their separation tore his stomach apart. When, late in his senior year, he decided to run away from everything that had been his life of eighteen years. In those, and other times, Amos found the solitude and holy aura of the Blessed Sacrament Church to be ideal for the meditation his spirit craved.

At the Assumption Catholic School, Amos had a fourth grade teacher named Sister Lucy. The diminutive Nun was easily the most spiritual person Amos had ever encountered. Her classroom was adorned with an assortment of pictures and knickknacks of various angels. And, the stories she could tell about them. Vivid stories of the Archangels— Michael and Gabriel— and of our 'Guardian Angel'; all of them miraculous and profoundly believable stories. Amos learned from Sister Lucy that his special angel would always be there for him...always!' There was a deep comfort in the faith Sister Lucy inspired.

On this Labor Day morning, Amos needed to talk to his angel.

~

"Captain DeJarlais, my name is Amos Moran," his voice was tight and trembled with pent emotion. "I need to talk to you."

Rudy DeJarlais had been playing catch with his teenage son in the back yard of their home on Turquoise Drive near McPherson Park when his wife,

Theresa, called him to the phone. He was tempted to tell her to get the caller's name and say that he'd get back later. Cops were always on call—holidays were no exception.

"Just a minute, Tee," he used his wife's familiar nickname.

Rudy overthrew the spiraling football, "Todd, back in two minutes," he told his son.

DeJarlais could recognize youth in the voice, and a measure of trepidation as well. "Can we do this on the phone?"

A long pause, "I'd much rather meet you in person, sir."

"What's this about, son?"

Rudy DeJarlais waited in the back booth of Dee Dee's where he and Begay had met with Heebie Henton on Saturday morning. It was Rudy's favorite place to have 'out of the office' conversations. Moran? The name was Irish, but not a familiar one in Flagstaff. The veteran officer knew nearly everyone in this growing community of more than thirty thousand. Rudy guessed the young man was an NAU student.

When Amos shook his hand and sat down across the table, DeJarlais waved to the waitress who brought another coffee cup, refilled his, and left a large, black decanter. The young man was good-looking, athletically built, and had the firm handshake of masculine influence.

"I'm scared as hell, sir." Were Amos' first words. "I'm new here...in Flagstaff, sir."

Rudy smiled, "Relax, son—Amos. For a cop, I'm a pretty easy guy to get along with. Where you from?" He knew better than to touch the nerve of what had precipitated this meeting right away. 'Know who you're talking to' was a simple credo and one that Rudy always followed. Tell me a little about yourself, Amos."

"Jeeze...it's a long story, are you sure...?" Amos spilled it all out. It took nearly fifteen minutes to explain his parents separation, running away from Hibbing, and some of the lies along the way. "What makes all this even more difficult, sir, is that my dad's a cop—like you, I'd imagine. I would be surprised if he's not out there somewhere right now, looking for me." He cleared his throat, "I hope that you will not involve him in this...this mess...for right now, anyhow. I really need to handle some things on my own."

DeJarlais looked up from his coffee, met Amos with a level gaze. Be careful of promises, he thought. "Amos, I can't promise you anything, except that we can talk in confidence, and that I'll protect you. That's the same level playing field I would give to anybody."

Amos liked the man. He was sure that his father would have said something similar. "Okay, I guess." He swallowed hard, "Last Friday night I met some friends at the 'L.Q.' and got home before twelve..." Amos explained everything he saw in careful detail. As he spoke, Amos could feel the intensity of DeJarlais's focus. The cop had steel-blue eyes that reminded him of Paul Newman—*Cool Hand Luke* was one of his favorite movies. "I'll never forget that tossle-cap," he concluded. He poured another cup of coffee, lit a cigarette, "Yesterday a girl friend of mine and I were walking around the campus..."

When Amos mentioned the name, Troy Tomlinson, he noticed that DeJarlais flinched. "It was the identical cap, sir; and the same tallish, lanky frame that I just described. I'm almost positive."

DeJarlais had been taking notes as Amos spoke. He underlined "almost positive" and flipped to a clean page, scribbled a capital 'Q' and 'A' at the top. "Let's start with the cap you mentioned. That's what really triggered your 'suspicions'—is that the right word, suspicions?"

Amos nodded with deliberate hesitation at the word DeJarlais used.

"The cap you've described might have been an NAU tossle. If that's the case, there may be a hundred of them out there."

"I've never seen one, sir."

"Take my word for it, Amos. I think my son has one somewhere in his closet at home. And at night you probably couldn't determine any colors or characteristics. Right?"

Amos nodded negative.

"Anyhow, the assailant was wearing a trench coat, or something similar—did I get that correct."

"Yes, sir. Dark-colored."

"Have you ever seen a similar-looking coat?"

"Oh, yes, sir. Lots of times."

"Nothing unusual about the coat, then?"

Amos could feel his story unraveling. He felt stupid and wanted to get out of there. "And, next you're going to ask how I could be certain that, under a trench coat, the assailant was tall and slender, right?"

"Is that a fair question, Amos? Look, I'm not your adversary and I'm not trying to trip you up. Everything you've told me seems honest. I've got a good sense for that. But—?" DeJarlais let the word hang between them.

Feeling defeated, Amos nodded, "I know what you mean, sir. I did not see anyone's face—not the guy with the knife, or either of his two friends. I didn't even see the knife for that matter. But, I'll swear on a stack of Bibles that the man who's being held, Mr. Yazzie, was not the perpetrator you're looking for. I'm positive of that. Absolutely."

"Do you know Sam? Can you describe him?"

Amos gave the description given to him by the old man in the Weatherford Hotel lobby the day before.

DeJarlais nodded. "I can't argue with that. Sam's not tall or lanky by any stretch. And, even from a distance, it would be hard not to recognize that pony tail of his."

Troy Tomlinson and Sam Yazzie were as different as cats from dogs and lived in two *very* different worlds.

19/ FISH

DeJarlais stopped by headquarters before returning home for what he hoped might be an uninterrupted remainder of the holiday afternoon with his family. He was troubled. The Tomlinson kid was a spoiled jerk; the son of an obnoxious and overbearing stepfather. Harold Tomlinson had made his sizable fortune in real estate. If Troy used drugs there was a possible link to the victim. But, how could there be any legitimate motive for *stealing* drugs when he could buy anything his spoiled heart desired? Much less pulling a knife on a dealer. He called Andy Platt, the department's best source of information on kids and drugs.

"He hangs with Brian Lofley, Rudy— another one of the rich and privileged. I think Brian was picked up once, a couple of years ago, with paraphernalia and a small amount of pot. Not certain, though. Might have been the James kid that the two of them hang around with. Nothing on record, I'm sure. Danny Olson is with those guys sometimes. He's bad news. I wouldn't be surprised if our young Mr. Tomlinson was a user from time to time. Speed, I'd guess." Platt, however, was concerned for the Captain. "Rudy, I don't know if you really want to go there. Troy would be a can of worms for you. Tomlinson and his old man! God Almighty, the Chief would shit his pants. Let me run Troy's name by 'Fish'." He laughed, "I know what you're going to say, Cap."

'FLAG'

Fish was Don Fisher, a veteran cop that DeJarlais and Begay were sometimes saddled with. The overweight, always amiable glad-hander, was much despised by most of those who knew him. It was common knowledge that Fish was an incompetent and an ass-kisser who had Chief Roth's ear and sometimes socialized with the City Council folks. "That numbskull! Don't bother trying to call him, Andy, I saw him down the hall a few minutes ago. I can check with him myself."

"I only mention Fish because he had campus supervision all summer, saw lots of the kids there."

"I know. It was the safest place to put him for three months—out of everyone's way."

"What's up, Captain?" Fish was up from his desk and thrusting his hand for DeJarlais to shake. "It's Labor Day for goodness sakes; you otta be home with Theresa and the kids." His face furrowed in apparent dismay over the Captain's missing deserved time off.

"You should be home, too, Don," DeJarlais said with a tinge of sympathy. Home for Fisher was a small apartment two blocks away where no family waited on his return. The veteran officer was a sad case. He was not pulling a scheduled duty yet here he was in full uniform with a crisply starched shirt and a tie knotted tightly about the fleshy folds of his substantial neck.

"Paperwork, Boss," Fisher said as he sat and leaned back in his chair. "Nothing to do at home," he added.

DeJarlais nodded understandingly, explained that he needed some scoop on a group of college kids. He fabricated a story about some vandalism late on Friday night. "Lady that called it in said she saw some college kids smoking pot near the property that was damaged. Hasn't been checked out yet. Anyhow, she gave us some names to look into. I thought that you're having been on the campus all summer might be of some help."

Fish nodded, feeling as if his boring three-month assignment might prove to be of some value after all. "Yeah, kept everything on the straight and narrow over there, too."

"Any of these names fit with pot smokers, potential trouble-makers— he rattled off several, including Troy Tomlinson."

Without much thought, Fish shook his head. "None of those guys. Good kids, Captain. Except for that Olson, Danny. He's a bad apple. These others here—Jeeze, they're some of our best." Fisher was puzzled but tried not to show it. He knew the Captain held him in low esteem. What was DeJarlais looking for? The alleged vandalism hadn't been investigated yet—three days after the fact—and wasn't the kind of matter that would bring the Captain into the office on a holiday.

DeJarlais low expectations of Fisher were surpassed by the cop's glowing response on the kids in question. "Just thought I'd check, Don."

Back in his office, DeJarlais poured over the notes from his conversation with Amos. He should call Troy Tomlinson but the phone staring at him was uninviting. If he was going to go fishing this afternoon, he'd have to open that 'can of worms'. "Damn!" A part of him would enjoy humbling that smart ass kid, and another part of him could see bright red flags fluttering before his eyes.

He would wait a few minutes, or until tomorrow. Undecided on what to do, DeJarlais decided to make a quick visit to Sam Yazzie's cell downstairs. He slipped his notebook into the top desk drawer before leaving the office. He passed Fish's open door, "Gonna go down and see how Yazzie's doing. Back in a few."

'FLAG'

Don Fisher was a snoop and a fink. He mused again, DeJarlais wouldn't be wasting a holiday afternoon visiting with the wino Indian...or checking on potheads and a vandalism report. Unless the vandalism was something far more serious than DeJarlais had reported. What was really going on?

DeJarlais would be away from his desk for a while—and Fish was awfully curious. The more he knew the better he might be able to help. There was nothing on the Captain's desk but the top drawer was not tightly closed. Perhaps the vandalism report was inside.

∼

Arlen Begay was passing the Birch Street station house and noticed Rudy's car parked out front. "What's he doing here this afternoon?" he mumbled to himself. He'd stop in and check. As he approached DeJarlais' office in the back of the overcrowded building, he caught a glimpse of Don Fisher slipping inside Rudy's office. Strange, DeJarlais despised the guy. At the open office door, Begay peeked inside without being noticed. Fish was rifling through Rudy's notebook splayed open on the Captain's desk. Where was Rudy? What was Fish up to?

Begay quietly walked back down the hall and around a corner. When Fish left the Captain's office, Begay bumped into him as if he had just come in from outside. "'S'cuse me, Fish... I'm lookin' for Rudy," he said.

"Downstairs with Yazzie," Fish blurted as he hurried past.

"Sam, I don't have to tell that you're in deep shit," DeJarlais said to the stocky Navajo. "I really want to believe your story about the money, but—?"

Earlier, Yazzie had explained that the money he was throwing around was a birthday gift from his sister, Betty, in Winslow. He stuck with the story through three hours of questioning the day before. Betty Yazzie had been contacted and confirmed that she sent him a check, but refused to

[112]

divulge any amount. "Quite a bit", was all she said. DeJarlais would follow up on that with the bank tomorrow. And Yazzie had stuck with his story about passing out in his apartment from late afternoon until nearly midnight on Friday. Living alone in a place off an alley, nobody had been found who could corroborate that flimsy alibi.

Sam Yazzie was stuck between a rock and a hard place. He knew his story would begin leaking like a sieve before too long. He knew even better that he would do serious time if he admitted to mugging the old woman on Friday afternoon. And, if that wasn't bad enough, he was looking at death row...or life in prison for the murder of Donuts Evering. One thing was certain, he had not murdered anybody, he would have to take his chances.

"Honest to God, I din't kill that guy, Captain. I din't even know him." Sam Yazzie, hung his big, pony-tailed head and cried. "I know I been in some fights cuz of my temper...but I ain't a murderer."

Sam had thought about his dismal circumstance for hours that day and the night before. Maybe he should tell DeJarlais that he found the purse in a trashcan. His sister Betty would do anything for him, including lying—but, she didn't have the kind of money that he had squandered at Joe's Place. If DeJarlais didn't already know that, he would find out soon enough.

"I only stopped by to see if you wanted to tell me truth, Sam. That's all. I hate to think of you spending the rest of your life rotting in prison. But we've got a corpse, and we think he had a wad of cash on his person, and we've got you—with a record of violent behavior— spending all that money that I think you're still lying about. Like I said, Sam—it spells deep shit any way you look at it!"

Sam rubbed the dirty sleeve of his denim shirt across his eyes, he didn't want to put Betty through a wringer. "Okay... I'll tell ya the truth 'bout that money, Captain." He related the story about finding a brown leather purse in a trashcan behind a white stucco house in the alley behind Hunt Avenue. "The purse is probably still there," he told DeJarlais.

"Can I talk to you for a minute, Rudy," Begay said from the doorway where he had been listening to Yazzie's story. He would tell Fish to check out the trashcans behind Hunt Avenue that afternoon. No garbage had been hauled over the holiday weekend. The purse, if was there, might belong to the Brown woman who lived a few blocks west of Hunt. "We'll look into that, Sam. Meantime, I need to visit with the Captain. You finished here, Rudy?"

DeJarlais put a hand on Yazzie's square shoulder, "Think about things, Sam...we've gotta see the judge tomorrow. Mayor Erwin is giving us a lot of heat, he wants this murder business cleared up by the end of the week.

Out in the hallway, DeJarlais said, "Strange as it might seem, I can't help feeling sorry for Sam. He's right on the edge of telling us the truth but can't quite get over it yet."

Begay nodded, still preoccupied with what he had witnessed upstairs. "You have Fish doing something for you in your office, Rudy?"

DeJarlais gave his friend a puzzled look, "What are you talking about, Arlen?"

Don Fisher had left the station without telling the desk clerk where he was going.

20/ ALIBI

When Troy Tomlinson hung up the phone his face was drained of color. The 'Fisherman's' call had sent a chill up his spine. "Brian, someone saw us!" He and Brian Lofley were playing pool in the spacious Tomlinson rec room. "Fish just called."

Lofley's mouth dropped. He and Marty James had been reluctant associates in Troy's crazy scheme to score some speed. A simple mugging that went awry. On Thursday night, the three boys found Donuts Evering where they had always found him. But Evering said *no* that night. He told them to find someone else. "I'm not selling anymore," Donuts said, "so get the hell outta here and don't come back."

Enraged, Tomlinson told his pals, "I'll get that son-of-a-bitch." The next night he did just that. Neither Brian nor Marty knew what Troy meant by 'getting that son-of-a-bitch'.

The three of them had been cruising in Troy's GTO sipping McDonald's coffee stiffened with Jack Daniels. They had planned to finish the Friday night with some beers at Bozo's Bus Stop downtown. Tomlinson spilled his coffee on the front of his shirt and wanted to go home and change clothes. He grabbed Brian's trench coat in the back seat instead. When Troy spotted Donuts Evering near the Orpheum alleyway he said, "Payback time, guys." They parked the car and Troy went into the trunk for something.

"Fuck! I can't believe it." Troy pulled out a Camel, lit up, and tossed the spent match toward an ashtray. "Somebody saw us."

"What are you talkin' about? Who the hell—? Those goddamn drunks never even woke up and there wasn't a soul on the street."

"Yeah, or so we thought. You know anybody by the name of Amos—Amos Moran? He's the one that saw us. Fish said that Moran talked to DeJarlais this morning. He got a glimpse of some notebook that DeJarlais has." Tomlinson cracked his cue against the side of the table in a fit of rage. "Fuck!"

"Moran?" Lofley shrugged.

"According to Fish he's from somewhere in fuckin' Minnesota. A student here, he thinks. He didn't have but a minute to see the notes. But Rudy asked Fish some questions about kids doin' drugs and raising hell in someone's yard on Friday night. Both our names came up. He thinks Rudy was bullshiting about the drugs though."

"My name came up!" Brian blurted. "Look, Troy, you know damn well—"

"Shut your fuckin' face, Bry," Tomlinson raged. Troy had a short fuse and a violent streak that went with it. He could be the greatest guy in the world one minute and an absolute psycho the next. "They probably don't have shit for evidence."

"They've got our fuckin' names, Troy. And they got a witness." Brian picked up a striped ball and whipped it across the room. "So what the hell *you* gonna do?"

"You mean, what are *we* going to do, Bry. Don't forget that—it was three of us."

"Yeah, three of us who were going to knock over the bastard for some stuff—not stab the fucker! That was your out-of-control goddamn temper. Me and Marty—"

Troy grabbed Brian's shirt, then let go. The impulse to shake his friend almost set him off. Almost. Troy knew *his problem*. The memory of that Friday night flashed through his thoughts. *Had he really meant to kill Evering?* Troy wasn't sure. At first thought, he had wanted to use the knife to establish his dominance over the despicable wino—but then he went berserk. For that fraction of a moment, Troy tasted a power he had never imagined: The power of life or death! "Listen, Donuts was a piece of shit, Bry. Nobody's gonna get hot and bothered over one less bum on the fuckin' street. Sunday paper said they've got a suspect in jail, some fuckin' drunk Indian."

Brian smoothed his shirt without comment. Troy intimidated him.

"Hey, man, don't get your ass in a bundle. Troy's gonna take care of things. Like he always does. I didn't hear any complaints from you or Marty when we split up the stuff. Hell, now we're set for a few weeks."

Troy's parents were in Phoenix for the holiday weekend. They left Friday afternoon and were not expected back until the next day. Troy slid his bottom onto the velvet table, "Hell, we were all here on Friday night. From around ten until...must have been two or three in the morning. Remember?"

Lofley smiled. "Yeah, I remember. A bunch of us. Not just us three, maybe eight or ten of us, right?"

The two of them hatched their story and began making some phone calls. The two college students had several good friends: friends who would vouch for the pool, ping-pong, and beer party. Troy's plan was simple. They told their friends that both of them had a little drug issue with the local cops—"We really need an alibi for Friday night."

Troy got Marty James on the phone. "Listen up..." he rehashed the information from Fish. "No fuckin' way they're gonna pin anything on us, Marty. No way in hell."

Marty James, however, did not share Tomlinson's bravado. His mouth had gone dry. "Look Troy, I had nothing to do with stabbing Donuts; neither did Bry."

Tomlinson fumed, pointed a stiff finger at Lofley's chest: "You gonna be able to prove that, Marty? We're gonna hang together or hang separately on this. Got it? Don't think for a fuckin' minute that you're not up to your eyeballs in the same shit I'm in!"

Marty James knew that to be true. Nevertheless, he felt a cold chill of resentment at Troy's reprimand. He stifled a provoking 'Fuck you'. "Okay, we were at your place all night. I was with my sister." Sally James was in her bedroom down the hall, "Sis, come here a minute," he called toward her open door. "Troy wants to talk to you."

"No sweat, we had a blast." Tom Hudley remembered being there along with his girlfriend, Brenda Lewis. Gary Greisdorff wanted a stipulation, "I won the pool tournament, okay?" Jason Bonetto remembered passing out, "I was with you guys but I can't remember much of what happened."

Brian called the girl he had been dating off and on. Sadie Kearney wasn't at home. "Thought she was with you this afternoon, Brian," Sadie's father said. "Must be that Jerry kid she's been talking about. They went hiking up to Elden for the afternoon."

"Jerry? Who's that Mr. Kearney?"

"Moran, I think she said. He's new here, a college student...from out of town. I haven't met him yet. Maybe she'll bring him by the house later."

"Bingo!" Brian shouted toward Troy. "I think we've just put an ID on the witness Fish told you about." He explained.

21/ HIKING MT. ELDEN

Sadie pulled her father's Chevrolet station wagon off the interstate and parked on a dirt road below Mount Elden.

"No sweat," Amos said as he looked up toward the top of the treeless peak. "In Colorado we call these foothills."

Sadie laughed. "So, the macho mountain-climber won't really be challenged by any of this?"

Amos was dressed in Levi shorts, a long-sleeved t-shirt with 'Dylan' across the front, and wore an old pair of black tennis shoes. He resolved to buy a pair of hiking boots like Sadie was wearing when he found time next week. He'd need to replenish his wardrobe with more than a few items. Most of his few clothes were in an odorous laundry box at the apartment.

Amos regarded the dirt pathway, "Contrary to the spirit of this great American holiday, I'm not going to *labor* very much on this hill. I could probably jog my way to the top."

"You're so very clever, Mr. Moran."

Amos took her hand and pulled her close, "Being with you puts me more in the holiday spirit than I can ever remember." Back in Hibbing, where labor unions had always possessed real muscle, Labor Day was a time of picnics and parades. "It's going to be a great afternoon, Sadie."

"Darn... I forgot my water bottle." Shielding her eyes against the sun, Sadie shook her her head in frustration. "I never forget to bring water."

Amos gave her a buss on the cheek, "I have that effect on women—they tend to become so enraptured that they forget things."

"Give me a break," she laughed. "You have nothing to do with it. As you will come to realize, I'd forget my head if it wasn't attached."

Amos was determined to put his meeting with DeJarlais earlier that day in the deep-freeze of his thoughts. He had kicked himself all the way back to his apartment that morning. He would have been much better off if he had let everything run its course. But, he couldn't do that. He couldn't let that Yazzie fellow take a murder rap.

'FLAG'

"Jerry?"

"What?"

"I lost you for a minute. You do that, you know. Drift off."

Midway along the steepening trail fringed with clusters of prickly pear and agave cactus, Amos and Sadie found a small rock shelf to sit on. The view of Flagstaff strung out below was awesome. Sadie pointed out the neighborhood where she lived, north and east of the campus. "And that's the hospital over there...that's where I'll be taking you if you have a heart attack from exertion. You've been panting pretty hard the last few minutes."

"You misunderstand my panting, Sadie. It's not from thirst or exertion."

Sadie winked and laughed, "Raging hormones?"

Thirsty but not spent, they held hands, and talked about the beginning of classes the next morning: Schedules, teachers, work-study assignments, and things related to college. "It's so much different from high school, Jerry," Sadie said. "Lots of free time to do your own thing. Do you plan on getting involved in any activities? The college drama program is fantastic, and sports...you'll see, NAU has just about everything you can imagine."

The Northern Arizona University moniker and mascot was a burly, axe wielding, lumberjack. The Northern Arizona University Lumberjacks were a source of great community pride. The nickname fit with Flagstaff's early history as a bustling logging town with several lumber mills and a network of railroads.

The lumberjack, however, would prove to be the undoing of Amos Moran's charade that lovely September first afternoon.

Ironic, Amos thought as he considered trying out for the NAU baseball team in the spring. Hibbing had played hockey and baseball *against* 'Lumberjack' teams back home. Basking in the sun without a care in the world, he began rambling without much thought.

He told Sadie about a hockey game in Bemidji during his junior year when he scored the winning goal against the *Lumberjacks*. And then about getting three hits against the Cloquet *Lumberjacks*. As Amos expounded on his athletic exploits he failed to see the expression on Sadie's face at the mention of Cloquet.

Sadie's heart skipped a beat. Cloquet? Her thoughts shot back to the young man from a place called Carlton in Minnesota—a small dot next to Cloquet in her atlas. Her brother Mikey's infantry buddy was from a small town near Cloquet. And, Hibbing? Jerry had mentioned the strange name once before but she couldn't remember where or when. An unusual name. She had let it pass. She had never heard of any place named Bemidji. Cloquet was an unusual name, as well—perhaps they were suburbs in the Denver area. Perhaps?

Sadie had the strangest feeling. As wonderful as Jerry was...she realized that she didn't really know much about him yet. And some of what she did know—like his running away— was still nagging in the back of her thoughts. She chose not to probe the Hibbing thing right now, nor inquire about the Lumberjack teams that Jerry had mentioned, but she would do some homework later. A weird premonition swept through her, her mouth went suddenly dry, a chill ran down her spine. What if Jerry had been lying to her? The story of leaving Denver because of family issues was certainly a plausible one—even if his admitted cowardice was perplexing. And, kids from all over the country had chosen NAU here in Flagstaff for their college training. Yet, sometimes Sadie believed things because she wanted to believe them. It was always easier that way. Blind trust, however, could lead one down a dark road. Lost in her doubts, Sadie missed the recap of most of Jerry's alleged high school heroics.

"So, I'm thinking about trying out for the baseball team in the spring," His laugh was modest: "I've got all the pitches, you know, and play a wicked first base as well. And I'll bet that the altitude here will give me some extra pop with the bat."

Sadie startled. The altitude here? Surely she had heard him correctly. Denver wasn't much different from Flagstaff. What was Jerry talking about?

"Jerry...let's finish the hike. It's getting awfully hot and if we rest too long it's hard for us to get back at it."

Amos could see that her smile was unusual, unnatural—even her face seemed a little peaked. "Jeeze, I'm sorry. I've been yakking for nearly twenty minutes. You okay? The sun getting to you? We don't have to keep going if you've had enough." Her eyes had lost the spark of earlier in the afternoon. "Would you like to call it a day, Sadie?" Amos didn't know much about women, but he did know that there was *a time* in every month. He would be discrete. "We can do this again another time."

Sadie stood, "Maybe that would be a good idea, Jerry. I'm feeling kinda drained for some reason. Almost fluish. Probably dehydration."

When she pulled to the curb at the corner of Aspen and Leroux, Sadie did not turn off the ignition. Amos had the strange feeling that something had soured between them—and it wasn't dehydration or fatigue. Had he been too boastful? Boring? Sadie had hardly said a word on the drive back into town, and that was very unusual. When he leaned over to give her a peck on the cheek, her face turned away from him.

"If I've got a flu, it might be catchy," she said defensively.

Amos didn't quite know what to say. "Drink lots of water when you get home, Sadie, and take a nap. I'm sure that whatever it is...well, it'll go away with some rest. Will I see you tomorrow?"

"I'm sure, Jerry. Sorry about everything." Was all that she could say.

∼

Two pairs of eyes watched the bearded young man close the passenger door on the Kearney station wagon. As Sadie drove away, they watched Amos Moran enter the doorway leading upstairs of the furniture store on the corner.

∼

Sadie easily located Cloquet only a quarter inch west of Duluth on the Minnesota page of her atlas. There was a Hibbing north of Cloquet. Running her index finger in a circle over the may, it took only a minute to find a place called Bemidji in northwestern Minnesota—in the Mississippi Headwaters State Forest. The large Greene plots on the map suggested that the area was timber country.

What did all this mean?

Sadie wept. Amos was not from Denver. Her tears were shed in anger, disappointment, and betrayal. Why had she been duped? What was Jerry trying to do?

22/ *DENVER EXIT*

The odometer indicated that they had traveled nearly six hundred miles on their second day. Pack and Maddie were approaching the outskirts of Denver. Despite the grim purpose of their mission, it had been a wonderful Labor

Day. True to her promise, Maddie had not cried—even through some very difficult conversation.

For the first time in a year, or maybe in years, the two of them had opened up to each other. From the time they left York, Nebraska, a noticeable thaw began to melt the walls of ice that had grown between them. Both acknowledged their pettiness and pride, stubbornness and inflexibility—each admitting to an empty existence with periods of profound loneliness. "You will never know how many times I wanted to call you, Pack...late at night...and tell you how sorry I was."

"But you just couldn't do it..." He smiled, "And I was probably waiting by the phone for a call I knew would never come: All the time hoping that I could find that ounce of courage to call you. I have been miserable beyond words."

Pack found Maddie's hand, resting in her lap, this time. He gave it a squeeze. "Despite everything that's happened between us, Maddie, I want you to know that I've never stopped loving you." Pack's eyes moistened with his revelation. "And this time we're spending together, regardless of the circumstance, is almost heaven-sent. It's been like rediscovering the love that we had when we made our trip out west...maybe even better because of all the years we've shared since."

The two of them had traveled from Hibbing to Sacramento to find Maddie's estranged father back in the fall of 1956. Along the way, they had had made love for the first time and later became engaged. That trip had been the stuff of dreams for both of them.

Maddie felt a rush of emotion. It would be easy and honest for her to make a similar profession, but she couldn't do that *yet*. This conversation was as inevitable as it was necessary. For too long their issues had been mountains neither of them could climb by themselves: Someone had to be their guide. Now, Pack had conveniently placed the ball in her court. How to get it back over the net between them? In reminding her of the trip they had taken nearly twenty years before, Pack had brought her back to the most wonderfully romantic time in her life. How many times in the past two days had she remembered the two of them—back then? A thousand? But, this time, her traveling companion was a man without the trappings of mystery and infatuation that characterized their courtship times. The veneer had been stripped away with the years. There had been moments when her husband evidenced the Pack Moran of old: sensitive, perceptive, animated, and resolute—qualities that first attracted her to him. The aloofness, brooding, self-absorption, and bluster—traits she had come to resent—had been kept in check since leaving Hibbing. There were times, however, when she wondered how much of this 'mission' was about finding Amos, and how much was an ego-challenge for him. There were times when she had to question: Who is this man?

Maddie broke the uncomfortable silence. "Who do you love, Pack? Is it the Maddie you took to Sacramento, or the Maddie I am now? They are two different women, you know. One had starry-eyed dreams with a dash of derring-doo, the other has wrinkles about her eyes and some heavy baggage."

Pack smiled, "Very good, Maddie. I think you know how much I loved the woman that I chose to marry. At least I hope you do. But the Maddie with a few wrinkles and baggage is the one I am talking about. Over all these years, every time I said 'I love you' I was saying it to a different Maddie. And, each time—I realize now—the love I felt was stronger than the time before. So, my answer to your question is simply, and honestly, and deeply—I love *you*."

Maddie looked away from his eyes and out the window at the flat, featureless, landscape of western Nebraska. Her eyes were tearing. She wanted to say that she liked the Maddie of years ago more than the Maddie of this moment. But she couldn't say that. And it wasn't fair to be talking about feelings when the issues that had separated them—her 'walls' and his 'space'— remained unresolved. She dabbed at her eyes, cleared her throat. There were years of history to deal with.

"Pack... Do you remember the names of our unborn children?"

Pack felt a tightness in his stomach, his hands gripped the steering wheel. Where was Maddie coming from with a question like that? "Amos' sister would have been Meghan...his brother Michael. We had those names chosen from the start—as soon as we learned you were pregnant. Why?"

"Where were you when they died?"

Pack's lip quivered. On each tragic occasion he had been away: a fishing trip with some fellow cops and a Twins baseball game in the Cities. The flowers and cards he had given her afterwards proved to be small consolations. Pack, not quite knowing what else to do, allowed his wife to find her own means of coping with the disappointment. But, it was more than simply *disappointment* to Maddie. She became despondent, inconsolable, and slipped into a shell. Pack allowed her to live there. In time, things seemed to get back to normal. In retrospect, maybe they had not. They were his children, too—what was she getting at with her question? He was confounded, "Why are you asking me that, Maddie?" He repeated his question.

"Pack, a part of me died with each of them. I needed you more than you could ever know...and you were not there. After Michael, maybe *we*, maybe the two of us as a couple, died. I do know that I felt so terribly alone that I needed to build walls—walls to give me a feeling, I don't know...maybe a feeling of safety, or—?"

Pack turned off the highway, flipped on his flashers, and parked with the engine idling. Maddie was struggling with something so important that he could not drive through it. "Talk to me, sweetheart. I've done something terribly wrong without even being aware of it. And saying that 'I'm sorry' seems almost trite." He searched for something consoling to say. "I would never do anything deliberate to hurt you. Never! I just didn't know what to do. And you couldn't tell me what you wanted."

Maddie was touched by the sincerity of his words, the hurt in his eyes. This was the man she fell in love with so many years ago. And, the man that she had deliberately walled out of her life. Like everything that comes between two people, there is blame to be shared. She fell into his arms and allowed the pent emotions of years to pour out of her body. Anger, grief, and denial had built her walls...firm and gentle hands could tear them down. "Thank you," was all that Maddie could say.

Having opened their hearts and souls to each other, the drive across eastern Colorado was a time of healing. Problems that had undermined their relationship for so long were aired with honest concern, compassion, tenderness. Pack laughed at one point, "I had no idea! None at all. You never told me how much it bothered you." The issue that Maddie had raised was the 'cottage' where Pack had been living the past several months. The Bunker Road house had been Pack's residence during his bachelor days. He had never sold the place, and often went out there to be by himself. He claimed that he needed the refuge from stresses of work and life in general. He planted gardens every spring, fed the birds, took long walks along deer paths in the woods. Maddie hadn't understood the part of his psyche that, like that of his beloved father, craved occasional solitude. Seen from Maddie's perspective, Pack could apprehend the mixed messages his retreats sent. Maddie had perceived his house in the country as a need to separate himself from her and Amos.

And they talked about how difficult the honest sharing of feelings had become over times of routine every day living—the 'ruts' of married life.

On several occasions one or the other expressed "Why didn't you tell me?" or "If I had known..." Between them there were countless "I'm sorry's".

While having a late lunch in Eastern Colorado, a place named Sterling off of I-76; Pack reached over the table and found Maddie's hands. "I've been thinking about all the things we've talked about...important things." He knew what he wanted to say but had difficulty in finding the right words. "When we *split up*—" He hated his choice of words, "I mean, you know—"

Maddie smiled, "Yes, I know. When *you left*...or—" Now, she laughed. Her words were no better than Pack's had been. "Just go on with what you were starting to say."

"Well, Maddie, you said we needed help—counseling, you said—to put things back together. I guess...well, I just couldn't swallow that idea. Pride, cop toughness, male ego stuff—maybe all of that. Anyhow, I'll do it. I mean, you know...see a shrink."

Maddie choked back tears. She had promised not to cry and wouldn't do so now. "You would do that, Pack?"

He felt as if a huge weight had been lifted, "For you...I mean, for *us*—Yes, I'll do that. Word of honor."

"Ooops, I think you've made a wrong turn," Maddie said. As they approached I-25, the major north-south artery in Denver, Pack exited on the north ramp. The sun was setting beyond the wall of majestic mountains that had loomed for hours of climbing the foothills of central Colorado.

"I need to find a phone, Maddie. Make a call back to headquarters and see if there's any news of Amos' whereabouts. With all the APB's I've put out and with five State Highway Patrols looking for Amos there might be something."

Maddie nodded, gesturing toward a large Amoco complex on the left. Pack seemingly oblivious, continued on past. He drove by other public phone opportunities as well. "Looking for a Shell station," was his feeble excuse. Pack hoped that his plan would not backfire, he was taking a huge chance.

A few miles north of the city, Pack found what he was looking for on the left side of I-25. Years before, the two of them has spent the night at a roadside motel named the 'Buena Vista Lodge'. It was there that he had proposed to Maddie.

Maddie gasped, then burst out laughing at her recognition, "Ohmigosh! It's still here. You schemer, you." An hour or two before she had thought of asking Pack if he remembered the motel. Obviously he had.

"I guess that your husband is an old romantic at heart, Maddie." He emphasized the 'old'. "What do you think...?"

Maddie met his eyes, "I think I'm scared to death, Pack." Maybe this was a case of too much— too soon. "I'm flattered, but...do you mind if we have separate rooms?"

Pack understood. He would disguise his disappointment: "No problem, honey. We probably still have a lot to resolve."

Sometime before midnight, Pack heard the light knock on his door. One unresolved matter would be resolved that night.

23/ PHONE CALLS

In his career as a law enforcement officer, Rudy DeJarlais had made his share of mistakes. He prayed often that sending the wrong person to prison had never been one of them. If Begay found the purse he was looking for, the money Sam Yazzie allegedly frittered away would have a logical explanation. Gertie Brown lived only two blocks from an alleyway behind Hunt Avenue.

He called home to apologize to his wife, promising that he'd be home for dinner and that he'd make it all up to her somehow. By now the holiday was nearly ruined. On his notepad were the names of two people he had to call before leaving the office.

Troy Tomlinson answered the phone. DeJarlais despised the arrogance in the young man's tone of voice. It seemed almost as if Tomlinson had anticipated his call. When asked about his whereabouts on Friday night, the alibi sounded carefully rehearsed. Rudy wrote down the names of several college students who were at his party. Familiar names from familiar and respected families. "You can call them *all*, officer," Tomlinson said with more confidence than seemed reasonable under the circumstances. DeJarlais would do just that.

The second call was long distance. He had found the phone number and name of the Chief of the Hibbing Police Department in a law enforcement directory. Understandably, Chief Sundval was not in. DeJarlais spoke to an officer Peloquin. Pack Moran, he learned, was out of town. "Something to do with his son," Peloquin said. Peloquin would leave a message to return the call and pass it on to Chief Sundval who would be in the next morning.

DeJarlais troubled over his betrayal of the confidence young Amos had placed in him. But he had told the young man he would make no promises. Police work caused problems in people's lives; could not be avoided. The boy's father was indeed a policeman in Hibbing. He had guessed that Officer Moran was out somewhere looking for his son. Conceivably, everything Amos had told him that morning was true. A nice kid, scared...what would the young man have to gain by making up the story? Hopefully this Chief Sundval would fill in some of the blanks on Tuesday.

Begay entered his office with a brown leather purse in his gloved right hand. "Found it right where Yazzie said it would be." He extracted the empty wallet, handed DeJarlais the driver's license of Gertrude Brown. "She told officer Loshe that the man who mugged her was 'mean and smelly'—kinda fits Sam Yazzie, doesn't it Captain?"

DeJarlais nodded, forced a laugh. "She didn't see him so she won't be able to make an ID. Have you ever heard of having a suspect put his arms around a witness so the witness can smell him?"

Begay shared the laugh.

"Let me get you up to speed on the Evering murder," DeJarlais said. "I got a call from a young man from Minnesota this morning." He explained his earlier conversation with Amos Moran, referring to his notepad as he reviewed the details. "So Fish would have seen my notes. I suspect he called Tomlinson."

Begay agreed, "We both know he's a fink, Rudy. Probably wanted to kiss the ass of the Tomlinsons. Too bad they weren't home when he called."

The two of them divided the eight names on the list Troy Tomlinson had provided. DeJarlais talked with Brian Lofley. His story matched Troy's perfectly. Sally James confirmed that she and her brother had been at the Tomlinson's during the precise timeframe both Lofley and Tomlinson had said. Tom Hudley arrived at 10:30 and left at about 2:30 in the morning.

"They must have all arrived at exactly the same time," DeJarlais said with the trace of a smirk.

"Lewis, Greisdorff, and Bonetto all said they were there. Sadie Kearney wasn't home."

DeJarlais scratched his head, dialed Benjamin Caddie who lived next door to the Tomlinson's. "Don't remember seeing any cars out there on Friday night, Rudy," Caddie said. "Can't remember any noise over there either. The Tomlinson's are out of town—Phoenix—you know."

Eloise Hutchins, across the street from the Tomlinson home, hadn't seen anything going on either. "I'm sure that Troy wouldn't have a party when his parents were gone, Mr. DeJarlais. His mother is quite strict about that, you know." Eloise did not trust the boy and knew he had been a problem for his mother. Mildred Tomlinson had once confided that Troy had, in her words, 'behavioral problems'.

"Looks like we're gonna have to bring them in one at a time and sit them down, Rudy. This all seems too convenient to me—what's the word—contrived?"

"I got the same impression. Tomorrow morning we'll spend some time on campus. Sometimes a kid's story will change a little when they're sitting in the back seat of a squad."

24/ BEATEN UP

Disappointed over the sour turn to his afternoon plans with Sadie, Amos took the last bottle of Coors from his fridge and snapped the cap. Something was bothering her and it wasn't just the flu. What had he done to turn a pleasant and promising day into such a rueful disappointment?

They had been having such a wonderful time. He smiled as he pictured her hiking up the trail ahead of him. What a wonderfully rounded bottom she had. He had hoped to see more of it this afternoon. Amos had even given his apartment a quick clean-up job before she picked him up. But everything changed while they were sitting on the ledge talking about school and—maybe, he thought, maybe he had been bragging a little too much about his high school athletic exploits. No, Sadie would have teased him unmercifully if he had tooted his horn too much. No, it was something else.

The door burst open!

Before Amos could turn completely around he felt a sting in his eyes and a powerful arm around his neck. Choking from the pressure, he struggled to breathe and to break the vice-like grip. In a panicked reflex, he clamped his teeth into the hand gripping his chin and mouth, tasted blood. The spray burned in his nostrils...his knees began to buckle. "Get your ass outta this town, Moran!" One of the assailants shouted. Then a crashing blow smacked across the side of his head. Splitting pain shot behind his eyes. Disoriented, he gasped...his throat was closed to any utterance. "Asshole!" growled a second voice. Amos flailed in hopeless self-defense as he was mercilessly pummeled in the ribs, arms, and back . Warm blood trickled along his ear, into his beard. A black cloud closed like a curtain across his eyes. Consciousness was rapidly slipping away.

On the floor, instinctively drawing his legs to his chest in a fetal position, he felt the crush of feet kicking at his side and legs and bottom. His last flash of memory was that he was going to die.

Sadie Kearney was choosing a skirt and light sweater for the first day of classes the next morning when her father called up the stairs toward her bedroom. "Some guy on the phone, Sadie. Can't tell which one anymore," Ed Kearney laughed. Her father had been "sipping", as he described his drinking, all afternoon. Sadie hoped it was Jerry, and hoped that it wasn't Jerry at the same time. If it was Jerry, would she hang up? She was torn.

It was Brian Lofley. "Hey, Sadie-girl, wa'cha been up to? Who's this guy I saw you with on Sunday?"

"Oh, just some freshman from—" What should she say? Colorado or Minnesota? She let the 'where' drop. "Name's Jerry. I gave him a little tour of the campus so he wouldn't get lost tomorrow."

Lofley didn't press for any more information. "Say, reason I'm calling is...well, Troy and me got a little problem." He went on to explain that some old lady had reported the two of them to the police. He lied, "We were out doin' a little hell-raisin' on Friday night. Had a couple of joints, made some noise, dumped her garbage can. All in fun, ya know." Brian explained that Troy would really be in trouble with his parents, "Will ya help us out, Sadie?" Her two friends needed her to firm up an alibi for Friday night.

But, Sadie had met Jerry at the 'L.Q." that night. "Did you say Sally was going to vouch for you guys?" Sally had been with her and Jerry.

"Yeah, both Sally and her brother were with us."

Sadie wanted to put Friday night and Jerry Moran out of her little history book. "Sure. I'm cool with that. What, 10:30 until 2:30, or so?"

After hanging up the phone and returning to her bedroom, Sadie plopped onto her bed. "Who are you, Jerry Moran?" she said to herself. "Where did you come from, and why are you here?" It was possible that Jerry had lived in Denver before, or even after, his senior year in high school. If that was the case, why hadn't he said so? She was angry with him, with herself. She had made the grand overture on Friday night—not him. Why? What was the attraction? She remembered watching him at registration, then later as he was walking down the street, not quite knowing where he wanted to go. She could not dismiss that there had been an immediate attraction. Or, that it was mutual. She could tell that immediately. His eyes never left her that night. "Those damn eyes!" she mumbled, squeezing her pillow. "Those damn eyes!" she repeated. "Lying eyes!"

Or, what if she was mistaken? Although she couldn't find a Hibbing or a Cloquet or Bemidji in the Denver inset map of her atlas: what if she didn't quite hear him right? What if these were local neighborhood names? If she was wrong, she would kick herself. She had thoughts of going up to Jerry's apartment after the hike. Hanging out there, and—? And, what? She knew exactly what. She was falling in love with this guy. It wasn't only that Jerry was great looking, well built, and could match her quick humor—shot for shot— he made her laugh. He had a subtle charm and innocence. And, he wasn't from Flagstaff. Why was that an attraction for her?

"Damn!" Sadie cussed. Jerry didn't have a telephone. She wanted to call him right now. Get things straight between them. If he had been lying, then she needed to know why? Maybe there was a good reason? People lie, they do. Even to those they love the most. She was going to lie to the police about Troy's party. What a hypocrite she was.

Sadie knew Jerry's schedule for the next morning. She resolved to locate him after his Western Civ class. There just had to be an explanation, or a misunderstanding. Jerry Moran, after all, was a decent guy. Sadie Kearney wouldn't be in love with him if he wasn't.

Before retiring, she called her best friend, Sally James, and poured out her heart. "You've got to clear things up with Jerry tomorrow, Sadie. He's a hunk if I do say so, myself."

25/ TUESDAY MORNING

The pain was overwhelming. Amos vomited into the small pool of blood. It took a colossal effort to raise his right arm and hand to feel the lump above his ear. The gash had scabbed. Most of the battering he had endured were crushing blows all over his body. Every part of his anatomy ached, his left eye was swollen half shut, and his head throbbed mercilessly.

Grimacing, Amos rolled from his side to his back, stretching out his legs. What was broken? His legs felt sore, but they would be okay. He lifted his arm toward the light that blinked garishly through the window. His wristwatch read 4:20 in the morning. Propping himself on an elbow he tried to get his legs under him, get to his feet. Fighting the pain, he stood upright. I know how Lazarus must have felt after being dead and buried, he tried to laugh at his 'Catholic school' memory. At his feet was the bottle of beer he had been drinking, spilled into the blood and vomit. Bending over to pick it up, he felt his cramped and bruised muscles begin to come to life. Miraculously, he was going to be able to walk and to function. The head wound might take some stitches, but nothing seemed broken. He hobbled toward the bathroom, flipped the light switch, and regarded himself in the medicine cabinet mirror. Bloodied and swollen but otherwise nothing looked too serious. Splashing cold water on his face and dabbing at the streak of ugly dried blood, Amos thanked God for being alive.

What had happened? At least two men had broken in. Mace or pepper spray? Whatever, the assailants had made their point. "Get out of Flagstaff!" one of them had said. Was it Sadie's boyfriend—Brian? Was the threat and beating motivated by some sick jealousy? He tried to remember Brian from the pick-up football game on Sunday afternoon. Solidly built, about Amos' size. Who was with him? Tomlinson?

The thought of Troy Tomlinson spawned a second theory. How could he know anything? The only one Amos had talked to was Captain DeJarlais. No, DeJarlais wouldn't have said a word. The cop was a straight shooter, like his dad. But, on the other hand, the Tomlinsons were an influential family in this town. Maybe they had a way of knowing everything that went on here. Maybe—

Amos considered three possible options: Shake it off and be more careful in the future, go to the police and file a report, or get out of Flagstaff? He wished he could talk to Sadie. Explain what had been going on in his life. Be honest with her for a first time. His lies had piled up and he had to begin unraveling them. Before it was too late. Sadie could be trusted. She knew this place and would know what to do and how to go about doing it.

But, so would his parents. Their advice had never been wrong. They loved him more than anybody else in the world. Maybe it was time to call them and explain the mess he had gotten himself into.

Amos dressed and crossed the street to the Weatherford Hotel. From the public phone in the lobby he asked the operator to connect a collect call to his mother. The phone rang and rang—fourteen times, fifteen, sixteen. No answer. Next, he tried the same with his father's number. Neither of them were home. Both were light sleepers and would have awakened. He considered calling Grampa Kevin in Hibbing. No, maybe later. He considered waking Captain DeJarlais. Sadie?

Back in his apartment Amos regarded his car keys resting on the desk. His decision was made. It took less than fifteen minutes to throw his things together and clean up the blood and vomit on the floor.

As the sun was rising in the east, Amos was cruising on I-40 between Winslow and Holbrook. Then, Albuquerque—probably two hundred and some miles ahead. He'd catch some rest there before heading north to Denver.

26/ LIES

The morning sun sent a shaft of light through a narrow gap in the curtains. Pack regarded Maddie at his side, smiled. The clock radio blinked 6:08. Brushing a lock of her blond hair to the side, he kissed her lightly on the forehead. Without opening her eyes, Maddie smiled, too. He was torn between getting up and getting aroused one more time. Maddie made the decision easy for him.

At seven, Pack got out of bed, showered, and walked to the motel's lobby for two cups of coffee and frosted cinnamon rolls. He and Maddie planned to be on the road before eight. Pack would make a few phone calls while Maddie was making herself more beautiful.

His first call roused Larry Quiggin from bed. Amos' high school buddy might have learned something since their last conversation. "No sir, I haven't," the Regis junior said. "I still find this all very hard to believe."

Pack asked the young man to call Chief Sundval in Hibbing if he had any contact with Amos. "The Chief will probably be the only one who knows where I am at any given time."

Quiggin promised to do so and wished Pack good luck.

His second call caught John Larson on his way out the door. "Glad you caught me, Pack," John said. The Visa Accounts Manager had taken time from his Labor Day to run a transaction check the night before. "Your son is both frugal and careful, Pack." The only transactions he had traced were from St. Paul—a Conoco gas station for $10.80 and a place called the Greene Mill on Hamlin and Grand for $13.97. "Nothing outside of St. Paul I'm afraid. But I'll keep on it, Pack. So check in every day when you get a chance."

Chief Sundval, usually one of the first day duty cops to arrive, was not in his office when Pack called. And Pack's partner, Peloquin, had just checked out from a night shift. Pack told Larry Beckers, the desk officer, that he would be traveling from Denver to Albuquerque that day, and that he would check in later. "We're headed toward I-40, then on to Phoenix."

What they would do when they reached Phoenix was still a shot in the dark. Pack hadn't talked with Mike Rapovich since Saturday night. He hoped he might catch the ASU student at his apartment. As with Larry Quiggin only minutes before, Rapovich was awakened by the early morning call. His voice was groggy, "Oh... Mr. Moran...give me a sec to get my bearings here."

Pack apologized, "Amos' mother and I are in Denver, Mike, and on our way to Phoenix. I've just talked with Larry Quiggin...thought I would check and see if you've heard anything—?"

Rap was not surprised to learn that the Morans were on the road looking for their son. "Still not a word from Amos, sir. Classes begin next week... I don't know what to say. I can't figger out what Amos is doing."

Pack gave Mike Rapovich the same instructions he had given Larry Quiggin. "We'll call when we get to Phoenix, Mike. Let's just hope and pray that we have some leads to follow when we get there."

Rapovich tried to laugh, "I hope you and Mrs. Moran know what you're in for out here. It was over a hundred again yesterday...but, the locals like to say it's a *dry heat*."

His last call was to his father in Hibbing. "Let's just pray that no news is good news, Son," Kevin said. Angie Moran wanted to know how things were going with Maddie. "Pretty good," Pack understated without trace of emotion.

'FLAG'

~

Chief Oscar Sundval saw the memo resting on the center of his desk. "What's this?" he shouted through his open door at Beckers. "Where's Peloquin?"

Sundval dialed Peloquin's home number. "Why and hell didn't you call me about this?" his tone frustrated. The note said simply: *'Call in from Captain Rudy DeJarlais, Flagstaff, AZ: re: Pack Moran.'*

Slamming down the phone, Sundval strolled to the front desk. "Where is Pack, Beckers? He's supposed to be calling in every morning."

"Just missed him, Chief," Beckers said. "He called from Denver only ten minutes ago."

"He had my job until he resigned about five years ago," Sundval told Rudy DeJarlais. "Damn good cop—one of the best I've ever worked with." The Chief would not add anything more to his description. No good would be served if he warned the Arizona cop about Pack's zealousness.

DeJarlais explained the Flagstaff circumstance to the Hibbing Chief. "I needed to check out young Amos Moran. Pleasant kid in an awkward situation right now."

Sundval explained the convoluted situation as he understood it. "So, Pack is somewhere south of Denver and heading toward Albuquerque on his way to Arizona. Thank God we know where Amos is now. Pack is thinking his son might be in Phoenix— put a capital 'T' on thinking. He's been flying in the dark so far . . he'll be damn happy you called, Captain. I expect he'll be checking in with me later today. I'll have him call you in Flagstaff as soon as I hear from him."

Oscar Sundval's next call was to the Colorado Highway Patrol. He gave the receptionist a description of Patrick Moran's Oldsmobile Cutlass along with its Minnesota license plate numbers. "Just a minute," the receptionist said, "There must be some mistake, sir. It's Amos Moran, Minnesota plate number LR 1053, that we're looking for. I'm confused."

Sundval remembered that Pack had made contacts with the highway patrols of several western states before leaving Hibbing: "Find'em both, then. There's no mistake, ma'am. Patrick is Pack Moran, Amos' father. He's a Hibbing police officer. Word that I have is that Pack left some place in Denver an hour or so ago. He's headed for Albuquerque."

~

Rudy DeJarlais and Arlen Begay left the station together. The NAU campus was only blocks away. George Breen of the NAU administration office had given the officers the class schedules of all nine students over the phone. DeJarlais had played hunches for years, developed instincts as well: the alibi these kids were floating was too contrived. He planned to save Tomlinson's interview until later in the day. That would give the others an opportunity to fill him in, maybe bolster his confidence or maybe make him sweat a little.

He found Brian Lofley taking with the Kearney girl. "Hop in the back seat, Lofley," DeJarlais called. "And you, young lady, hang around. I've got some questions for you, too."

Lofley was nonplused, too sure of himself. Sitting in a squad car should make anybody nervous. Exceptions were rare, but Lofley didn't squirm. He had his Friday night story down pat, admitted to "trying pot a couple of times", and assured DeJarlais he wouldn't lie—"not even for a friend."

"What happened to your hand?" DeJarlais asked. The back of Lofley's hand was bandaged.

"Playing football with the guys on Sunday afternoon," Lofley's smile was a crooked line across a smug face. "Anything else, Captain? My team won, if you care to know."

Sadie Kearney, unlike her friend Brian, was nervous, distracted. DeJarlais guessed that she had been crying earlier. "What's wrong, Sadie?" He knew she had a tough situation at home.

"Nothing," she said.

"You been crying?" DeJarlais liked the girl, gave her credit for keeping her family together through some very difficult times. "Your dad's problem making things kinda rough at home?"

"No." Everybody's apparent knowledge of the Kearney's *situation* made her angry. "We're all doing just fine, thanks!"

DeJarlais fumbled for his notebook resting on the dashboard and searched his shirt pocket for a ballpoint pen. There was attitude in Sadie's comment.

Sadie looked away. It had been Rudy DeJarlais who brought the news of her sister's tragic death. Sadie remembered his staying at their home for nearly an hour and offering sincere solace to her traumatized parents: far beyond the 'call of duty'. That recall triggered another that went back to her childhood. She and her sister had set up a Kool Aid stand at the corner of Eldon and Birch one hot summer afternoon. DeJarlais had pulled his squad car to the curb and walked over to their table. He bought two nickel Dixie cups of grape Kool Aid and gave the girls a fifty-cent piece. Sadie remembered Maggie's infatuation with the handsome cop.

"I'm glad to hear that." DeJarlais noted the lapse in the pretty girl's attention. He was going to let the family matter drop, when Sadie explained. "I've been upset. My boyfriend. We had a quarrel of sorts. Nothing serious."

DeJarlais offered his condolences, "I know that's hard," then proceeded with his questions about Friday night. Sadie did not make forthright eye contact, looking away uncomfortably two or three times. But her story was identical to all the others he had heard. He concluded with a standard: "Would you lie to cover for a friend, Sadie?"

Sadie cast a level gaze at the officer, "I might. You know that, Mr. DeJarlais. Who wouldn't?"

DeJarlais had the feeling that this answer was the only honest one he might get that morning.

Upon leaving the squad car, Sadie had a pang of guilt. What's this *really* about, she wondered? Drugs and horseplay? If the issue were something more serious, she would never lie to DeJarlais.

27/ AN EMPTY APARTMENT

Back at police headquarters, DeJarlais found a Seven-Up in his small office fridge, and opened the lunch bag his wife had packed. Peanut butter and jelly, Theresa DeJarlais was paying him back for ruining their Labor Day afternoon plans. He gave her a call. "Just wanted you to know how much I love you, sweetheart. And I can taste your love for me in this absolutely delicious sandwich."

Rudy and Tee DeJarlais had a wonderful marriage—sustained by daily humor and expressions of love. Theresa said, "It was either peanut butter or leftover baron-of-beef, hon. I know how much you love peanut butter."

"For you, Rudy," Arlen Begay had taken a call on the other line. "Long distance, Colorado."

"Gotta run," DeJarlais told his wife. "Love ya, Tee."

The Captain and the caller talked for nearly fifteen minutes. "I'll swing over to his apartment after classes this afternoon," Rudy said. "I'll look forward to meeting you when you get here."

After lunch, DeJarlais and Begay compared notes on their campus interviews. "They've all read the same script, Rudy—like lines from a class play." Arlen Begay shook his head. "The only one who seemed even a little bit shaky was Sally James. But she swore up and down that she was at the Tomlinson place."

DeJarlais knew that Sally and Sadie were best friends. "Let's visit with both girls again tomorrow, or Thursday," he said.

Begay looked at the wall clock, "Well, it's after two, what say we pay a visit to young Mr. Tomlinson. He's had a few hours to get his briefing from the cast and crew of his stage production."

DeJarlais smiled at his partner, "Which of us is going to be the 'bad cop'?" The two of them had teamed-up in more than a hundred interrogations over the years. "I think it's my turn, Arlen."

Troy Tomlinson was quick to seize the offensive. "My parents are going to be home this afternoon, and they are going to be really pissed-off at you guys. I called Mr. Morrow an hour ago and told him that the cops were harassing all of my friends. He told me to say I had a party and nothing more. Said if we have any questions that we should meet in his office."

DeJarlais should have expected the lawyer card to be played by one of the kids. Morrow was easily the best-known attorney in Flagstaff and represented the Tomlinson family's business affairs. He was probably checking with the police department already and would learn that the charges were a fabrication. DeJarlais was going to be in trouble. Again. But, this rich punk wasn't going to call the shots. He had the Amos Moran account in his notebook, and if Fisher had relayed that information to Troy, then the matter at hand was far more serious than smoking pot on Friday night. He would call Troy's bluff.

"Let's go downtown then. We'll continue our little conversation with Jim Morrow present to advise you. Of course, the issue of Friday night's activities will need to be expanded beyond pot smoking and vandalism. We had a murder in Flagstaff that same night. And I'm going to talk with every person in this town if I have to— until I damn well find out what happened to a guy named Axel Evering. Let's go."

Tomlinson flinched. The allusion to the Evering murder was far more than he had bargained for. Fisher had told him about the Amos Moran report. DeJarlais was not someone he wanted to play any more games with. He needed to backtrack, "I'm sorry, Officer DeJarlais. My folks always told me to call Mr. Morrow if I found myself in any kind of trouble. So, I did just that. No need to bother him this afternoon, I'm sure he's got more important things to do."

"No problem. Jimmy Morrow and me go way back. And he's probably got a pot of coffee somewhere in that suite of offices of his. Arlen, you need a cup of coffee?"

"Dyin' for coffee, Captain." Begay amused over Tomlinson's suddenly contrite demeanor.

"Just a minute. I told you I was sorry. I really don't want any lawyers involved in this...this, what...vandalism thing? It's like all my friends have already told you, we had a party at my parent's house. They were out of town and I'm probably in hot water with them already. I'd rather not get in any deeper."

DeJarlais nodded without reply.

"You're going to tell my mom and Harry about the party, aren't you, sir?" Troy never referred to his stepfather as Dad.

DeJarlais weighed his options. Before meeting with Morrow, and probably Troy's parents as well, he wanted to have a better hand to play. He needed to find the Moran boy and go through the story one more time. "Yes, I intend to talk with your parents when they get back." He looked at his watch, "When might that be?"

A deeply troubled Troy Tomlinson departed the squad car to meet his friend, Brian Lofley, who was waiting out of sight near the end of the block. His fifteen minutes with DeJarlais and Begay left him drained and scared. Nobody Troy knew had seen the Moran kid that day—hopefully he had taken their advice and left Flagstaff. The El Camino with Minnesota plates was no longer parked behind the furniture store.

~

The unique relationship between DeJarlais and Begay had the solid foundation of mutual and unequivocal trust. It was contrary to established procedure for a Captain to spend most of his time in the field. It was even more unusual for a Captain to have a partner. The job description for DeJarlais' position enumerated three pages of administrative duties. An 'unofficial' trade-off of assignments between Rudy and Chief Roth had worked well for everybody in the department for several years.

DeJarlais had said nothing about his midday telephone conversation. Begay was curious but non-intrusive—knowing that his partner had never kept him in the dark about anything of importance. At the same time, each respected the other's privacy. Almost as an aside, Rudy commented: "Guess who called me from Colorado—?"

DeJarlais parked his squad across from the Weatherford Hotel on the north curb of Aspen. The yellow tape was still in place across the street. He and Begay climbed the stairs and knocked on the cheap pine door. The door was unlocked. The sparkly furnished apartment was empty. A quick walk through found an empty dresser and closets with naked wire hangers. "Kinds looks like our boy has flown the coop."

Having checked the desk drawers, Begay went to the window. "A pretty good view of the crime scene tape from here."

DeJarlais joined him. "He could have seen it all. Let's talk with Levitt downstairs. See what he knows."

As DeJarlais was about to pull the door closed, Begay caught his elbow. "Just a sec, Rudy. Look over there...by the rug." He walked over and lifted an edge of the cheap floor covering. "Blood stains." Bending down, he put his fingers over his nose. "Smells like vomit."

"What are you thinking, Arlen?"

"Your guess is as good as mine."

DeJarlais entered the unimpressive furniture store and found Jake Levitt in the back. "We're looking for one of your tenants, Jake."

Levitt hadn't seen the Moran boy. "Kid in trouble already? Only been here a 'cupla days."

"Not that I know of. We were just upstairs a minute ago. His apartment looks deserted." DeJarlais said.

"I ain't seen'um...probly not since Sataday mornin', I'm guessin'. Boy's paid up fer the month tho'...cash he gave me."

"Any kinds of disturbance going on up there lately, Jake?" Begay asked.

Jake Levitt shrugged, "Nothin' I heard 'bout. Corse, I close up my shop 'bout five usely. Other tenants ain't said nothin' bad."

DeJarlais wondered how the disheveled man could remain in business selling the shoddy merchandise haphazardly displayed in the musty store. "We're wondering if the Moran boy might have seen something last Friday night. His window has quite a view of the alleyway by the Orpheum where Evering was murdered."

DeJarlais had talked with Levitt on Saturday morning. "Thought maybe the two of you have talked about what happened."

"Nope. Nothin' since I talked with 'em that morning. Ask'd 'em if'n he'd seen somtin from upstairs. Said he din't, said he'd been out late the night before. Said he'd had too much ta drink."

DeJarlais' eyelids raised, "Run that by me again, Jake."

"Sez he was drunk."

Outside Begay gave the Captain a dubious look. "Kinda shoots the Amos Moran eyewitness story in the foot."

DeJarlais shook his head, "Somehow I don't think so. Amos was a scared kid when I talked to him. Why would he make up a story that would only make his life here miserable?"

Begay pondered the question, "Maybe so you would do something he didn't have the courage to do...call his parents."

"Good point."

28/ *FLAGSTAFF P.D.*

"Oh, Oh...was I speeding, Maddie?" Pack heard the siren, then saw flashing lights in his rearview mirror. He had stopped speeding motorists countless times but had never been pulled over himself. "God, this is a terrible feeling," he said.

The Colorado Highway Patrolman was overweight and puffing after racing from his squad to Pack's Oldsmobile. "Patrick Moran?" he said. "I've got an urgent message for you."

Pack tensed. Maddie gasped: "Amos!" she cried. "Something's happened to Amos!" Pack reached for her hand, "Stay calm, Maddie."

Officer Robert Dorsher explained that Pack was to call an Oscar Sundval in Hibbing, Minnesota. "That's all I know sir." He smiled, "You're a cop, aren't you? Keep an eye on your speedometer, okay? The New Mexico 'fuzz' are pretty tough."

They had just driven through Colorado Springs, a town named Fountain was six miles further down on I-25. "Will do. Thanks, Officer."

Oscar Sundval had been waiting for Pack's call all morning. It was approaching noon and he had his Rotary luncheon meeting to get to. As he was almost out the door, Beckers called from the front desk. "It's Pack, sir."

Sundval said, "Pack, we've got a location. Amos is in Flagstaff. He's just fine; tell Maddie not to worry." Sundval cleared his throat, "There's something going on out there that your son is involved in. I don't really have any details but there's a cop in Flagstaff that would like to talk to you." He gave Pack the name DeJarlais and phone number.

While Pack talked with Rudy DeJarlais from a Burger King pay phone, Maddie paced behind him. "He's a good kid, Captain DeJarlais. Believe him. And, please keep an eye on him until we get there. My wife and I will probably drive straight through from here. Should be there by this time tomorrow morning."

DeJarlais smiled to himself. Amos had told him that he had run away, in part, because his parents had separated. But now they were together. He was happy for them both. It must be the hardest thing in the world for any parent to go through...what would he and Theresa ever do if something happened to their son, Todd? "Classes at the college started today. I'll swing by his apartment this afternoon. Everything will be fine...can I call you Pack? Your son says everybody does."

"Absolutely...Rudy. And thanks. Thanks a helluvalot."

∼

Amos had only driven about ninety miles before the aches became so bad he had to turn off the highway in Holbrook. His greatest pain, however was in his throbbing head. "What in the hell are you doing, Amos?" he slammed the palm of his hand against the steering wheel. "Running like a coward?" For nearly two hours he had been in absolute torment.

In front of the small convenience store where he parked, he bought a Coke from the vending machine, and popped four more Bufferin. He was sweating from the morning heat, but the sun felt good on his shoulders. His breathing had been labored and he wondered about broken ribs. What else was wrong? He considered finding a local doctor and getting checked out.

Yet, through all the pain he endured, his thoughts were preoccupied with Sadie more than anything else. He had to make things right with her. Amos looked back at the highway he had traveled. Regret and guilt and shame were on the highway ahead. His mind was made up.

It was just after noon when Amos arrived back in Flagstaff. He had an afternoon English 101, but decided to skip it. His first day was going to be a washout. Rather than go back to his apartment, he decided to take a room at a Pony Soldier. For the first time since leaving St. Paul, he used his Visa card. He didn't care anymore. The charade was over with—once and for all. From here on, Amos was going to be Amos!

Sadie had classes from one until three that afternoon so he'd call her later. He considered going to the police department and reporting last night's assault to DeJarlais, but that could wait, too. Instead, he called back to Hibbing—first his mother's number, then his father's. Again, no answer at either place. Where could they be? He dropped onto the queen-sized bed, closed his eyes, thought of Sadie.

As the air-conditioner whirred, Amos slept.

It was nearly seven when he awoke. He dialed. Sadie answered.

"Jerry, where were you all day?" She had been worried that her behavior of yesterday had scared him away. She didn't want that to happen.

The sound of her voice sent shivers down Amos' neck. "I need to talk to you, Sadie."

A long pause, "Honest talk, Jerry?"

"Yes."

"There hasn't been much of that between us, has there?"

"Some...but not enough. Sadie, I think..." Amos stammered, although he wanted to, he couldn't finish the 'I love you'... "Sadie, I'm crazy about you. And...well, I need you to forgive me. That's the most important thing in the world to me right now."

"Forgive what, Jerry?"

"A thousand things, Sadie. Lies..."

Sadie could hear the emotion in his voice. She wanted to see him more than anything, too. "I've got tons of homework, Jerry," her tease was inappropriate and she realized it immediately. Jerry was hurting. "But then—what's more important, grades...or love?"

Amos' heart fluttered at the word *love*, which was almost lost in Sadie's familiar tease. "Grades, of course," he said. "Grades are a foundation for one's future success in life... But, grades have an entire semester for repairs— don't they?... Love, on the other hand—love can't wait." Amos blushed over what he had just said.

"Did I hear you say, or imply anyhow, that you're in love—?"

Amos welcomed her question, "Yes, I love you."

"Give me fifteen minutes to put on my face. No, forgive my face— I've been crying all day. Give me five minutes to get over there."

"Oh...Sadie, I'm not at my apartment."

"Why not? Where are you?"

Amos explained that there was much he needed to tell her. "I'm at the Pony Soldier Motel on the east side."

Sadie giggled, "Jerry Moran, how sleazy!"

"The place isn't bad, Sadie. Kinda nice in fact."

"I don't mean where you're staying...it's just: Do you expect me to sneak into a motel room after dark, like a wanton woman?"

"We could meet in the coffee shop, Sadie." His voice had the serious tone of innocence.

"Wouldn't think of it, Jerry. This all sounds much too intriguing and risqué for me to pass up. Room 212 in ten."

Amos had a wide smile as he hung up the phone. How great it was going to feel to shed *Jerry* once and for all!

29/ ROOM 212

"Jerry! Oh my God! What happened to you?" Sadie gasped as she rushed into the room. Delicately, she touched her finger to the purple gash above his ear. "This should have been stitched right away."

Amos put his arms around her shoulders and pulled her into him. She melted into his chest; he kissed her lightly on the top of her forehead, lifter her chin and kissed her again on the mouth. Again she smelled of strawberries. "I've missed you so, Sadie," was the best he could say.

Sadie found his deep Greene eyes. "And I've missed you. Now, tell me about it. Tell me everything." She fought back tears.

"The cuts and bruises are near the end of the story, Sadie. And I want to get everything right this time. I've been wrong for too long."

She took his elbow, sat him down on the bed, nestled beside him. "It's going to be a long story, then." Smiling, she swallowed hard. "Somehow I have the feeling that I'm not in love with Jerry Moran. Am I right for openers?"

Amos hung his head for a long moment, then found her eyes. He knew that the time had come to take the greatest risk of his life. He would tell the girl he loved that he was a liar—there could be no sugarcoating on that reality. "Let me say that I'm sorry...with all my heart... I'm sorry—before I even begin.

Sadie felt a flutter in her stomach. "I'm a big girl," she said. "I've had my fair share of bad news along the way."

Amos swallowed hard, began his story, his lengthy apology, by taking Sadie back to Hibbing the year before. "I've already told you that my Mom and Dad split up last year..." His voice tightened with emotion. "...And about my rebellion. Obviously, I didn't handle the pain of all that very well. Running away was irresponsible and cowardly."

"I agree on both counts, Jerry. We've been over that once before."

"I know...but...I left out some important things."

Sadie frowned without reply. Her stomach twinged again with an anticipation of something hurtful.

"I didn't *just* run away from home. I put a whole pattern of lies into motion. Before I knew it, the lies really started to snowball on me, Sadie. My parents were only the first in a long line of people that I deceived." He described how his friends conspired with him, his flight from Minnesota, and his, almost accidental, discovery of Flagstaff only the week before. "Everything seemed to fall into place when I got here. Registering at the college, locating an apartment I could afford, and then meeting you last Friday night." He told her about introducing himself to Billy on campus when he was registering. "I used my middle name, Jerry. I guess that was like my beard and everything else, part of the cover I was creating. This whole experience was going to become a new beginning for me."

Jerry had been talking nonstop for nearly twenty minutes. Sadie finally interrupted, "If you're not *Jerry Moran*, who are you?"

He forced a weak laugh "...I am *a* Moran, and I am Irish—like I told you from the very start. But...my *real* name is Amos. Kinda strange, isn't it? Amos. Amos Gerald Moran."

Sadie laughed a full laugh for the first time. "Amos! I love it. I've never met anybody named Amos before. Jerry's are a dime a dozen. There's got to be a story behind that, too."

"There is, but I'm going to save it for later—okay?"

"I can't wait, but yes. Back to Flagstaff. You've registered, met this Greene guy, found an apartment which I haven't been allowed to see yet, and met this tantalizing brunette. Or, has your story pretty much been told... Amos. Oh, I just love it—Amos!" She repeated his name and gave him a kiss on his beard. "Do you have a razor?"

Amos gave her a puzzled look. "Why?"

"After your story, I want to shave it off—the beard. That's Jerry stuff, that's history now. I'll bet that Amos was a clean-shaven and a clean-living kind of guy. I mean before he became a deceitful, conniving, unscrupulous—give me some more adjectives," she jested, giving him a light jab in the ribs.

Amos winced, "Ouch! I got myself pretty well beaten up last night, Sadie. My entire body is one huge ache right now."

"Sorry. Your story wasn't quite over yet, was it? When that part's over...maybe some TLC will help you forget."

"There's a lot more, Sadie..." Amos continued, beginning after meeting her at the 'L.Q.' last Friday night and returning to his apartment on Aspen Avenue later. "I saw it from my window, Sadie. I thought it was a mugging and went to bed." He described the assailant without giving a name. "The next morning I heard a commotion outside and went down to see what was going on." He explained his torment of Saturday and being too bummed-out to meet her at the Quarter.

"Then I read the Sunday morning *Sun*..." He told her about his conversation with the old gentleman in the lobby of the Weatherford. About a guy named Sam Yazzie sitting in jail.

"When we were walking across the campus that afternoon I saw the guy—the one who killed that transient, Evering. Sadie, I was positive! And from that moment my life has been a living hell. The next morning I went to church and prayed about what to do. Then I called DeJarlais; the two of us met for an hour or so—before you picked me up to go hiking."

Sadie's face was drawn and pale. She remembered their campus stroll and stopping to chat with her friends. Amos had seemed distracted, but he had gotten over it rather quickly. "You saw him when we stopped to watch the football game?" Her question was more a statement. "Was it one of my friends, Amos? Brian Lofley?"

"I would be surprised if Brian wasn't one of the two guys that I couldn't really see. The ones who were on my side of the street."

"Troy?"

"Yes. Troy Tomlinson. It was that unusual tossel-cap he was wearing. I nearly froze when I saw it—saw him. Everything matched. Tall, kinda lanky, and that cap!"

Sadie got up from the bed, walked toward the draped window. With her back to Amos she began to cry. "You told DeJarlais?"

"Everything, Sadie. I don't think he took me seriously, though. He poked holes in just about everything I said. And it didn't help that I was a runaway kid from Minnesota. I felt like an ass."

"You said you were positive, Amos," her back still to him. "I've grown up with Troy and Brian , , , and Marty James. If Troy and Brian did anything, Marty would have been with them. The Three Musketeers—the Cherry Hill Chums we call them—it's always been the three of them."

Amos didn't know what to say. He had the sinking feeling that his story had struck a very sorry note with Sadie.

She turned to face him, "I'm going to have to think about what you've just told me for a while. Amos, I'm blown away by all this. I mean my friends—not the rest of it, not your parents or your rebellion or your coming here to Flag...and not even what you saw on Friday night. And certainly not the two of us." She began to sob, "Damn! Love can really be a downer. Amos, I love you...but...but, these guys are some of my best friends—kids I've grown up with. And you, an outsider in every way...you blow into Flag and tell me they are murderers. This is devastating!" Her tone was indignant, and laden with sadness.

Amos held her close to him, let her cry for a few long moments. "I can feel for you, your hurt and your confusion. You don't know how many times I've wished that I hadn't seen anything that night. But wishing doesn't make it go away. I was there and I saw it. And a guy's in jail—a total stranger to me—accused of a murder he didn't commit. Maybe it wasn't your friends: I don't know them any more than that guy in jail or anybody else here."

He sighed, trying to release the stress of the moment, "I only did what I thought was right. My conscience was absolutely killing me, I prayed on it. And now, I'm in this horrendous mess. A mess that I almost ran away from today, like a coward. But, I couldn't do that. I turned around in Holbrook and came back here. I had to see you. I had to make things right between us. I love you, Sadie. I love you like crazy...even if I don't *really* know you yet, either. God, sometimes I don't even know myself."

Sadie pushed away, looked into his reddened eyes. Amos seemed about to cry. She puzzled over what he had said. Running like a coward? Going to Holbrook? "You are not a coward, Amos. Under the circumstances, I wonder if I would have had the courage to do what you did. I'd like to think so, but—" She knew there was still more. "You're saving the worst for last, aren't you?"

"Sadie, last night after you dropped me off—and, by the way, I was miserable about how our afternoon ended up—two guys broke into my apartment. They caught me by surprise, maced me—I think—and beat the living hell out me. They were crazed, like drug-crazed! They told me to get my ass out of Flagstaff as they were pounding and kicking me. I got zonked on the head and passed out. When I came to early this morning, I packed my bags and headed out of town. These guys were going to destroy whatever life I hoped to make for myself. And they knew my name and where I lived. Without even knowing the game I was in here, I was convinced that they had won and I had lost.

"As I said, I ran like a chicken. At Holbrook I turned around. I realized that I had to finish what I had started here. I had to deal with all the garbage—but, even more importantly, I had to share it all with you. No, you're right, Sadie, I'm not a coward, but I'm not a fool, either. I think I know who beat me up but I'm not going after them. Doing that would only dig my hole a little deeper."

Sadie was emotionally drained. "And it's deep enough already, isn't it, Amos? I'm sorry—really. I laid a guilt trip on you that you did nothing to deserve. You're not making love easy for me. But I just can't deny my feelings. And that means I've got to be by your side through all this—this mess as you've called it."

Amos leveled his eyes on her, "Sadie, don't get pissed at me for asking, but I've got know what I'm up against...are Brian and those guys users? Pot, or speed, or whatever the hell else is out there?"

Sadie had tried pot and speed herself: a couple of times with Brian, and with Sally and Marty James. But not for months now. "Who doesn't, Amos? Yes, on weekends they sometimes do...yes! I don't think any of them are addicts or anything like that."

It was nearly eleven and they had talked for more than two hours. Sadie rested her head on Amos' chest, gripped his strong arms. There was a feeling of reassurance in his embrace. She needed to be at one with him as much as he needed that connection with her. She wanted him, too. Only the intimacy of the bed on which they were sitting might give her the bond she had to have. In a way, they were still both strangers. In all their time together she had not shared very much of her life with him. That, she was certain, was going to happen in a manner and time of her choosing. But not right now—not here.

Sadie's mind was racing in Amos' quiet embrace. He was giving her time to digest all he had shared. She considered things she had wanted to tell him, her geography work in the atlas and figuring out where he was from. How much that truth had hurt. And her complicity in the Tomlinson alibi. Her interrogation by DeJarlais that morning. There were so many things still hanging in her closet of remorse...but, at this time, there were more important things to do. Things that would bind their exhausted spirits far more deeply than any words could do.

Sadie's hands moved under his T-shirt, up his bare back. "I want you to love me, Amos Moran," she whispered in his swollen ear. "More than anything else right now...we need to make love."

30/ TAKING TURNS AT THE WHEEL

Amos stirred slightly as Sadie got out of bed and dressed. In the glow from the neon outside she could see the smile on Amos' bruised face. She lightly kissed the gash on his head then gathered her clothing from the floor and dressed. Before leaving she scribbled a brief note. The door closed softly behind her.

It was one-thirty when she pulled into the narrow garage alongside her home. Dad was sleeping on the living room sofa with the television blinking a rerun of *I Love Lucy*. Upstairs, Mom was snoring ever so gently. The anti-depressants had done their job.

But Sadie could not sleep. Touching her groin, the tingle was still there. Amos was so wonderful. So troubled. So in need of her love and friendship. She smiled, maybe she had helped some of his pain go away.

What was she going to do? Sadie remembered her conversation with DeJarlais the morning before—it seemed so long ago already. She had lied to him; and, strangely, she had the feeling that he knew she had. He was a decent cop. Then she thought of Amos' father—also a cop. What was he like? And Maddie? From what Amos had told her, Maddie was beautiful. Maybe that's where Amos got his good looks. She had wanted to shave his beard that night, to see what he really looked like under his 'Jerry' hair.

Mostly, she wanted Amos to know who she was. The Sadie behind the masks that were her disguise. Amos had opened up to her...but she remained closed to him. She loved her parents deeply, but there was a mixture of shame and sadness that kept her from talking about them.

After tossing and turning until three, she drifted to sleep. Her final resolve was clear in her thoughts. She would visit DeJarlais during a break between classes the next day.

The alarm clock woke Amos at six-thirty. Not surprising, Sadie was gone. He pulled her pillow to his face and breathed in the lingering scent, smiled at the memory of their lovemaking only hours before. The feeling of wonderment was beyond any words he could imagine. Sadie!

Placing one foot gingerly on the floor he realized that his battered body was noticeably improved. In the bathroom he plunged his face in a sink of cold water. "You still look like absolute hell," he told himself. "But Sadie loves you and that's all that matters right now." He smiled again at the memory of the night before, still in almost disbelief over what had happened. "You're head-over-heels in love," he spoke to the face grinning at him from the mirror. After showering and brushing his teeth, Amos searched his duffle bag for anything still clean enough to wear again. "Aha." He found a white Gant dress shirt that wasn't too badly wrinkled, a pair of khaki Guess shorts he hadn't worn since registration, and his last pair of clean socks, but no clean underwear. "Oh well, who will know?" He pulled on the shorts sans underwear.

On the desk near the door, Amos found Sadie's note:

> *"I'm with you all the way, 'Gopher'.*
> *I know you'll be feeling better this morning.*
> *The most wonderful night of my life.*
> *Meet you outside Gammage around eleven.*
> *Love*
> *S*

Amos gave the note a kiss, tucked it in his shirt pocket, and headed for the NAU campus. He'd try to catch each of his professor's before class and attempt to explain his absence from the first day of class. He'd have to conjure another lie—hopefully the last one for a long time.

~

Pack and Maddie had been running on adrenalin and caffeine for nearly twenty hours. They shared the driving, each taking four hour shifts while the other tried to catch some sleep in the back seat. Although Pack had not kept an eye on his speedometer, as promised, the night was free of New Mexico 'fuzz'. "Two or three more hours, sweetheart," Pack said. It was after eight in the morning when they crossed into Arizona.

Highway fatigue had curtailed their conversation through the long night, but hundreds of smiles passed between them. "I can't wait to see our Amos," Maddie said. "It's only been a few weeks and I need to check his picture to remember what he looks like." Maddie had tucked one of Amos' wallet-sized graduation pictures under the sun visor and stared at it often.

"I hope he's all right. I got the impression that he's mixed up in something that the police in Flagstaff are working on. I pray that it's not drugs, Maddie. They're everywhere these days.

"He's got a good head on his shoulders, Pack."

"I've got to believe that—despite the troubles he's put us through. Don't forget that the crowd he's been hanging out with over the past year is not the same bunch he grew up with. I've met a few of them."

Maddie did not reply.

∼

Sadie watched Amos approach. "Hey, Jerry," she called.

Amos heard her but didn't lift his head in acknowledgement.

"Amos!"

He looked up, smiled widely.

He stepped close, flung out his arms to embrace her.

Sadie stepped away, "Public displays of affection are frowned upon here at NAU." Then she dropped her canvas book bag and gave him a big hug. "Let's break all the rules. Do you still love me, Amos Moran?"

"More than ever, Miss Sadie Marie Kearney."

Amos took her hand. "Can I buy you lunch?"

Sadie gave him a serious look. She hadn't told him about the Tomlinson party alibi and her meeting with DeJarlais the day before. "Maybe later...but...there's something else I have to do first. I'll tell you all about it while we walk to the police station."

Amos shook his head as she told him her story. Everything was fitting together. Tomlinson, Lofley, James...and several others were involved in a cover-up.

"So I lied, Amos. And I didn't sleep much last night."

"Do you want me to go in with you when you talk to DeJarlais?"

Sadie considered the benefit of his moral support. "I don't think so. It's my lie and I don't want to give DeJarlais the impression that you put me up to confessing it. That might look bad for both of us, don't you think?" She took his hand in hers, "But please do come along with me, Amos. You can wait outside the office."

Amos found a chair in the hallway opposite DeJarlais' office door. Sadie went inside by herself.

DeJarlais stood, offered his hand, gestured toward the chair beside his desk. "Good morning, Sadie. What can I do for you?"

Sadie sat. "I've come to apologize, Mr. DeJarlais. I lied to you about the Tomlinson party. If there was a party, I wasn't there."

DeJarlais wasn't the least surprised. "Tell me about it."

She explained the call from Brian Lofley, the promise to go along with the party story. "On Friday night I was with Amos Moran and some friends. We were at the Quarter until it closed at one." Sadie hesitated over her next admission. 'The whole truth', she reminded herself "Sally James was with us."

DeJarlais' eyes widened imperceptibly at the name of Amos Moran. "Amos Moran?" he asked.

Sadie said, "Yes."

"Until closing?"

"Oh, no. Amos left earlier. Just after...about eleven-thirty, I think. But Sally stayed."

DeJarlais was writing in his notebook. "Sally James, huh?" Another bogus party alibi he thought. Both he and Begay had been almost positive from the start that the Tomlinson party story was a sham. "So Brian Lofley called you on Monday night?"

Sadie nodded. She could feel herself sinking into the hole that Amos had begun digging for both of them. If he hadn't gone forward with his story none of this would be happening. But Amos had done the right thing and there was no turning back now.

Begay entered the room. When the door swung open, DeJarlais spotted Amos sitting outside. He was relieved to see the boy. The bloodstains on Amos' living room floor had caused him grave concerns. "Arlen, you remember Miss Kearney?"

Begay nodded, said "good morning", and pulled a second chair next to the Captain. The three of them talked for a few minutes more. "Thanks, Sadie. You've done the right thing by coming here," DeJarlais smiled. "Do you mind if I ask Amos to join us for a few minutes? I saw him sitting outside."

Sadie shook her head, "Not at all, that's fine with me."

Begay opened the door, waved Amos into the room. "What happened to you, young man?" he said. "You've had me and the Captain a little worried." Amos found another chair and slid it next to Sadie.

"Tell me what happened to you, Amos," DeJarlais said from his place behind the desk.

Amos explained everything in detail. "They put a darn good beating on me, sir. All I got in was a good bite of somebody's hand."

"Once again, Amos, you didn't see anybody's face?" DeJarlais frowned, but remembered Brian Lofley's bandaged hand. The young man's story made sense. DeJarlais' feelings were mixed: Excited to have some leads to follow, yet apprehensive about where these leads were taking him. He was going to have to meet with the influential Tomlinson's and their arrogant son. And, without a doubt, their high-powered attorney as well. He smiled inwardly at the challenge.

"Amos?" DeJarlais' eyes leveled at the young man. "You didn't see any faces..."

Amos, dismayed over not being able to offer much help, nodded, "No sir. I didn't get a good look. My eyes were burning from the mace, or whatever they sprayed in my face."

DeJarlais' phone rang. He listened to the receptionist without betraying any emotion. "...about five minutes, okay." He hung up, leaned over and whispered something in Begay's ear.

31/ TOGETHER AT LAST

Pack and Maddie paced outside the door marked Captain Rudolph DeJarlais. Neither spoke.

A tall, clean-shaven Indian with broad shoulders and looking smart in his pressed Flagstaff police uniform opened the door. His smile was pleasant. "Come in, folks," he said.

Amos' jaw dropped! His eyes tearet as he leaped from his chair and wrapped his arms around the lovely blond woman standing speechless in the doorway.

Sadie knew immediately who she was. And the handsome man at her side was a picture of Amos. But even better looking.

"Mom...I can't believe it," he sobbed. "And Dad! The two of you— together!" Pack joined his son in a three-person embrace. "Oh my God I can't believe this."

Everybody in the room was swept into the emotion of the moment.

Amos stood back from his parents, dabbed his shirtsleeve at his eyes and shook his head. "This is a dream come true." He turned to Sadie and took her hand. "Sadie, these are my parents."

Sadie shook hands with Pack and gave Maddie a brief hug. "I'm Amos' *friend*."

"Friend?" Amos put his arm around Sadie's shoulder and pulled her close to his side, "That's putting it mildly— Mom, Dad, she might not know it yet, but I'm going to do everything I can to make Sadie a Moran some day."

Maddie's jaw dropped as she looked from Sadie to Amos and back to the equally startled young woman. "My goodness," she beamed.

Sadie's face flushed, "Amos, what on earth—?"

Maddie's arm encircled Sadie as the family hug added a fourth member.

Pack, concerned about his son's conspicuous injuries, was the first to step away, "What happened to you, Amos?"

"Nothing too bad. I'll tell you about it later."

Maddie touched his swollen eyebrow, "A fight?"

"Yeah, kinda. I'm okay, Mom." Amos, still overwhelmed by the moment, was at a loss for words. "There's so much..."

"I know," Maddie agreed, giving him a soft kiss on the cheek. "And what's with the beard?"

Amos said, "It'll be gone tomorrow, Sadie's anxious to see what I really look like."

They all shared a laugh over the beard. But caught together at this moment in the Flagstaff police department and under circumstances so completely unexpected was awkward for each of them in different ways. Pack was concerned about a 'problem' he didn't yet understand, Maddie over her son's appearance, and Sadie about where she belonged in mix.

Amos shook his head in disbelief. "I can't tell you how happy I am to see the two of you together. I've prayed my heart out. What happened?"

Pack smiled, winked, met Maddie's eyes. "As hard as we tried, the separation just didn't work"

The laughs, however, were as strained as the situation.

"Oh, excuse me," Amos said, turning away from his parents, "This is Captain DeJarlais, Officer Begay."

They all shook hands. "I can't thank you fellows enough," Pack said with emotion in his voice. "This is just about the happiest day of my life."

Amos said, "You called them, didn't you, Captain?"

DeJarlais nodded, "I called the Hibbing police, Amos. But I understand that your parents were already headed in our direction."

Maddie thanked the two Flagstaff officers as well, "We're deeply indebted."

"We were pulled over in Colorado," Pack said. "The patrolman told us that we had a message from my Chief in Hibbing. Now we're here."

Amos reached for the Captain's hand, "Thanks, Mr. DeJarlais. Even though I asked you not to...in my heart I was hoping you would."

All of the introductions made and emotions spent, there was an awkward moment among them. Sadie broke the ice, "Mrs. Moran, I hope that you'll be staying in Flagstaff for a while."

"I would hope to, Sadie. We've all got a lot of catching up to do." She brushed back her hair, then smoothed the wrinkles in her satin blouse, "Hopefully we can find a motel room pretty soon. We've driven straight through from Denver."

Pack leveled his eyes toward DeJarlais, "I'd like to spend some time with you, Captain—if that's possible." Meeting his son and Sadie sitting in the Flagstaff police station spoke volumes about something. "I understand that my son has some sort of problem."

"It's more like *we*, Begay and myself, have a problem. It would by my pleasure to bring you up-to-speed, Mr. Moran...Pack."

Sadie tugged at Maddie's elbow, leaned toward her ear. "Amos' car is just down the street, Mrs. Moran. I'd be happy to take you out to the Pony Soldier Motel. Seems the men have things to talk about."

"Maddie, please, Sadie." She smiled at Sadie's offer, looked at Pack, "I'd really love to find a place, dear. You and Amos could join us later."

"Take our car, Maddie," Pack said. "Amos and I will meet you in a little while. If that's okay with you, Sadie? Afterwards, the four of us can go out to dinner."

32/ GETTING DOWN TO BUSINESS

DeJarlais, Begay and Pack Moran had much in common. All were veteran cops and none were very good at small talk pleasantries. "Lets get down to business, Pack," DeJarlais suggested. "We've got a homicide on our hands here."

Amos sat off to the side, brimming with pride at seeing his father sitting shoulder to shoulder with DeJarlais—one cop to another. It was almost beyond belief: His dad, here in Flagstaff, to help clean up what had become a messy chapter in his young life. But, more than anything else, his spirit was buoyed by something much more important— his parents were back together! His life was finally back in order.

DeJarlais began with the Friday homicide. His depiction was detailed and expressed with professional articulation. At times the Flagstaff Captain asked his partner to add to the picture being painted. On his desk, he folded open the coroner's report and outlined the salient facts:

- *Approximate time of death between Eleven PM (Friday) and One AM (Saturday);*
- *Single stab wound punctured aortic artery below the rib cage and between the spleen and liver;*
- *Weapon presumably, a filet knife with a six-inch blade, thrust delivered with considerable force. Angle of blade suggests assailant was right-handed.*

Twenty minutes later, DeJarlais turned to Pack. "Your son and Sadie Kearney have helped us a great deal so far. Amos, as I've said, is the only witness we have so far. Naturally, we're scouring the neighborhood, but nothing's come up yet." He scratched his head, "And, *if* the Tomlinson boy is involved in this...well, we're going to have to walk through fire. Believe me...Pack." He explained who the wealthy Tomlinson's were.

Begay added, "Harold Tomlinson's attorney is a guy named Jim Morrow and he's a handful, too. Plus, Judge Howard Flynn. Our Flagstaff judge and Tomlinson are golf buddies at their private club—Harry and Howie, as the locals often call them, are tight."

Pack regarded his son, "You did what you should have done, Amos. And, as you can see, you've given some very fine officers a very big headache."

Amos warmed to the compliment," If I wasn't certain that the wrong man was in jail...I don't know if I would have had the courage to contact Captain DeJarlais when I did."

"I'm inclined to agree with your son, Pack. Sam Yazzie, down in Number 4 cell, has some other issues. We're pretty certain that he mugged an old lady, stole her purse and more than two hundred dollars with it." He laughed weakly, "I hope you don't get the impression that Flagstaff has a lot of crime. We don't really. But, with major railroads and Interstate highways running through town, we get our share of transients. And, like everywhere in America, we got some drug problems, too."

Pack considered what DeJarlais had just said. His gut instinct was that the murder was drug related. DeJarlais and Begay had treated him like a colleague, but— Pack had no legal authority in this jurisdiction. How might he be of assistance without getting in the way or stepping on toes? The two cops struck him as being highly competent and fair-minded. In capital cases like this one, complicated by the local power structure, he believed that the solution might only come from breaking someone down: probably an accomplice to the crime. "Are you going to talk further with this Loflin boy, and Marty James?"

"Lofley," DeJarlais corrected. "Yes, later today. They have classes this afternoon so we'll pay them a visit at home."

"Tough kids?" Pack asked.

"Never in trouble with us," Begay said.

"Potheads, users?"

"We have suspicions, but nothing on record. Some of our people are looking into that," DeJarlais said. "Like you, I have no doubt that drugs are involved."

Pack nodded. He had a good picture of where things stood. "Rudy, I'm out of my bailiwick here, but I'd like to help in any way I can. I've been given a 'blank check' leave from my Chief in Hibbing. I'd like to see this through."

DeJarlais and Begay stood, offered their handshakes. "Pack, without raising any eyebrows around here, I'd like to consider you...what should I say...? A professional consultant?"

"I'd be privileged, sir. Arlen, Rudy, thanks again. I don't know where my wife and I would be right now if you hadn't called Hibbing."

Outside police headquarters, Amos bumped his father's shoulder. "I'm so damn happy I could cry, Dad. You just don't know how great it feels to see you and Mom together."

"I guess you had everything to do with that, Amos. I should be thanking you for running away and for all the hoops and headaches that you put us through. It's been quite the escapade, hasn't it, son?"

Amos smiled at his father's choice of words: escapade. "Where would you and Mom be if DeJarlais hadn't called back home? I asked him not to do that, you know."

"We were headed to Phoenix. To see Mike Rapovich."

Amos laughed heartily, "You're pretty good, Dad. How did you figure that out?"

Pack explained all that had happened on his end of the so-called escapade—from his trip to St. Thomas the previous weekend to getting pulled over in Colorado the day before. "You've covered your tracks pretty well, Amos."

"A worthy adversary, right?"

Pack gave his son a light punch on the shoulder. "I'd use the word rebel."

Amos winced at the pain, "Ouch...let me tell you, they sure know how to beat a guy up around here. My body is one huge bruise. I thought I was going to die on the floor of my apartment."

Pack considered the thrashing his son had endured. "We both know who did it, don't we? Well, the ones who laugh last laugh best. We're going to get to the bottom of all this."

33/ FEMALE BONDING

Sadie and Maddie bonded quickly. "That's the north edge of the campus," Sadie gestured from behind the wheel of the Moran's Oldsmobile. Her offer to drive across town was graciously accepted.

"Did you meet Amos on campus?" Maddie inquired.

Sadie maneuvered through the Santa Fe traffic, eastward toward the strip of restaurants and motels. "No, we were walking down the street last

Friday night," she laughed easily. "Truth be told, I sauntered up next to him and asked if he'd buy me a drink. Not very ladylike by any means. But I could tell by the way he was walking that the town was new to him. I've lived in Flag all my life. We hit it off immediately."

"I would think so. Amos' eyes were sparkling when he introduced you. And...his pronouncement...about your not knowing that you were going to be his wife—well, that really caught me off guard."

"Me, too." Sadie wondered how she would respond to Maddie's surprise. "Do you believe in love at first sight, Maddie?"

"Absolutely—from experience, no less. I think I knew from the first that Pack was the one for me. At least I hoped so. His younger sister, her name's Mary, was my best friend."

"Like father, like son."

Sadie had become so comfortable with this attractive and vibrant woman beside her that she was unafraid to be open and honest. "When we met, Amos told me his name was Jerry. It wasn't until yesterday that I got the truth out of him. You see, he was trying to live his life incognito: thus the beard, the name Jerry, and a Denver home address. He was pretty good at first, but without his knowing it, I tripped him up." She explained Amos' few slips and her trusty atlas.

Maddie shook her head, considered her next words. "His father and I are responsible for all that, you know. We broke his heart. He ran away. Over the past few days, Pack and I have finally talked about the consequences of what we've done. They have been wonderful days—but not without a lot of pain for both of us. A lot of healing happened once we became truly honest with each other."

Sadie smiled inside at the truth of what Maddie had just said.

In ten minutes they pulled into the motel lot.

"I hope you can stay until the men get back, Sadie. I'll shower quickly and we can visit some more. Will that be okay?"

"I'd enjoy that. Don't rush on my account." Sadie called home, got her mother on the phone. "Mom, I won't be home to make supper for you and Dad. Will you be able to find something? I think there's still some leftover meatloaf in the fridge."

Dorothy Kearney's voice was groggy, "I think so. I'll check later, your daddy's taking a nap right now. I didn't get to the dishes today and had hoped you could do the laundry when you got home."

"Maybe later, Mom. Why don't you take a nap, too? I won't be too late." She added a lie, "A group of us are going to the library to begin working on a sociology project."

The inevitable comparison of her parents with those of Amos brought a grimace of apprehension to her drawn face. An alcoholic and debilitated father and a chronically depressed and usually over-sedated mother would hardly be appropriate social company for the Morans. If Amos had lied to her about his past, perhaps her shameful deception was even greater. Pack and Maddie were handsome, affluent, intelligent, gregarious...all the qualities that her parents had once been and, in recent years, seldom were. Even more candidly, perhaps, the Morans possessed qualities that her parents had squandered. How often had Sadie wondered *what might have been* since the tragic deaths of her brother and sister? A million and more?

Yet, on good days—and there were some of those, too—her parents could be charming people. Despite her regimen of meds, Dorothy was an avid reader and enjoyed talking about books. Edward devoured the sports pages and could discuss any sport with even the most knowledgeable fan. Sadie hoped that if ever the Morans and Kearneys met, Edward and Dorothy would be having a *good day*. Despite their disabilities, both were loving and caring people.

"I'll only be another minute or two," Maddie called cheerfully from the bathroom.

∼

Troy Tomlinson skipped his afternoon classes. DeJarlais had shaken him. In his mind, Troy was replaying the cop's accusations and threats. Maybe he had been foolish to involve his stepfather's attorney friend, Jim Morrow. He would get home before his parents arrived from their weekend in Phoenix and make the downstairs rec room look as if there had been a drinking party. He would empty all the beer bottles from a case that Harry had stored in the garage, transfer cigarette butts from the ashtrays in his car into ashtrays in the basement, find some potato chip boxes in the kitchen, and make the place look as 'college kids' messy as possible. And, if he was going to create some tracks, he was going to erase some others.

Back at the house, Troy raced downstairs to the hamper below the laundry chute, rummaged through three days of dirty clothing. Thank God, Marjorie, the Tomlinson's maid, had been given the holiday weekend off. He found the jeans he wore on Friday night. Sure enough, there were tiny stains of blood on the lower legs and cuffs. He stuffed the pants in a plastic garbage bag along with two pair of dark socks and the navy Polo shirt with a dark coffee stain on the front. In the hall closet upstairs he found the brown loafers he had been wearing over the weekend. Without examining them, he added a pair of shoes to the bag. He remembered that he had been wearing Brian's trench coat on Friday night. If his pants had bloodstains, so would the coat. His mind was racing. He'd have to tell Brian to get rid of the coat as soon as possible. Burn it!

The stabbing of Evering that night had been more of a thrill than an angry outrage over drugs. The knife he wielded was intended to scare the shit out of the grungy scumbag. But—the thought of killing overwhelmed him. One powerful thrust! The memory was vividly etched in his memory.

Before he could get the plastic bag out to the outside garbage can, he heard the Lincoln entering the attached three-stall garage. "Fuck!" he cussed out loud. There was no time to create the party scene. He tossed the bag toward the back of the walk-in closet. His temples had beads of nervous sweat when his parents entered the kitchen entry from the garage with shopping bags and luggage.

"Hi Mom," Troy crossed the room to give Mildred Tomlinson a hug and kiss. "Harry," he said without enthusiasm toward his stepfather. "How was the trip?"

Mildred dropped her purse on the table, set the bags on the ceramic-tiled floor. "We're both exhausted, Son. Me from shopping and your father from golf. But, a good time all the same. How are you? Did your first day of classes go well?"

Troy small-talked with this mother while Harold unpacked the trunk.

When his parents had sufficiently unloaded and Harold Tomlinson had mixed martini's for him and his wife, Troy told them to join him in the living room. "Something I've got to tell both you about." He had rehearsed his story since leaving DeJarlais hours before.

Troy was masterfully contrite while explaining his having a few friends over to play ping-pong and pool at the house on Friday night. "I know you've told me not to do that when you're gone, but I tried to get away with something. It's been bothering my conscience." He dropped names of some friends then added, "But Brian and Marty helped me clean up everything so you wouldn't even notice."

Mildred smiled her approval, "I'm glad you told me. "I guess if there was no trouble—"

"None at all, Mom. We all behaved." Troy went on to explain the 'misunderstandings' and harassment of Captain DeJarlais that morning. "The cops thought that some of us had done some vandalism that night. You know I don't do drugs, Mom." Troy focused the story on his mother. Anything that upset her was certain to upset his stepfather. He turned to Harold, "I spoke with Mr. Morrow like you've told me to do if ever there was a problem, Harry."

Harold Tomlinson nodded his approval. "What did Howie have to say, Son?"

Troy winced at the reference. He hated when his stepfather called him *Son*. "Not to worry about it. Tell you everything when you got home. That's about all," Troy said.

Harold drained his martini, "Then, don't worry about it. I'll probably see him at the club tonight." Both men were charter members of the exclusive Continental Country Club. "I'll let you two visit while I shower." He tousled Troy's hair as he walked past him toward the stairway leading to the second level of the large three-storied estate.

Later, Brian Lofley answered Troy's call. "Yeah, I'll take care of it, Troy," he promised. "Tomorrow." Troy was always telling everybody what to do and how to do it. Brian had always hated that. His friendship with Troy was something he never quite understood. Both he and Marty James had talked about Troy's power trip stuff: How Tomlinson called all the shots. Maybe, over time, a subtle fear cultivated the warped relationship among them. However he might rationalize the circumstances, Troy's dominance and manipulation were the tight knots that bound the trio together.

Troy explained DeJarlais' interrogation. "So, *we've* got a little problem, Brian. The Captain didn't say much, but the way he looked at me when he said he was going to talk to everybody in Flagstaff about the Evering *thing* (he could not bring himself to use the word *murder*) made me feel like you and me and Marty were near the top of his list. The asshole made me nervous."

The mention of Evering's name made Brian even more nervous. He would have to talk with Marty later. Just the two of them. Troy was leading them into a pool of quicksand.

"Don't forget to take care of it," Troy insisted. "Tomorrow, Brian!" He decided to burn the plastic bag with his own clothes.

Ten minutes later, Brian held the trench coat up to the light. He could see some obvious stains. "Damn you, Tomlinson!" He remembered how Troy had grabbed his coat without asking, then tossed it in the back seat of the car later that evening. "Bullshit," he grumbled. Brian had paid twenty-five dollars for the coat the previous spring. Rather than throw it away, he'd bring it to the cleaners later in the week.

When Troy had gone up to his bedroom to study and Harold had left for the golf course, Mildred went out to her front yard and turned on the spigot for her garden hose. The weekend had been hot and dry and her flowers looked withered.

"Mildred. How was your trip?" Eloise Hutchins called from across the street and walked over.

"Just fine," was all she said. Eloise was difficult to tolerate. Her neighbor was an incessant yakker, a gossip, and a busybody who simply had to know everybody else's business.

"Just thought you'd like to know that your son didn't have the party—in case the police have any questions for you."

"Oh—!"

"Yes, that DeJarlais from the police called me. I told him that you were very strict about that...when you and Harold are out of town, I mean."

Mildred was curious, "You mean on Friday night?"

"Yes. The neighborhood was as quiet a mouse."

Mildred Tomlinson had inspected the basement rec room before going outside. It looked much the same as it had when they left for Phoenix. She stiffened, "The police called you?"

Eloise explained. "So as far as I know Troy was a good boy while you were gone."

Back inside, Mildred poured a Manhattan from her husband's decanter. Troy had made up his story about a party. Why? What had he really done? What were the police checking on? Another lie...there had been so many that she had trouble believing anything he said. Troy, she had feared since his early childhood, had a sociopathic personality. Lying didn't bother him. He also had a temper. Mildred Tomlinson was terrified of her only son. When he was eleven, he had kicked and slapped her for making him return a baseball glove he had stolen from a sports store. When he was fifteen he slashed the tires on her car for not letting him go to the movies with friends. Fear of reprisal kept her from telling anybody about Troy's behavioral problems.

∼

On campus Wednesday morning, Brian Lofley looked for Sadie Kearney. She had a third period sociology class in Liberal Arts. When he spotted her, she was walking hurriedly toward Grammage. Brian followed at a distance. "Son-of-a-bitch," he cussed. Waiting for Sadie was the Moran kid. Obviously, he and Troy had not scared him off.

Brian trailed them as they left the campus and headed downtown. When they entered the police station, Brian turned back. He'd find Troy and tell him about what he had seen.

34/ FATHER AND SON

Amos closed the door on his El Camino, turned toward his dad, "Let me give you a little tour of Flag before we head over to the motel. That will give Mom and Sadie a little more time to get to know each other."

Pack, however, had slipped deeply into thought as he surveyed all that was around him. "Sure," he mumbled.

Amos recognized his father's rumination, allowed him time to put the past two hours into some kind of perspective. He was a cop through and through.

In two minutes, Amos was pulling into the north lot of the campus. "Let's take a five minute stroll, Dad. I really like it here...I think my classes are going to be great." He knew he'd be having a conversation about his future plans when they all got together later. Amos planned to say here for a while.

As they walked, Amos identified the red stone buildings and mentioned those where he and Sadie had classes. "Have you heard a word I've said, Dad?" Pack hadn't spoken in several minutes.

"Sorry, Son. I'm still in my 'cop mode' I guess. All kinds of things running through my mind. Nice campus," he added absently.

"What kind of things, Dad?"

Pack laughed weakly, "It's not that I don't have confidence in DeJarlais and Begay, because I'm very impressed with both of them...it's just that I'm trying to figure out what I would do if the case were mine. That's all."

"They're pretty good cops, Dad. And this is turf they know like the back of their hands. Is there something I'm missing? I mean, I thought you and them were on the same page."

"Oh, we are, for sure." He placed his hand on Amos' shoulder. "You got the absolute hell beaten out of you the other night: those hoodlums could've killed you, Amos. Why?"

"Like I said, I'm almost positive it was this Tomlinson kid, and Brian Lofley. I think Brian is an old boyfriend of Sadie's."

Pack shook his head, "No. If Lofley's a jealous former boyfriend, he calls you out where others can see the encounter. That's the macho thing to do. You were maced and cold-cocked by two guys: not the manly thing for a spurned lover to do."

Amos did not reply. One-on-one he could handle Brian Lofley.

As if he'd read his son's thoughts, Pack said, "I'd like to see that kid call you out in a fair fight." He laughed, "I'll bet my last dollar that you'd take pretty good care of yourself."

They walked back toward the car without saying anything more. Both were lodged in unshared thoughts of their own. Amos was already missing Sadie and anxious to see how she and his mom were getting along.

Pack was making a mental list of all the things he would want to take up with DeJarlais and Begay the next day. Later he would go over every detail of Amos' story. Every tiny detail! He would poke every hole he could. Amos had been out drinking shortly before witnessing the murder. His sobriety was an important factor. Who in this strange town had their fingers on the pulse of the drug scene? The victim was a drifter and transients were not likely mugging suspects—unless they had money. And the only two sources of money were pimping and drugs. Who was dealing? Who was buying? More than anything else, where was the weapon—the knife? He would want to examine the coroner's report for himself.

More than anything else, Pack wanted to see the Tomlinson and Lofley kids. Eyeball-to-eyeball. Early the next morning, he'd find the address and do some surveillance of the Tomlinson house. He needed a 'feeling' to get things started. This town was probably like Hibbing in more ways than not. Crimes committed by the wealthy and influential were ball-busters for law enforcement. The playing field was never level: rich kid murders street riffraff—this was going be tough, very tough. Throw in a Clarence Darrow-type lawyer, and a boozing-buddy judge into the mix...? He remembered the DeJarlais off-hand reference to country-clubbers 'Harry and Howie'.

~

The four of them, Amos and Sadie, Pack and Maddie, enjoyed a bottle of champagne with a delicious prime rib and shrimp dinner along with animated conversation.

Amos was careful to integrate Sadie into the family reunion. "Do all the Minnesota male Morans have unusual names?' Sadie recalled that Amos had promised to tell her the origins of his name. "I'm so happy that my Amos is not really an every-day, plain-and-simple, Jerry...and Pack; how unusual that is. I can't help thinking of wolves and cigarettes."

They all laughed at her observation. "My mother still despises the nickname," Pack confessed. "For the same reasons as you. I'm Patrick Anthony Claude...my dad helped me come up with 'Pack' when I was a kid. I had a crush on a girl named Patty and wanted something more masculine than Pat. I might add that my mother has never—not once—called me Pack. I'll always be Patrick to her." Pack reached across the table and took Sadie's hand, "You'll love Amos' grandmother. I can't wait for you to meet her."

Sadie's heart skipped a beat at the affectionate gesture. Pack Moran was the most handsome and charming man she had ever met. She blushed, looked toward Maddie. "Maddie must be...let me guess... Madeline?"

Maddie nodded. "My grandmother was a Madeline. I struggled with it as a little girl, but Maddie has become comfortable." Maddie offered a brief family biography. Like Sadie's, hers was a dysfunctional family.

When Maddie finished her story, eyes were upon Sadie. She felt a chill. Out of respect for the Morans, she would be honest. She explained how wonderful things were when she was growing up. Then, everything fell apart a few years ago when she was fifteen. Sadie teared as she recalled Mikey's death in Vietnam, and her sister Maggie's tragic accident while hiking in a nearby canyon. "I'm the only survivor of all that. Edward, my dear father—" she told of her parents decline without a trace of self-pity or remorse. "Sometimes, bad things happen to good people. Despite sometimes feeling ashamed about how they cope with things... I love them both dearly."

Amos sat spellbound. He had not known any of this. His heart ached for the girl he loved. Maddie had a small well of tears in the corner of her eyes. "I hope we will be able to meet them both one of these days," she said. "My father was an alcoholic for most of his adult life. And I've almost lost connection with my mother over the years. Pack's family has become my family." She did not say a word about her personal tragedies: the loss of her Meghan and Michael.

Sadie felt as if an enormous burden had been lifted. Amos was squeezing her hand under the table and his deep Greene eyes were softer than she had ever seen them.

Amos cleared his throat, "I guess it's my turn to do the name game." Then he turned to his father. "Maybe I should let you do it, Dad. You tell the Amos story much better than I do."

Pack warmed to the opportunity. "Which story, Son" There have been a few."

Amos laughed, "The first one. Start with when I came home from first grade with tears in my eyes." One of his classmates at Assumption School had teased him—"Amos is for cookies, not real people." Another had added, "Let's call him Amy, for short." Amos, however, was quick to squelch the *Amy* moniker. Uncharacteristically, but in no uncertain terms, he warned the second boy: "Say that one more time and you'll be missing some teeth."

Pack sat back in a reminiscent posture, "Well, we talked about his name that night. I told him that many Catholics chose the names of great saints for their children. I wanted to do better than that. 'You have been named after a great prophet' I told him. Then I got out our family Bible and told him the story of Amos, a shepard and a poet and a man of divine judgment. I think he was reasonably impressed."

They all chuckled at Pack's telling of the story.

"There is more than one story, Patrick?" Sadie used Pack's given name to spark a reaction. Pack smiled, "A woman after my mother's heart."

Amos chimed in. "Sadie, when I was older, Dad told me that the reason for Amos was that he and Mom were going to have twenty-six children. And, they were going to go through the entire alphabet."

After a sherbet dessert, the table was cleared. It was nearly ten; three hours had flown by. "I'm sure everybody's pretty worn out after the day we've had," Pack said. After a long pause, he continued. "Maddie and I are going to stay in Flagstaff until this matter is cleared up."

Maddie nodded. Her intuition told her where her husband was going before he explained.

"We're all involved in this unfortunate business. I have every confidence in DeJarlais and Begay, and I am really limited in what I can do to help. But—" Pack unraveled a plan that had been evolving in his thoughts all evening. He expounded at length how each of them, in a surreptitious manner, could help out. "I want to get a feeling for this young Tomlinson. He doesn't know me from Adam, so I can keep an eye on everything he does, every place he goes. I'm pretty good at that. Amos, both you and Sadie have classes during the day and need to go about your lives as if nothing had happened. But, Sadie, if you could hang around the Lofley boy as much as possible during the day. He's an old friend of yours so that might be easier for you to do than any of us." He turned to Maddie, "Maybe you could spell Sadie from time to time. Especially after school. Maybe she could show you where Brian lives."

Amos said, "What about me?"

"As best you can, keep tabs on this Marty James. That way we've got all of them under a surveillance of sorts without raising any eyebrows in the process. We'll get a pretty good idea about their relationships and contacts. If drugs are a part of all this, maybe we can even spot a dealer."

It all made sense. Sadie giggled, "My role is going to be easy. Brian's always been crazy about me. Amos might get awfully jealous if he sees me holding hands with Brian."

Maddie giggled as well, "I will give you a time-out, Sadie— so you and Amos can have some time together."

Amos added, "I'm going to shave and get a haircut and wear sun glasses. A whole new look. Maybe Sadie won't even recognize me while I'm spying on her and Brian."

Amos drove Sadie home. He would spend another night at the Pony Soldier and move back to his downtown apartment the next day. Sadie was bubbly over his parents. "I've already got a huge crush on your dad," she said. "He's much better looking than you."

"I can beat him at one-on-one hoops every time...and I'm much smarter than he is. As you now have learned, I'm even prophetic."

After a long silence, Sadie's voice was subdued, serious: "Are you planning to go back to Hibbing after your parents leave...when this stuff's all over with here, Amos?"

They were approaching Sadie's house. "I've thought about going back for Christmas. But...*only* if you'll go with me."

Sadie smiled and kissed him on his swollen ear. "A perfect answer, a prophetic answer. Because if you go—I go."

Amos parked, put his arm around her shoulders. "Looks like we're going to have to lay low for a few days." Pack had outlined their fate. "I'm going to miss you terribly."

Sadie leaned into his long kiss, then pushed herself away. "I just remembered something. I know it's late but I have this...this obsession, Amos. I've just got to do something before we say goodnight.

"Was I really that good last night?"

"Let's just say I saw some potential and leave it at that. Come with me, this will only take a few minutes." Sadie opened her car door and stepped outside. All the lights were off inside her house. "Come on, Amos. My parents are already sleeping."

They tiptoed up the staircase. "Where are you taking me?" Amos was becoming confused.

"Shhhh, in here," Sadie whispered as she turned on the bathroom light switch. "Sit on the stool." She draped a towel over his shoulders, turned on the hot water, and opened the medicine cabinet.

Amos could hardly contain a laugh. "You're not going to—?"

"Only take a few minutes. Don't worry I'll be as careful as a surgeon."

Twenty minutes later, Sadie kissed him at her front door. "Now that wasn't so bad, was it?" she said as she ran her fingers over his smooth face.

35/ SURVEILLANCE

At six-thirty on Thursday morning a dark-colored Oldsmobile Cutlass was parked on Hutcheson Street in the posh Cherry Hill neighborhood. At seven-twenty, Troy Tomlinson backed his '65 GTO out of the garage and headed down Bertrand toward the campus.

Pack followed at a safe distance.

~

Rudy DeJarlais and Arlen Begay met for breakfast at the downtown cafe where they had a reserved booth every morning. In the back corner of Dee Dee's Diner the two cops would routinely share their daily agendas and bounce ideas off each other.

"Sleep well last night, Cap?" Begay knew that his partner was an insomniac and asked that very question almost every morning. DeJarlais usually lied.

"Not bad." He removed his cap, placed it on the vinyl seat beside him. "Wasn't that something yesterday? The family reunion, I mean. Everybody back together again. Heartwarming."

Begay nodded, smiled, "What did you think of this Pack guy?"

"I liked him. He didn't tell us what he thought we should be doing and kept his ideas pretty much to himself. Most cops like to let you know how damn good they are."

"I felt the same. He'd like to help, but what can he do?"

"What are we going to do is a better question, Arlen." He pulled out his notebook and scribbled the date, September 4, at the top of a blank page. Below he wrote the name Amos Moran. "The Moran kid was pretty beaten up wasn't he? What's your read on him?"

Begay pulled the shade against the sun, looked out the window. "Believable. Dad's a cop, so he's got good blood."

They both ordered English muffins.

"Think Tomlinson beat him up?"

DeJarlais scratched his head, "I wouldn't doubt it. He and Lofley. Might have been over the girl, Sadie...but I think not. Tomlinson!" The name had kept him from sleep the night before. He leaned over the table, "Arlen, have you met this new guy on the force, Loshe?"

"The one with the crew cut?"

"Yeah. Anyhow, I was thinking that we could give him a plain-clothes assignment. Put him on Tomlinson's tail. My gut instinct is that Evering was killed over some kind of drug dealing. Had to be! Nothing else makes much sense. Street people don't kill each other—they just move somewhere else when they have problems. I'm going to talk some more with Heebie Henton—see what he can find out for us." The most perplexing question was *motive*. Why would a few rich kids kill a transient? Kicks? Revenge for something? Drugs—that was the only plausible explanation.

"Sounds like a plan. What else?"

"I'd like to see Judge Flynn..."

"Just a minute, Rudy. We don't have a snowball's chance in hell of getting a search warrant if that's what your thinking. What young Moran says that he saw, and his getting himself beaten up, doesn't amount to a hill of beans."

"I can't argue that. But we've got to get into Tomlinson's house and look around. The longer we wait the more likely any evidence is going to disappear. He was damn scared when I mentioned the murder yesterday."

"Finding the weapon, the knife—that's going to be like finding a needle out there in the damn desert. Even an idiot would get rid of a knife."

"Maybe so. But there's got to be blood from the stabbing on someone's clothes, shoes. A punctured aorta is a gusher."

The two of them had thoroughly checked Sam Yazzie's clothes already. Nothing.

"According to Amos, the assailant was wearing a tossle cap and a dark trench coat. It was that damn tossel cap that stuck out most in his mind. I'd like to go through Tomlinson's wardrobe."

"How much does the Chief know about all this?"

"He's my first meeting this morning. He's probably going to shit his pants, Arlen...but we're damn lucky that Roth always sees the big picture. I'm sure he'll have some ideas of his own."

~

Pack followed the GTO, keeping at an inconspicuous distance. Tomlinson parked in a lot on the eastern perimeter of the campus, then walked toward a red-bricked building with a tall chimney. He had a backpack slung over his shoulder and textbooks under his arm. At a side door, Tomlinson entered the building.

Pack got out of his car and wandered to the shadowed corner of another building where he could better view the side entry door. Ten minutes passed. Was there another exit? Pack moved to a different vantage place. The side door swung open. Tomlinson hurried away toward the center of the campus. A minute later, Tomlinson had joined a group of friends.

"Shit!" Pack cussed. Tomlinson didn't have the backpack. He raced toward the building. A small sign near the door caused his heart to drop into the bowels of his stomach. 'Incineration & Heating Plant'. Inside he felt a wash of heat on his face. "Hey...anybody here?" he shouted. He saw a railing-lined stairway heading downstairs. Leaping three stairs at a time, he headed into the basement chamber. The roar of a furnace struck his ears. He hollered again, "Anyone here?"

A stout man in a Greene uniform came around the corner. "What the hell you doing in here? This is a restricted area—can't you read the signs?"

The name patch read 'Kolbe' the red face read anger. "Get the hell outta here before I call security."

Pack stifled his anger, "Did you see the young man in here...just a few minutes ago?"

"Nobody's been down here. Like I said, this is restricted. Now, are you going to leave, or—?"

"Mr. Kolbe, I don't want any trouble with you. But, I'm looking for someone who came into your building, then left by the side door upstairs a few minutes later. A tall, lanky kid. A student here. He had a backpack with him. And, I suspect, he tossed it in the furnace."

Kolbe shook his head, "Can't be. I would have seen anyone around the furnace. I'm the Boiler Technician here—nobody trespasses."

Acknowledging that he hadn't been watching the furnace would only get Kolbe into trouble. Pack knew defeat when he faced it. He asked a stupid question anyway. "You've got the furnace fired-up, don't you?"

∼

"Hey, Bry!" Sadie called from a few feet away. "Wait up."

Brian Lofley gave her a strange look. He was positive that his former girlfriend had turned on him—hanging out with this Moran jerk, talking to the police. He needed to know what her visit to the police station yesterday was all about.

"Sadie, what you been up to?" He smiled, flung his arm about her shoulders as if nothing had happened between them. "Ain't seen you around much lately. You goin' out with that new kid?"

Sadie would be careful. "I was. That's history now."

"You talked with DeJarlais about last Friday yet? You know, Troy's party?" He winked.

"Oh yeah, he's a real jerk, don't you think?"

"What did you tell him?"

"Same as you and everybody else, I guess. Arrived about ten-thirty, left about two. Played some pool. Why?"

"Just asking. Someone said you and what's-his-name went to the police station yesterday. Thought that was kinda strange. Most of us got questioned here on campus on Tuesday."

Sadie tried to check her surprise, "Oh, that was this guy—Jerry Moran—he had a parking ticket to take care of. I went along. It was just after that when he, Jerry I mean, tried to feel me up in his car. That was it! I slapped him a good one."

"Someone else slapped him pretty good, too." Lofley laughed. "The pervert must be striking out with our Flag girls, right?"

Sadie felt very uncomfortable. 'Sure looks that way. Say, Bry, how are the classes going?" She would divert the conversation. "You got Doc Schultz for Soc?"

"No. I lucked out. Got Lang instead. So, you were saying that this Jerry guy was paying a parking ticket?" He'd call the 'Fish' later and check that out. Don Fisher was the inside guy.

"Yeah."

Brian Lofley withdrew his arm, "Gotta run, Sadie-girl. Maybe see ya at the 'L.Q.' tomorrow night. Dollar pitchers of Coors, remember?"

Sadie considered the plan she and Maddie had arranged by phone earlier that morning. "What are you doing later, let's say...about three?"

Brian paused in mid-step. Was Sadie really showing some interest? "Why?"

"I'll buy you a cup of coffee at the Java Joint. Okay?"

He would play it cool, "Maybe. We'll see." Turning away, he smiled to himself. For three years he had tried to get into her pants. He never got close; but he never got slapped, either. Maybe it took an asshole like this Jerry to make her realize what a catch Brian Lofley really was.

∼

When Amos awoke that morning, he felt strange. It took ten minutes for him to realize what the peculiar feeling was about. "Not too bad," he said to himself in the mirror as he splashed cold water on his newly-shaven face. "Not too bad at all." He grinned at the memory of Sadie's scissor cutting, lathering, and Gillette blue-blading his face.

Amos saw Marty James twice that Thursday morning. Once talking with his sister, Sally, and later as he entered the Liberal Arts Building for a class. James was barrel-chested with weight-lifter arms and short, thick legs. He looked like a linebacker. Amos wondered if James was one of the two men who beat him up. For two days he had totally ignored his class work and had to catch up on his reading. He wandered toward the library. It was going to hard on him to avoid having any contact with Sadie.

In the library, he spotted Billy Greenee for the first time since the previous Friday. He sat across the table from his friend. Greenee looked up, frowned as if some private space of his had been rudely invaded, then returned his attention to the book he was studying.

"Hmmm...hmmm." Amos cleared his throat.

Greenee looked up disturbed, then back to his book—then: "Jerry?"

"In the flesh, amigo."

"Jeeze, I hardly recognized you." He squinted, "Sadie Kearney do that to you, Jerry? Or Brian Lofley? " He laughed, "I saw Bry this morning, if it was him... you didn't leave a mark on his pretty face."

"I dumped my cycle," Amos lied.

Greenee puzzled, Jerry's arms were not skinned up. "None of my business, but Sadie's been Brian's girl. Thought I should tell you that."

Amos shrugged, "He can have her."

Greenee shrugged, none of his business. "Something else...what is it, Jerry?"

"The beard."

Later, Amos nearly bumped into Troy. There was no sign of recognition. Amos smiled inwardly, rubbed his smooth face, pulled down his baseball cap, and slid his sunglasses up on his nose.

Maddie Moran could almost pass for a college student in her tennis shoes, jeans and open-necked, short-sleeved white blouse. She had spent the morning wandering around downtown and was crossing Santa Fe Avenue, heading for the NAU campus. She wanted to get a good feeling for this new place. Comparisons with Hibbing were unavoidable. Flagstaff appeared much busier, more commercially prosperous, and definitely more youthful. Few empty storefronts along the sidewalks, more foreign cars (mostly Hondas and Toyotas) on the streets, and a busyness in general.

At the Chamber office she picked up maps of the city and campus along with brochures about the city's history and tourist attractions. She was simply killing time and looking around for now. At three she would meet

Sadie at a coffee shop called the Java Joint on Benton. If everything went as hoped, Sadie would have Brian Lofley with her and would introduce Maddie to him as her aunt from Denver.

36/ *CHIEF ROTH*

Chief of Police, Leon Roth, surveyed the stack of reports, files, and office memos on his desk. Paperwork was the bane of administration—he hated pushing paper as much as he hated meetings and committees: City council, municipal financial planning, NAU campus expansion oversight, Chamber Pro-action Task Force, and twenty other annoying civic responsibilities. Most of the time the corpulent chief felt more like a bureaucrat than a cop. It was no wonder his new navy colored trousers had a 42-inch waist.

He scanned last night's reports: three drunk drivers, three domestics, two 'suspicious' character reports—one a peeper, the other a prowler— a materials theft at the Madison construction site, another assault outside of Joe's Place (three or four every week), an indecent exposure on Franklin Avenue. "Bullshit," he cussed into his empty office. His yellow daily report indicated five people in lockup downstairs. He'd be talking to DeJarlais in a few minutes about what to do with Sam Yazzie. Roth was of the opinion that they could make a reasonably good circumstantial evidence case for homicide...or, maybe, get a clear confession of robbery in the yet unresolved Gertrude Brown matter. Maybe both.

Taped to his desk lamp was an 8x10 sheet of red paper with the name *Evering* penned in bold black marker pen. The murder was priority one and nearly a week later nothing was happening. Mayor Bill Erwin had called again last night. For the umpteenth time all Roth could tell him was that things were moving slowly. Although the story had been relegated to page two of the *Sun*, it remained in the reading public's eye every day. Thursday nights were when the Flagstaff City Council met and Roth would be called upon for a progress report. "Shit," his expletive brought him back to where he had started minutes ago: shuffling papers from one side of his desk to the other and fuming over the all the crapola he was responsible for.

"Four more months," he mumbled. 'Come hell or high water', when he retired next January, he was going to leave a clean slate for the next guy.

Rudy DeJarlais never shook hands with the Chief. He simply plopped in the leather chair in front of Roth's large mahogany desk. As always, he opened his notebook. Rudy was organized and to-the-point. "I think you're going to be very disappointed to learn that we've got a solid lead on the Evering matter, Chief." He went on to explain the Amos Moran information.

"Holy Jesus!" Roth straightened in his chair at the name of Troy Tomlinson. "Harry's kid? You've got to be pulling my leg, Rudy. Harry Tomlinson's son!"

"I knew that wasn't going to set well, Chief. But, I'm almost positive that Sam Yazzie's not our guy. We're thinking about charging him with assault, battery, robbery—whatever fits. Begay's certain that Sam's going to confess to that Brown purse-snatching episode last week. Arlen's going to visit with him this morning. So—?" DeJarlais gave his boss a 'what next' shrug.

Roth frowned and sent DeJarlais a dismissive wave of his wide hand. He was almost as certain as his captain that Yazzie was not a murderer. "So, what? You think I've got any answers, Rudy? Some kid from...where did you say it was?...in Minnesota? comes in and tells you that he saw Troy Tomlinson murder Evering. That's a real pipe-full, Rudy."

"A real can of worms, Chief. I know it. But we can't sit on our hands—time is wasting away."

Feeling the familiar symptoms of a migraine, Leon Roth leaned back in his chair. What should have been good news was bad news in disguise. It wouldn't be that difficult to bring charges against Sam Yazzie for the Evering murder. The notorious wino had a violent record and a bad reputation in Flagstaff. A good prosecutor would give any jury, and Judge Flynn, plenty to think about. With a conviction, Mayor Erwin would get his kudos from the city council, the department would be vindicated, and any lingering public concern would be conveniently appeased. But, that would be railroading. The Chief knew that cops had done worse things before, but not in Flagstaff and not on Roth's watch. And DeJarlais would be over his desk and at his throat if he so much as hinted at a frame job. 'A can of worms...' what an understatement of reality!

Roth shook his head. "What's your plan, Rudy? I know you've got something up your sleeve. Troy Tomlinson!" he mumbled the name in obvious distaste for the third time in five minutes. Roth would be in a foursome with Harold Tomlinson in the Club's annual fundraising tournament this coming weekend.

DeJarlais explained his strategy from clearly outlined notes:

- *the new cop, Roland Loshe would go undercover; "He's only been here a few weeks and isn't known to anybody on the campus..."*
- *Heebie Henton would hang out in the Orpheum neighborhood and look for the guys from LA who dropped by periodically... "I doubt if the Evering murder has made the LA papers so the suppliers don't have a clue yet... and Henton is a non-threatening face on the street."*

- *Send 'Fish' down to Phoenix for a week or two to find any connection between the drug traffic down there and in Flagstaff, "He's pretty good with the college kids..."*
- *DeJarlais would not suggest to Roth that Fisher was a leak and could screw up everything he was trying to do. It was Begay's idea to get Fish out of town on some trumped-up assignment.*

DeJarlais saved the toughest issue for last. He would count on the experience and wisdom of his boss. "I'd like to pay a visit to Judge Flynn. We will need a warrant to do any searching at the Tomlinson place. And I'll need you to be one hundred percent behind me on this. You and Howie Flynn go way back, Chief."

Roth grimaced, "Do you really think you're going to find anything? It's been, what—six days, already?" His wide forehead furrowed, "No. A bad idea. We'd only stir up a hornet's nest, Rudy. If the kid actually did it— which I seriously doubt— and he's stupid enough to hang his clothes back in the closet, and put the knife back in the kitchen drawer...then, there's no pressing urgency in doing a search today."

DeJarlais expected the rejection and was almost relieved when he got it. The courts had constrained police work so much that cops were handcuffed in nearly every aspect of investigative work. Miranda rights, search and seizure limitations—the Earl Warren Court had gone much too far in codling criminals. Fortunately, the Captain was pretty damn good at old-fashioned police stuff.

"You've got to come up with something more substantial and less circumstantial, Rudy. If we're going after Troy Tomlinson I want to be loaded for bear."

While DeJarlais was meeting with Chief Roth upstairs, Begay visited the small basement cell where Sam Yazzie suffered through his fifth day of withdrawl from booze. His fellow Navajo clansman wore an expression that spoke volumes of utter desperation and defeat. A cold sweat beaded on his broad brow as he fought through another episode of shakes.

"How you doing this morning, Sam?" Begay offered a woeful smile. The desk had told him that Yazzie wanted to talk to him.

"Not so good, Arlen." Sam used Begay's first name. "Thanks for comin' down ta see me. I ain't too well, ya know. Shakin' alla time, and vomitin' all the food I gets."

Begay sat at the end of the metal bunk without reply. Sam looked absolutely pathetic and smelled even worse.

"I wanned to talk with ya about things. Needin' a favor if'n I kin ask ya fer one."

Begay noticed the beginnings of tears in Yazzie's eyes. "What can I do for you, Sam?"

Sam Yazzie began to cry. "I need two hunnerd bucks, Arlen. Can ya loan me the money?"

Arlen Begay knew why Yazzie wanted that amount of money. He nodded, "I can help you with that, Sam...but only on one condition."

Yazzie rubbed away the stream of tears on his stubbled face. "I get me some kinda treatment...right?"

Sam Yazzie explained what he had done. "I wanna give her da money myself, Arlen...an tell'er I'm sorry fer doin' it."

'FLAG'

~

"Just blend in. Don't push, Roland." DeJarlais explained to the rookie Officer. Roland Loshe, twenty-two, was from Kingman and had logged only twenty-three days on the Flagstaff force. Most of his work had been learning the procedural ropes in the office. DeJarlais finished his briefing. "I've set everything up with the college. You'll be in three of Tomlinson's classes. Meet him, befriend him if you can, follow him—he and his pals hang out at the Latin Quarter, play pick-up at the football field on weekends and pool down at the Cue Ball a couple of times a week, along with all the other stuff college kids do."

Loshe, who could easily pass for a freshman, smiled easily. "Should be fun, sir. I just finished college at UNLV in June, so blending into campus life again will be a cake walk."

"Remember, don't push...just let things happen as they might." DeJarlais stressed.

~

Heebie Henton met Begay at the familiar coffee shop for a late morning piece of pie and milkshake. "Ten bucks a day? For hangin' around with 'Mo-Joe', Funk, and Willie Dunn, and dem other guys down at da Weatherford. I know 'em all. An 'memmer t'was me that tol'ya about the hoods from LA in da first place. If'n they show up agin I'll get plate nummers."

"That would help us a lot, Heebie. And, see what you can find out about any college kids you suspect might be looking for drugs." Begay had hoped to set up the snitch with a few bags to sell himself, but DeJarlais had nixed the idea. "We'll meet here early tomorrow morning."

Mid-afternoon. Maddie chuckled to herself. She had walked past her husband who was having a cigarette while visiting with two attractive coeds on a bench near the library. "Hmmm," she said, rolling her eyes. One of them, a shapely redhead wearing a tight burgundy sweater, was really interested in what her husband had to say. Pack had glanced up and away as if he didn't even know her. What an operator he was. She couldn't contain a wide smile as she checked her wristwatch: 2:45. Maddie strolled off the campus toward the Java Joint to meet Sadie for mid-afternoon coffee.

37/ JAVA JOINT

Sadie slid into the chair across from Maddie. "I had to look twice when I came in the door. Jeeze, with your hair back and that outfit you're wearing, you look just like one of us." Sadie's exaggeration was not far from the truth. Maddie looked years younger than – what? She could only guess: Maybe forty?

Maddie smiled at the compliment, sipped her Coke: "I think I could be a perpetual student. My college years at St. Scholastica, back in Minnesota, were among the best of my life. I still take a class at our local Community College every now and then. Art, literature, psych—whatever looks interesting at the time."

"What did you think of our campus, Maddie?"

"My goodness, I'd never heard of NAU until two days ago—it's lovely, and the new construction going on everywhere...well, I am impressed to say the least. How many students are enrolled here?"

"More than ten thousand I've heard." Sadie ordered coffee. "I talked to Brian this morning. Really strange. I got some strong 'I don't trust you' vibes. He asked about Amos. Saw the two of us go the police station yesterday...he must have been following us. How ironic, everybody following everybody else!" Sadie laughed at the notion. "I told him that Amos and I had split—under embarrassing circumstances." She explained the story she had given him.

Maddie laughed, "You didn't!" She remembered Randy Skalko, the first boy who tried to 'feel her up' back in ninth grade. Maddie had enjoyed it, but pushed his hands away with a reluctant 'don't you dare'.

Sadie laughed, too. Leaning over the table she said, "A pretty good comeback for spur-of-the moment' wouldn't you say? And, please don't ask me if Amos ever tried."

Maddie chuckled, "My Amos?"

"Anyhow, things didn't go too well with Bry."

"So, you'd be surprised if Brian shows up this afternoon?"

"I would." Sadie brooded for a moment, "He sure wasn't the same Brian I've known all my life. C'est l'vie, I guess."

"Sadie-girl."

The voice was familiar, Sadie looked up in surprise. Brian Lofley was approaching. "I didn't think you were going to show up." Sadie pushed a third chair out from the table and smiled "...Bry, this is my aunt from Denver—Maddie Loiselle. Have a chair and join us."

Maddie offered her hand, "Nice to meet you, Brian. Sadie was just talking about you, told me that she wanted me to get to know her friends while I'm visiting. Said she hoped you might be able to join us." She studied the man she would be watching these next few days. Brian was nice-looking, well dressed in a preppy way, and wore his dark hair in tightly-permed curls.

He looked more high schoolish than college-aged and probably didn't shave often.

"So, you're from out of town?" Brian commented as he nudged his chair closer to Sadie's.

"Denver, actually. On my way to Los Angeles for a job interview," Maddie said. "Haven't seen my niece in almost three years."

"Cool. So, are you staying in Flag for a while, or just passing through?"

"My interview is next week, so I'm just playing things by ear right now."

"Oh, I want you to stay, Maddie. At least through the weekend," Sadie pleaded.

Brian noticed Maddie's wedding ring, said nothing. "Coffee, Louise," he called to the obese, aproned, waitress. "Cream and sugar, too." Smiling at Sadie, "You're buying, right?"

Sadie nodded, leaned into Brian's shoulder in an obvious flirt. She tried to pick up the conversation of earlier that day, "So, is Lang piling on the homework yet? I've heard his tests are killers, and he's one of those research paper fanatics. Maybe you should have taken Schultz's class."

Brian dismissed Sadie's bait with a shrug instead of a comment. He seemed to be studying her aunt with more than casual interest. "I'm swamped with reading for Lit...three Steinbeck short stories for tomorrow," she tried again.

"What kind of job?" The question was posed to Maddie.

Maddie had noticed the intensity of Brian's stare. It made her uncomfortable. "Elementary school principal, I'm a teacher—finished my administration masters this summer."

"Uh-huh. Nothing open in Denver these days?"

Maddie puzzled, why was Brian ignoring Sadie? "My son, Sadie's cousin, is a student at UCLA. It would be nice for me to be closer...he might not agree, though."

Brian laughed, "You ain't old enough to have kids our age. Right Sadie-girl?" He poked her with his elbow.

Maddie was relieved to see Brian turn away from her and toward Sadie for the first time in a long minute. On the floor beside his chair and only inches from Maddie's knee was a brown grocery bag. Inside the bag, she thought, were items of laundry. What caught her attention was what looked like the collar of a trench coat, barely sticking out from the top of the sack. Her mind was racing.

Brian interrupted her thoughts. "Me and Sadie used to go out... Maddie. But, lately things have kinda gone sour—ya know?"

Sadie nestled her head on Brian's chest. "That's what you say, Bry. I told you, I'm free as a bird."

With eye contact between Sadie and Brian finally established, Maddie brushed the napkin from her lap, bent down to retrieve it. Keep his attention, Sadie, she said a quick prayer. Quickly she spread the top of the bag enough to get a better look inside. She felt a chill.

"Another cup, Brian." Maddie had straightened in her chair.

"Nah, cuttin' back on the caffeine. I gotta run, anyhow."

"Where you off to, Bry? You just got here," Sadie pouted.

"Errands." He stood, hung his hand over the table for Maddie. "Nice to've met you, Maddie. Hang around a while. Have Sadie take ya over to the Quarter tomorrow night."

Maddie took his hand, smiled, "I might just do that, Brian. Nice to have met you, too."

Maddie watched Brian walk out the front door and turn west toward Beaver Street. "Sadie, follow him. This minute!" Her voice had the sharp edge of urgency. "See where he's going with his errands. I can't explain why right now, okay?"

Sadie could read the fervor in Maddie's widened eyes. "Sure...you going to wait here for me?"

"Yes. Just hurry, Sadie!"

∼

Amos dreaded returning to his apartment. There was an empty feeling of gloom there and nothing but bad memories lurking within its dreary plaster walls. He parked behind McMahan's Furniture Store and began unloading his few belongings. Sadie had promised that she would help him do some decorating and make the place 'funky' was the word she used. He smiled at the inspiring thought.

It was only four in the afternoon and Amos had promised to join his parents for dinner at the motel around six. He would call Sadie from their motel room. Both he and Sadie had agreed to avoid seeing each other for the next few days. That was going be hard for them to do. But, necessary. And each had schoolwork to catch up on before falling hopelessly behind.

Pack had been beating himself up over the incinerator episode all day. He was convinced that key evidence had vanished into the thin mountain atmosphere of Flagstaff. By three in the afternoon he had become comfortable with his new persona (borrowing a page from his son's act) and an expert at NAU campus geography as well. He was, to those who were at all curious, a demography professor from the University of North Dakota who was doing population research in the Southwestern States— "everybody's leaving the rust belt for the sun belt" was a favorite line in his repertoire. Being Professor Howard Street was a fun cover for him to be acting out. Nobody that he had met that day seemed to have a clue as to what demography was all about. When he explained population pattern studies, all were highly impressed. Two coeds, obviously attracted to his fabricated intellect, wished he would consider teaching at their University. "It's really important stuff, Professor Street" they insisted. "If you need any help with your project..."

Troy Tomlinson's trail led nowhere: four classes, lunch in the campus cafeteria, an hour pretending to be studious in the library. Pack did little more than meet students, memorize faces, and get a feeling for the dynamics of the campus. At three-thirty he followed Troy's GTO back to the affluent and pine-shrouded Cherry Hill neighborhood.

38/ THE TRENCH COAT

Maddie waited impatiently for Sadie to return. Twenty minutes passed. All the while she had been rehashing Amos' description of what he had seen from his window that Friday night. A dark-colored trench coat! She was positive about that detail.

Sadie returned, hunched her shoulders: "So...what was following Brian supposed to be all about?"

"Where did he go from here?"

Still confused, Sadie explained: "He picked up a newspaper at the magazine shop, dropped off his bag at the dry cleaners on Beaver, got into his car and drove away. Probably headed home from there."

Maddie had been eyeing a coat rack near the Java Joint's front door. An old, beige, waist-length men's jacket hung by itself. Her survey of the few students in the shop led her to surmise that the jacket didn't belong to any of the customers. "Sadie, I'm going to do something I've never done before. Let's go."

Sadie's expression remained vague. "Okay?"

Maddie left two dollars on the table, took Sadie's elbow, and walked toward the door. Deftly, she snatched the jacket off the hook, draped it over her shoulders, and stepped to the sidewalk outside.

"It's not mine, Sadie. I'm only *borrowing* it for now. Where's the dry cleaners?"

Sadie rolled her eyes at the frumpy jacket and gestured across the street without making any comment. Whatever Maddie was doing simply baffled her. Maddie had her by the elbow and was steering her toward the cleaners in a half-run. "We've got to hurry," she said.

Inside the Quick and Clean, Maddie stepped to the counter, waited. A small Asian woman was putting plastic-sealed garments on a nearby rack. "Vith you in minute," she called."

Maddie spotted Brian's bag on the floor behind the counter. When the woman was finished, she asked, "Can I help you?"

"There's been a mistake," Maddie said in a strained voice. "My son was just here with our cleaning. That's his bag right there," she pointed. "He took the wrong jacket. My husband wanted this one cleaned," she handed the woman the beige jacket she had been wearing. "The one in the bag doesn't need cleaning just yet."

The woman picked up the bag, placed it on the counter, and took out the dark trench coat. "You vant dis back, den?"

"Yes, please."

"Dis is same cost, okay?"

"That's fine."

Sadie was finally getting the picture. Clever, she thought. Maddie was really on the ball.

"Here, you take back dis, den. Okay?" The woman slid the coat toward Maddie.

Maddie hesitated as she tucked the trench coat under her arm. "Could you rewrite the ticket...for Brian...Brian Lofley?"

"Juz give you my receete here, okay? Same ting." She tore out the top page of the Quick and Clean receipt book with Brian's name and address on the top, and scribbled signature below. "Bring back receete on Tuesday."

Outside, Sadie gave Maddie a pat on the back. "You just put Nancy Drew to shame, Maddie. That was a stroke of genius!"

They both laughed at the coup. "Pack will know what to do with Brian's jacket."

"You're so good I'm tempted to take you with me and do some shoplifting," Sadie said, taking Maddie's free hand.

Every minute she spent with Sadie Kearney more deeply confirmed how Amos had become so captivated by this remarkable girl. Not only was she pretty and smart, she was great fun to be with. She squeezed the small hand in hers: "Sadie, we're going to be a great team, you and me— I can just feel it."

Sadie returned her wide smile, "So can I. But, despite an obvious talent, you're not up to a female crime spree, are you?"

∼

Pack checked his wristwatch: 3:45. He had told DeJarlais that he would check in on Thursday afternoon. He also needed to call Oscar Sundval in Hibbing and tell his Chief that he would be spending some additional time in Flagstaff.

DeJarlais smiled as Pack came through the door. "Good to see you, Pack. Have a chair, I'll let you know what we've been up to today."

DeJarlais explained his meeting with Roth and the strategy that was now in place. "Loshe will do a good job on campus, and Heebies' been invaluable to Arlen and me for years."

Pack nodded, "You folks are good, Rudy. I think we would have done the same back home. Your Chief, like mine, seems to have a good perspective on things." He chose not mention that he had been a police chief for many years.

"So, what have you been up to today, Pack? Somehow, I'll bet you haven't been a casual tourist in our fair city."

Pack considered how he would answer. He did not want to give the impression that what he, and his family were doing, might be undermining what the Flagstaff police were trying to accomplish. "As you know, Rudy, a cop can't just sit on his hands and watch and wait for something to happen. I was up early this morning..." He explained his surveillance of Troy Tomlinson.

DeJarlais was an intent listener. Pack Moran, he believed, was a lot like himself. "Damn! It all went up in smoke then? What did you do?"

"Not much I could do. I apologized for the intrusion, and left. I didn't give boiler man any names—mine or Tomlinson's. No sense in making waves. I think this guy, Kolbe, would have told me if anyone had been down there."

DeJarlais nodded his agreement and approval. "Pack, I have no problem whatsoever if all of you continue what you've been doing." He handed Pack a photo of Roland Loshe, "This is what our guy looks like if you should run into him."

Pack remembered faces, "I saw him this afternoon. In fact, I know he saw me, too." He laughed in amusement of the irony, "I think he was suspicious of me, kept me under some kind of surveillance of his own."

DeJarlais stood from his chair, "I wouldn't be surprised." He checked his wristwatch, "If I don't get home in time for supper tonight, my wife is going to kill me. A justifiable homicide, I'm afraid."

"I'll stop by tomorrow, if that's okay, Rudy. If you'd allow me to, I'd like to see the coroner's report."

"Not a problem, Pack."

~

"Don't trust the bitch," Troy Tomlinson barked. "Sounds like a pile of bullshit to me." He cupped the mouthpiece of his phone in his large hands. "Parking ticket, crap! She and that fuckin' Moran are up to something."

"Maybe you're right, Troy. I tried to check that out with the Fish, but he wasn't in. Lady I talked to at the station said our favorite cop was goin' to Phoenix for a few days."

Troy asked, "You see Jerry Moran anywhere today?"

"No, and I looked for him, too."

"Did you get rid of that trench coat like I told you to?" He had been plagued with second thoughts all day. Maybe he had made a mistake in that regard. If things got really bad for him at some point, he planned to pin the murder on Brian. His friend's bloodstained trench coat might be all that it would take. Marty James could be coerced into corroborating any version of the story that Troy wanted. Marty was weak... Brian was simple—perfect colleagues if the shit ever hit the fan!

Troy explained his own exploits of that morning. "I dumped all my clothes and shoes in the incinerator at the college." He laughed, "Ole man Kolbe was dozing with a porno magazine plopped in his lap."

Brian Lofley wasn't going to trash a perfectly good coat. Troy could go out and buy all the clothes he wanted. He lied, "Yeah, I got rid of it this afternoon."

Amos rearranged his desk. Instead of the separate pictures of his parents, he displayed one that had the two of them together. He looked around the bleak room. Awfully sparce. But, now he would be able to use his Visa card without worry. It would be fun for him and Sadie to redecorate: a television set in that corner, a stereo near the tattered sofa, some posters on the wall, a new rug for the living room floor. He would trash the small rag rug with the bloodstains and replace it with something colorful.

Amos imagined spending evenings with Sadie in the refurbished apartment. Watching movies on TV with a bowl of popcorn, listening to music—maybe even spending the night together. He'd replace the sagging mattress and fix up the bedroom, too. Sadie. All day his thoughts were consumed with her. That melting smile, the lilt of her voice, her quick wit, her firm body. That night in the motel had replayed itself a thousand times in his thoughts. How his every pain simply washed away. Had she had sex before? With Brian? Had Amos done everything right? Did women make comparisons when they made love?

He laughed at himself. The only way he'd find answers to these questions was to ask Sadie herself. If he could ask her those things, he could ask her anything. He could even tell her that he had never done it before.

Amos looked at his textbooks. He was behind in everything. At the moment, however, he would slough it off—catch up on his reading later tonight. He was anxious to see his parents and find out what they had been up to all day. He'd call Sadie from their room. He imagined her voice.

Roland Loshe had spent several hours on the campus that day. He hadn't made any contact with Troy Tomlinson. As he reviewed his notes over coffee at the Java Joint he remembered the stranger. A man in his forties, good looking, just hanging around and talking to people. Somehow the man looked out of place: A dealer? "He's a college teacher from North Dakota," a coed had told him. Loshe would contact DeJarlais about the stranger later.

Heebie Henton was ashamed of himself. On his first day of surveillance, he had disappointed DeJarlais. Willie Dunn, one of the winos who hung around the Orpheum had a bottle of Old Crow. 'Heebie got drunk. If any of the LA hoodlums had been in the neighborhood, he would have missed seeing them.

39/ HIBBING HEART...OR NOT?

Arms folded behind his head, Amos lay on his bed reflecting on the past ten days of his life in Flagstaff. Tomorrow would be the first week anniversary of his and Sadie's relationship. One week! So much had happened, and happened so fast it almost made his head swim. He realized that, despite all the turmoil in his life, the headaches that had bothered him for months had gone away.

The night before, Sadie had asked him if he was going to return to Minnesota now that his parents were back together. He would be dishonest if he didn't admit to thinking about going home. Everything familiar and comfortable and safe was back there. Or, was it? Amos had felt no more than a slight twinge of remorse when leaving it all behind only weeks before. He often thought of Hibbing's most famous son, Bob Dylan. More than fifteen years ago, Dylan, like Amos, had turned his back on the familiar environs of Hibbing to make a life that the Iron Range could never hope to offer. Yet, Amos wondered, did the former Bob Zimmerman have what his father had called a *Hibbing Heart*? Was there still some arcane attraction, some hematite magnetism that inexorably tugged at the spirits of her sons and daughters? He remembered hearing from his Uncle Steven that Dylan had been in Hibbing that very summer although many locals knew nothing about the visit. Dylan's negative feelings about his old hometown had become almost legendary.

Amos pondered: what was most important in his life at this precise moment in time: Education? Experience? Freedom? Adventure? Love? Probably all of these and more, in some combination yet unresolved. Essentially, Amos was searching for his self. Had he found any real sense of self while living in Hibbing? If he had done so, it was reasonable to believe that Hibbing was where he truly belonged. Or, maybe it was a matter of *timing*. Maybe his time there had been completed, at least for now. The red earth roots of home had given rise to the tree; now the tree was being drawn toward the sun. The analogy gave him pause. Must we grow where planted? What is *our soil*? How much are we defined by family and factors of nurture? And what role did location actually play? It did seem to Amos, at this time in his young life, that here in Flagstaff he was getting more in touch with what he was really about than ever before. Somehow, he had to tie his past and his future together. Such could only be done by understanding the present.

    When compared to one-industry dependent Hibbing, where iron ore and taconite mining defined all aspects of life, Flag appeared to be far more diverse and vibrant and youthful. Hibbing and the Iron Range were experiencing a 'brain drain' as it's well-educated youth migrated to lucrative jobs and opportunities in the Twin Cities metro area. The Range population was graying, property values slowly declining. Whatever catalysts necessary for changing the status quo remained elusive to those in position to effect an upturn.

In contemplating *there* and *here*, as Amos had been doing for days now, he found his perspectives shifting back and forth. Perhaps, more than any other single factor, NAU was the accelerator that fueled the engine of Flagstaff. The highly respected university was expanding in every direction, drawing thousands of young people like a magnet. The Lowell Observatory, where the ninth planet—Pluto— was discovered back in 1930, had given the city an international reputation in astronomy. New construction projects—commercial and residential—were everywhere in evidence. Add climate to the mix. The sun graced almost every day and winter was no more than a brief discomfort. And Phoenix was little more than two hours of freeway away if Flag got too chilly in January. If placed on a scale, Flagstaff and Hibbing appeared clearly out of balance. But—

Yet, a Northern Minnesota summer day could be breathtaking. The pristine lakes, abundant forests, and air so fresh it made one's lungs sing. Or, even a cold, clear, crisp December day at his grandparent's house on Maple Hill with snowflakes the size of quarters. Sadie would love it.

No matter where his thoughts strayed, Sadie reined them in. Amos smiled at her picture in his mind. Sadie. How he would love to take her home, if even for a visit. All things honestly considered, however, Amos was going to stay here for a while. Maybe, for quite a while. Once again he wondered, how can a person become so deeply in love in such a short time?

~

Maddie and Sadie got whistles from a cluster of college-age boys sitting on a bench outside of the Latin Quarter Bar. "That's where I hustled-up your son, Maddie," Sadie pointed. "It will be our one-week anniversary tomorrow… and I won't be able to be with him. Damn it!" Sadie grinned, "Ooops, I'm sorry."

"No need to apologize, I'd say 'damn' myself if I were in your shoes," Maddie offered. "Maybe we can come up with a plan of some kind."

"That would be swell with me." Sadie remembered her promise to join Brian and the group at the 'L.Q' on Friday night. It would be beyond hard to be there without Amos...especially on their 'anniversary' night.

Maddie looked perplexed. "Speaking of plans, after all the planning we've done, here we are: stranded downtown without a car. I have no idea where Pack might be and Amos is resettling his apartment. We probably should stay away from there or the police station. How about waving a taxi?"

"My place is only a ten-minute walk from here, Maddie. I can borrow my dad's car and give you a ride to the motel. But, after that, I'll have to hurry back home to make supper and take care of my chores."

∼

Maddie was stepping out of the shower when she heard Pack's room key in the door. Wrapping a towel around herself she stepped into the room, anxious to tell Pack what she had found. "You won't believe..."

Pack didn't let her finish. Pointing his index finger at her in mock gun arrest, he commanded: "Drop the towel and get your hands in the air!"

Maddie's story was put on hold for nearly an hour.

Pack's eyes widened as Maddie explained everything that had happened that afternoon. "Maddie, that was amazing! What quick thinking... I wouldn't have pulled it off as well as you did. My God, this coat might be the break we needed. Look here," he held the coat to the light, "these are blood stains. I'd bet my life on it."

Maddie smiled, then frowned, "I did something illegal though, didn't I Pack? It's not legal evidence, is it?"

"Makes no difference, Maddie. This is exactly what we need to break those kids down. Whether or not it can be used in court isn't important right now." Pack laid the wrinkled coat on the bed, "Lofley will piss in his pants when he sees his blood-stained coat and the signed receipt you picked up."

"But Amos was certain that the Tomlinson boy was—"

"If this blood matches that of Evering... Brian Lofley's got a huge problem."

Maddie frowned at the thought. The Lofley boy had not seemed to her as the type capable of doing anything so heinous. Maybe cocky, maybe a bit full of himself, but...?

"I can't wait for Amos to get here. I can't wait to see DeJarlais in the morning." Pack was almost hyper with enthusiasm as he paced back and forth across the small room. "This is such an enormous stroke of good fortune, Maddie...Maddie my lovely, my clever, and my oh so wonderful partner." Pack slid next to her on the bed, put his arm around her shoulders. "I just thank God that we are together again."

Maddie smiled, "He's answered our prayers, hasn't He?"

Pack kissed her full mouth then met her eyes, "saying that 'I love you' almost seems inadequate: but I do love you...more than you can possibly imagine."

"Mom, you are spectacular!" Amos gave her a big hug and a kiss on the forehead.

"Well, your girlfriend was sure impressed with me." Maddie smiled. She had retold the story of how she and Sadie and Brian met that afternoon.

"Do you like Sadie, Mom? I mean, really?" Maddie's approval seemed more important to him at this moment than the trench coat.

"Amos, if I were to try and find you a perfect match, I don't think I could do better than Sadie. She's an absolute delight. She's the daughter I never had. Yes, I like Sadie. Yes, I *really* like Sadie."

Amos turned to his father with eyes that asked the same question. "I couldn't agree more. I'm looking forward to getting to know her better, son. Sadie's surely a good-looker and she's funny, too. And, the *funny part* will be far more important than great looks in years to come. I really like your Sadie."

Amos leaned back in the booth with a satisfied 'I knew it' expression washing across his face. How could anybody not like his Sadie? They had finished their meal and Amos was getting antsy. His dad would take care of the Lofley business with DeJarlais so Amos could put that out of his thoughts for now. He *knew* Tomlinson was the perpetrator, but it would be perfectly fine with him to let the professionals get to the bottom of everything. Amos wanted to talk to Sadie right now much more than with his beloved parents. That reality surprised him.

"A penny for your thoughts, son." Maddie interrupted Amos' reverie of the moment.

Amos considered his next words, "Mom...Dad...when all this stuff is over...I'm not going back."

A long and silent minute passed across the table.

"I don't mean *never*. But for now, I've got to be here in Flagstaff. I feel like I fit here better than I would at home. I've really thought a lot about that—" He let the sentence drop without further sentiment.

"I think we'd both be surprised if you wanted to come home right now," Maddie's smile caught Pack's eyes. "Sometimes, I think, God puts us where we belong and keeps us there until we're ready to go some place else." She could have shared the story of her and Pack's time in Sacramento before Amos was born, but Amos already knew that story.

"I don't have to tell you that you will have our blessing, Son...whatever you decide to do. You've been on your own for a while now, and I'm proud of the decisions you've made. Even the bad ones," Pack could not contain his laugh. "The bad ones had a lot to do with—" his eyes moistened, "I think you know what I mean."

Amos nodded with heavy emotion of his own.

40/ THE WAKE

Arlen Begay noticed the obituary in the Thursday *Sun*. Ingrid Solderholm had passed at the age of seventy-three. He leaned back in his chair as memories flooded back. Ingrid's daughter, Marva, had been his first and only love. So many years ago. The two of them dated, as secretly as they possibly could, for nearly five years. His proposal of marriage was refused. Although Marva had never said as much, Arlen knew the problem. He was a Navajo, she a Swede. How many times had Marva Solderholm told him that her mother must never see them together? A hundred?

Eventually, the two of them went their separate ways. Since Flagstaff was a relatively small town, their paths occasionally crossed. When they did, both seemed almost embarrassed by the encounter. Marva had gone on to become an accountant, Arlen a cop. Neither of them had ever married.

Arlen wondered to himself: Should he go to the wake scheduled for that evening, see Marva, offer his condolences? He also considered that Ingrid's death would mean a significant barrier was gone. He smiled. How wonderful it would be see Marva again, despite the circumstances. It had been months since their chance meeting at a local grocery store: the end of May, the twenty-eighth, he was cop-certain of dates.

"I'm so very sorry, Marva." The right things to say at a wake always troubled Arlen. He wanted to give her a consoling hug but kept an arm's length away. "Was your mother's health bad?"

Marva stepped into the space her old friend had established between them, "Arlen, how nice of you to come." She gave him an ungraceful embrace.

Feeling as if his hands were all thumbs, Arlen softly rubbed her back touching some bare skin below her neck. Marva's scent was almost intoxicating. "I'm sorry," he mumbled in repetition of his first remarks.

Marva stepped away, met his eyes: "She's been ailing since last winter, had a stroke last Friday. I brought her to the hospital. She hung on for a few days, died on Labor Day morning. I guess it was a good death."

"She's in a far better place now," Arlen said, wondering if that was a proper thing to say.

"I believe that, Arlen," Marva smiled approvingly. "Will you join me for a few minutes?" She gestured toward a sofa toward the back of the viewing chapel.

"It's pretty quiet over here. My mother didn't have many friends, and to be perfectly honest, had become pretty much a recluse. It's sad for me, but—" She let the unpleasant thought drop.

Sitting down, Arlen ventured to change a topic he found bothersome. Deep down he secretly loathed the deceased woman whose bigotry had kept her daughter and him apart. "So, how's work going, Marva?"

In generalities, she explained a project she was working on and admitted that September was a slow time for her firm. "How about you, Arlen? I'm sure that things are always busy at the P.D."

"They are that," he admitted. "Hardly ever a dull moment."

She laughed, "I almost called you the other night...to register a complaint, no less. Isn't there a curfew for the kids in this town? I almost ran someone over." Marva explained how she had taken her mother to the hospital on Friday and stayed with her until nearly midnight. The nurses told her she should go home and get some sleep, "There's nothing you can possibly do here," they said. "Anyhow, it was late as I said, and I was crying my head off as I headed home. Then, out of nowhere, these kids come racing across San Francisco. One of them stopped within a few feet of my front fender."

Arlen shook his head at the near tragedy, explained that Flagstaff did in fact have a curfew. "I'd be the first to admit that it's not very well enforced—especially on weekends." Then it struck him! "Did you say this happened on Friday night?" Arlen straightened in his chair. "Late last Friday night?" he repeated.

Marva nodded.

"What time was that, again?"

"Somewhere around midnight...a little after, I suppose."

Arlen was unable to subdue the excitement in his voice, "Where? I mean, where exactly on San Francisco? Can you remember?"

"Must have been at Aspen. Yes, Aspen."

Arlen's eyes widened, "Did you say one boy?"

"No. I think three boys. I'm not sure. Two or three."

"Can you remember what they looked like? Any details?"

Marva placed her hands on Arlen's, "What's the matter? You seem out of sorts, Arlen."

Arlen smiled, tried to relax. "I'm sorry, Marva. What you're telling me might coincide with a case I'm working on."

"Did I do something wrong?"

"Not at all. But it would help me if you could tell me anything you remember about the boys."

~

"It was the strangest feeling, Sadie." Amos borrowed the phone in his parent's motel room while they shared a nightcap in the motel lounge. "As much as I love them both, I was chomping at the bit to get away so I could call you."

"What's so strange about that, Amos? I'm adorable."

Amos laughed, "And so very modest, too."

"Actually, my good qualities are endless." Sadie was picturing his face. Giving him a shave and haircut the night before had been an erotic experience for her: almost like undressing him. Amos was even more handsome than she first thought. "Do you have any good qualities, Amos?" She loved to tease and enjoyed his retorts even more.

"Beyond good looks, intelligence, wit, and candor?"

"Your dad is much better looking than you, Amos. And, I think Maddie is a lot smarter."

He laughed. "Probably true." Amos was anxious to share what his parents had said, "They both love you, Sadie. I asked them."

"They wouldn't want to hurt your feelings."

"No. Seriously. We were talking the other night when you called your parents, Mom said she couldn't find anyone more perfect for me."

Sadie was flattered. "I love them, too. Really! But, Amos, I love you more than anyone—even myself."

"Please Sadie, don't ever say that. You are the most lovable person in the world. Give yourself a hug right now...and say, 'I love you Sadie Kearney'. Okay?"

41/ FRIDAY MORNING

In the back corner of Dee Dee's Cafe, Arlen Begay checked his watch: DeJarlais was five minutes late. It always seemed that when he had something exciting and important to share, it had to wait on someone else's time.

"Before you ask, I slept marvelously well last night." DeJarlais slid into his place opposite Begay. "Theresa gave me this backrub that . ."

"You'll let me imagine, right Captain?"

"Took the words right out of my mouth, Arlen," he laughed. Years of familiarity led him to believe that his friend had something on his mind. Begay had added an extra spoonful of sugar to his coffee and twisted his napkin into a knot "Anyhow, you're looking quite chipper this morning, yourself. Ahaa, the life of a bachelor," he teased. "So, why all the sugar? What were you up to last night?

Begay stirred his coffee, met DeJarlais' smile with one of his own. "The bachelor went to a wake last night."

"That explains everything."

"Yes, my friend, it really does!"

"Anyone I know?"

"Probably not." Begay leaned over the table. "But get this..." Begay told his story in a near breathless rush. "Two or three young men...probably college age...running like hell...time coincides perfectly...and the location, a block-and-a-half east of the crime scene... But, there's more. The tall one, running behind the man that Marva almost hit...well, believe it or not, he was wearing a dark trench coat! So, what do you think, Rudy?"

Rudy shook his head, "I think you should go to more wakes." Behind half-closed eyelids, DeJarlais processed the new information. For a long minute he said nothing more.

"This gives the Moran boy's story some credibility, doesn't it?" Begay said.

"It does that. Good job. Some corroboration of what Amos told us, however circumstantial, has been a critical missing piece to the puzzle. Now it looks like we've got our work cut out for us."

"Back to the campus, Captain?"

"Yep, back to the campus." DeJarlais shook his head in mild self-reproach. He should have pressed harder in the first place. Worse, he felt as if he'd been played for a fool. "Arlen, we're going to break down those flimsy alibis we've been fed and do some heavy leaning on some screwed-up kids. Beginning with Sadie Kearney's friend, Sally James. She wasn't in two places at the same time and Miss Kearney has put her in the 'L.Q.' on Friday night."

"Should we tell Sally and the others that Sadie folded?"

"Whatever it takes."

The two men swallowed the last of their coffee and headed to the office to retrieve the class schedules of the NAU students who they had interviewed earlier in the week.

Upon their arrival, DeJarlais saw Pack Moran sitting in the chair next to his desk. A cop on a case was always up early and usually without much sleep the night before. Pack Moran was all cop. "I've got some good news, Pack," he said while sliding his bottom across the corner of the desk... "Arlen has had an unexpected bit of luck." He gave Begay a grin and a solid clap on the back.

"So do I, Rudy, Arlen. Some damn good news." Pack stood, handed DeJarlais the folded trench coat.

"What's this?"

"Something my wife picked up at the dry cleaners yesterday. Belongs to Brian Lofley, Rudy—here's the signed receipt."

Begay was a man who rarely used profanity, "Son-of-a-bitch!" he said, loud enough to be heard down the hallway.

Pack went on to explain what Maddie had done.

The minds of veteran cops seem to run on parallel tracks. All three men were in quick and complete agreement about the strategy to be employed. Rudy would first inform his Chief, "Never want to leave the boss out of the loop," he said. DeJarlais remembered being told that Pack Moran had been a police chief himself. "You'll like Roth," he said.

Pack had yet to meet the Flagstaff Chief. Surely Roth would want to get the coat to a crime lab for blood-type analysis. He swallowed the thought. These guys knew what steps to take.

"We'll have to get the coat over to the campus at some point. We've got a State lab over there," DeJarlais said. "For the moment, we'll use it as bait."

Pack understood.

"Lets pay a visit to the Chief before we do anything," DeJarlais said.

Roth impressed Pack as being conservative and thorough. The large man listened attentively, raised questions, and took notes. It was agreed that DeJarlais and Begay would pick-up Brian Lofley and bring him to the station for questioning. They would read him his Miranda Rights and make certain that an attorney was present.

"Lofley's folks probably have an attorney, Chief. Should I get in touch with them?" DeJarlais asked.

Roth pondered, "Hmmm...maybe not right now. Let me take care of that. I'll call the DA, see if Hendricks can come in. By the time you get back here I'll have everything set up."

When Roth stood, the three cops knew the meeting was over. "Nice to meet you, Pack," Roth smiled over a parting handshake. "What are you going to do while my men are on campus?"

"I'd like to look over the coroner's report if that's okay."

Roth nodded, "I know where you're going. Evering's blood type is B-Positive, am I right, Rudy?"

"Fortunately for us, it is, Chief."

"About ten percent of the male population if I remember correctly," Pack said.

Roth gave him a thumbs-up. "Close enough!"

Pack would take a back seat for the duration of events and wait in DeJarlais' office. As the Captain and Begay were leaving, DeJarlais turned and said: "You've baited the hook for us, Pack. Now Arlen and me are going to go out and catch something."

Pack smiled, "You sound like two Minnesotans."

∼

Amos stepped into the between-class student traffic in the second floor hallway of the Liberal Arts Building. He had read four chapters of Western Civ the night before and finally felt comfortable with the Phoenicians naval exploits described in Dr. Young's lecture. If he was lucky, he might catch a glimpse of Sadie outside the building. He had her schedule memorized and guessed she'd be heading toward the Blome Building.

The sudden jolt to his chest sent his books flying from under his arm. Looking up, he saw the scowling face of Troy Tomlinson. "Watch where the fuck you're going, asshole."

Amos considered the taunt and made a quick judgment. "Sorry," he apologized as he stooped to retrieve his books and scattered papers.

"Watch out!" a voice hollered from someone nearby.

Amos glanced up quickly enough to see a foot swinging toward his outstretched arm. He grabbed at the blur of an ankle and twisted sharply. Tomlinson kicked free, lost his balance, but didn't fall.

Amos stood, "Take it easy. I said 'I'm sorry'."

Letting the apology stand would be humiliating to Troy Tomlinson. "You started it, Moran. Ran right into me." His hands fisted as he postured for a fight.

Several students formed a ring around the two men in anxious anticipation. "Com'on asshole," Tomlinson provoked.

Two apologies were more than enough for Amos. He raised his own fists and moved away from the wall and toward the center of the corridor. Tomlinson was a full two inches taller than he was and had an advantage in reach. Amos' last fight had been on an ice sheet while wearing skates at the Memorial Arena while in the ninth grade. He wasn't sure what he should do now. Tomlinson was circling and inching closer. Amos would let him be the aggressor and wait for any opportunity to retaliate.

Tomlinson swung wildly with his right hand, missing Amos' face by inches. With athletic agility, Amos stepped back from the errant roundhouse. He watched the hooded eyes of his adversary as well as the right hand he favored. The second swing grazed Amos' chin but left the taller man's midsection exposed. Amos caught Tomlinson below the ribcage with a solid right of his own. The impact caused Tomlinson to gasp for breath while causing the taller man to drop the left hand that had been guarding his face.

Amos surged with a straight left to Tomlinson's face, catching him flush on the jaw. Tomlinson staggered backward a few feet but both hands instinctively raised to prevent a second blow to his face. Amos jabbed with everything he had—a right and then a left to Tomlinson's midsection. Tomlinson tumbled backward and landed on his butt.

"Break it up! Right this minute! Both of you!" Professor Young had broken through the cluster of students. "Enough!" He pushed Amos to the side and peered down at Tomlinson on the floor.

"Tomlinson started it," shouted a girl near the professor. "This other kid was minding his own business."

A chorus of voices agreed. "Yeah. Tomlinson wanted to fight."

Amos smiled weakly at the support he was hearing. There was not a familiar face in the crowd.

"He was only defending himself, Dr. Young," said another bystander.

Young looked angrily at Tomlinson, then to Amos. "Is this business over with?" he said.

Amos nodded, "I'll shake hands, sir."

"Tomlinson. Get on your feet and shake hands," Young demanded.

Troy only glared. "We'll talk about this later, Moran." He got to his feet and brushed by Amos without another word.

Sadie saw the crowd leaving the Liberal Arts Building. Amos was in the center, getting pats on the back from those surrounding him. One of those at his elbow was Karen Waite, a Lumberjack cheerleader: a tall, shapely, blond cheerleader that every girl on campus loved to hate. A pang of jealousy perked in the pit of her stomach. Sadie wanted to rush over and see what the commotion was all about, but that was not something she could do. They both had to stick to the plan.

Several feet behind Amos' group were another cluster: Brian Lofley, Marty James, and two guys with letterman's jackets. Troy Tomlinson was in the center of that group. "Damn!" Sadie cussed under her voice, "What did I miss?"

~

Doctor Lang was explaining the concept of 'cultural inertia' to his Sociology 101 class when he was interrupted by a knock at the door. Obviously disgruntled, the portly man removed his reading glasses and waddled toward the back of the lecture hall in a huff.

Heads craned at the hushed voices from the hallway outside. Lang stepped back inside, "Mr. Lofley, collect your things and go with these gentlemen," he said. None of the students could see who the gentlemen were.

Closing the door behind him, Brian growled: "What's this about?"

"Outside Lofley," said DeJarlais in an even tone of voice. He and Begay each had an elbow as they escorted him toward the entry door.

On the outside steps, Begay raised the clipboard he was holding and began reading: *"You have the right to remain silent..."* from the sheet of paper held out for both of them to see. When he finished the four-part Miranda guarantees, he offered his ballpoint pen to Lofley. "...just sign this line," he pointed to the blank space below the text.

"I ain't signin' nothin', Begay," he blurted. Drops of spittle dotted the sheet.

"Let's go downtown and talk about it," said DeJarlais.

42/ INTERROGATION

Barry Hendricks was serving his tenure as the Coconino County Public Defender, a job that none of the local attorneys relished. Chief Roth had been unusually vague when calling him earlier that morning. He was told that the matter concerned the Evering murder last week, but wasn't given the name of the suspect he would be representing. Hendricks could only assume that he would be defending Sam Yazzie.

Hendricks was a natty dresser and his tailored suit looked well on his tall, slender frame. The salt-and-pepper goatee that lengthened his narrow face was new this summer. He waited in the first floor interrogation room where a tape recorder rested near the center of a large mahogany table with five matching chairs. Extra chairs lined the south wall. A pot of fresh coffee had been set out on a card table near the double entry doors, the lights had been turned on because the windows were draped behind a heavy purple curtain. A two-way mirror hung on the north wall. Hendricks wondered who was in the closet-like room behind the looking glass.

As in all public facilities, a portrait of President Gerald Ford was displayed. Hendricks regarded the vigilant eyes of the accidental Chief Executive in a guild-framed portrait looking over the room's otherwise sparse furnishings. (Ironically, on this September fifth morning, in Sacramento Gerald Ford would be the target of an attempted assassination. Lynette ''Squeeky' Fromme, a destitute drifter and former Charles Manson follower, went to Sacramento's Capitol Park to plead with the President about the man-made destruction of the earth. Her loaded .45 automatic Colt held four bullets but none in the firing chamber. She was swiftly disarmed and arrested by Secret Service agents at the scene).

"Barry, thanks for joining us on short notice," Chief Roth stretched out his fleshy hand, covering his firm grip with his left hand. "Something unexpected turned up this morning and we're bringing in a suspect for some questioning." Roth said. "At this point I want to cover our collective asses. Just make sure that we don't screw up anything. Okay?"

"Who is your suspect, Chief?"

"I can hear him in the hallway outside right now."

As both were seating themselves, an angry-looking young man walked between DeJarlais and Begay into the room.

"Let's all get comfortable," Roth said pleasantly, gesturing toward empty chairs as he leaned forward at the head of the table.

"Mr. Hendricks, this young man's name is Brian Lofley...you already know officers DeJarlais and Begay." Roth introduced.

Hendricks nodded, offered a handshake to Lofley. "I'm Barry Hendricks, the public defender."

Lofley's hands remained folded on the table.

"Brian," Roth would attempt to make the scowling young man feel more at ease, "We have a few questions for you. Before we go any further, however, if you would like us to..." he cleared his throat. "...We can contact your parents and allow them to provide you with legal representation of their choosing. Do you want us to do that before we proceed with this?"

Lofley grimaced, shook his head negative.

DeJarlais watched Lofley's eyes as Begay laid the dark trench coat on the edge of the table as if it were his own. He saw an instant dilation of fear as the young man made a quick recognition.

Roth would lead the meeting. He slid Begay's clipboard with its unsigned Miranda page near the center of the table next to the tape recorder. "You understand your rights, Mr. Lofley?"

Brian cleared his throat but his affirmative was barely audible.

"Did you say yes?"

"Uh-huh...yes."

Turning to the attorney, Roth said: "Mr. Hendricks, I'm going to record our conversation. Do you have any problem with that?"

Hendricks tried to meet Lofley's eyes but the young man was focused on the mirror across from where he was sitting. "Brian?"

Lofley ignored him. "Standard procedure," the lawyer said in the direction of his recalcitrant client.

Roth pushed the play button, "One...two...three...testing..." He stopped the machine, rewound, and pushed play again. The recorder was working. "The tape is good for three hours, gentlemen...but I seriously doubt if we'll be here that long." He asked each in the room to identify themselves on the tape and suggested that each do the same each time they spoke. All but Lofley nodded agreement. When Lofley's turn came he mumbled toward the microphone.

Roth was a stickler for every procedural detail. He turned to Begay, "Officer Begay—Arlen Begay," he spoke toward the recorder: "Did you read the rights guaranteed in the Miranda ruling to Mr. Brian Lofley here present?"

Begay leaned forward, "Yes, sir...Chief Roth, I did so. On the clipboard before you, sir, I have noted the time of 10:17 AM on this date of September 5, 1975, on the top of the page, sir."

"Did Mr. Lofley sign the statement of understanding, Officer Begay?"

"No sir, he did not."

Roth reread the rights and asked Lofley if he understood them.

Lofley nodded belligerently.

"Speak into the microphone, Mr. Lofley, please."

Brian mumbled, "Yeah."

"Please respond 'Yes' in a clear voice, Mr. Lofley. And identify yourself when you do so."

"Yes. My name is Brian Lofley."

"Do you have a middle name? If so, will you please add that for the record of this proceeding.

"Brian John Lofley," he said.

After several more minutes of preliminary procedure, Roth asked Officer DeJarlais to provide a detailed explanation of the murder of Axel Evering on the Friday night of August 29, 1975.

DeJarlais complied, handing the manila folder with the coroner's autopsy report to Hendricks. "Mr. Hendricks, the murder was witnessed by Amos Gerald Moran, a student at Northern Arizona University." He went on to report on the Moran testimony. DeJarlais was selective in the data he reported. No mention was made of the assailant's size, nor of the tossel cap. "A man wearing a dark-colored trench coat..." was all he said.

Brian stared at his folded hands during the entire DeJarlais report.

"Officer Begay has a second witness report, Chief Roth and Mr. Hendricks. Arlen..."

Begay explained the signed statement that Marva Solderholm had provided to the police.

Hendricks cleared his throat, "Nothing that you gentlemen have presented so far has any clear connection to Mr. Lofley. Everything is speculative and hardly within the parameters of legitimate circumstantial contention." Seemingly satisfied with his presentation of legal mumbo-jumbo, he regarded his client, "Brian, do you have anything to say?"

"It's all bullshit. I was at a party on Friday night and I got plenty of proof of that. These cops have checked that with all my friends, too. I was at Tomlinson's party from ten until after two in the morning."

Hendricks shrugged, looked toward DeJarlais for clarification. "Fill me in, Officer."

"We've talked with the following students about that alleged party, Mr. Hendricks. To date these are the names of those who have verified being there..." He slid a copy toward Hendricks then read off the names. "However, since Tuesday, one of the students has recanted and told us that a second member of the alleged group was also lying about being at the Tomlinson's residence on the Friday night in question. In light of that we intend to interview all of them again." He explained the revised testimony from Sadie Kearney.

Brian was shaken. If Sadie and Sally caved, others would do the same. Tomlinson had been so fuckin' confident. Where was he right now? Why did everybody do what Troy wanted them to? Troy was a fuckin' sociopath. He'd hang Brian out to dry in a heartbeat. The picture being framed in his thoughts was a dire one.

Out of the corner of his eyes, Lofley had been staring at the folded black trench coat on the table at Begay's elbow. He was certain that it was the coat he had dropped off at the cleaners only yesterday.

"I'm hoping you have something more credible than what this Moran boy and Ms. Solderholm have given you. And, until clearly demonstrated otherwise, there are six other students who have told you that they were, in fact, at the Tomlinson's party from Friday evening until early Saturday. If you don't have anything else, I think that both Mr. Lofley and I have better things to do than listen to innuendo and conjecture." He offered Brian a confident smile, closed his attaché case, and pushed away from the table.

Chief Roth said, "Mr. Hendricks, please don't be in any great hurry to dismiss us all. What we have done so far is simply to review where everything stood prior to this morning. As you know, counsel, *most* police work is conjecture in its early stages. If we're really good at our jobs we get something tangible to support our theories. In this case, however, we've been far more lucky than good."

Hendricks frowned, "What else have you got?"

"Officer Begay, what's that near your elbow on the table?" Roth asked.

43/ CONFUSION

With the rush of post-fight adrenalin and lingering notoriety pulsing like drumbeats through his veins, Amos hadn't noticed Sadie watching only fifty feet from the congregation of congratulators outside of the Liberal Arts Building. He was feeling a bit 'full of himself'. If there was another confrontation with Troy Tomlinson, and Amos expected there would be, he might not be so fortunate. Thank goodness, Dr. Young arrived when he did and broke things up. Tomlinson, he was certain, would have fought like a cornered tiger until his last ounce of energy was spent. It could have been a dirty brawl with a far different outcome.

Self-conscious over all the attention, Amos split from the crowd at the first opportunity and hustled to his next class.

The Friday morning was glorious: another cloudless blue sky, with a refreshing breeze wafting a subtle scent of pine, and temps in the low seventies. At eleven both he and Sadie had a two-hour break. Regardless of his father's caution to keep to themselves for now, Amos needed to see her.

It was their anniversary after all. The two if them could slip away, maybe go for a ride somewhere, without being seen. Or, Sadie still hadn't been to his apartment and he was anxious to have her give him some idea about what to do with it. Over the past few days they had had so little time together and his desire to see her was more longing than wanting. In his heart he knew that Sadie must be trying to cope with similar feelings.

He spotted Sadie walking toward the library and slipped behind her without notice. Amos reached around and placed his hands over her eyes, "I know you're not supposed to see me, but I've got to break the rules."

"Do I get three guesses?"

"Only one." Amos removed his hands and stepped into pace at her side. "Happy one-week anniversary."

Sadie smiled without eye contact. "Anniversaries are dates that girls remember, Amos. What kind of guy are you, anyhow?"

"Well, quite a macho guy, most would say. Even a tough guy."

"The kind of guy that Karen Waite would be attracted to? So, what was that all about?" Sadie's face wore her pouting frown of obvious disapproval. "Just an hour ago I saw you...and your pack of new friends."

"Who's Karen Waite? What in the world are you talking about, Sadie?"

Sadie stopped and met Amos' eyes, "This morning. Leaving Liberal Arts. Seemed to me like you had the key to everyone's final exam in your pocket. Mister 'Big Man on Campus'. Strutting like a banty rooster."

Amos laughed, "Oh...that!" He took her by the elbow and suggested they sit on the grass where there was a patch of shade. He explained his encounter with Troy Tomlinson. "Honest to God, Sadie, I didn't start it and I apologized twice. If there was any way I could have avoided it, I would have."

Sadie felt as if her familiar and comfortable world was coming apart at the seams. She had grown up with stormy, but often charming, Troy Tomlinson. She had dated Brian Lofley. Her best friend, Sally, was Marty James' sister. Now...it was like a fence had dropped between her and all of them. In the space of one week, old friends were becoming sworn enemies.

In these past few days, Sadie found herself in love with a stranger from two thousand miles away, tangled in a murder investigation, and thrust into an unexpected family reunion. This bizarre concoction of experiences had sent her mind spinning.

She thought ruefully. Along the bottom line of her otherwise mundane life, this had been an overwhelming week—a week that started and ended with Amos: alias Jerry Moran.

Sadie Kearney was feeling almost bowled-over and swept away by the dramatic turn of events—and even more confused and frightened by their potentially devastating impact. Was this all a colossal mistake? Had she fallen too hard and too fast? Would she wake up some morning and find Amos gone—back to Minnesota...or, wherever else his whimsical travels might take him? Could she really trust him? This swirl of doubts was tormenting Sadie Kearney more than she had been willing to admit.

Sitting beside her, Amos knew something was seriously 'un-Sadie' beyond the unreadable silence hanging in the warm breeze. When he had described the Tomlinson episode, Sadie seemed caught in a cloud of remote contemplation. What had he said, or done, that caused this obvious rift? "I'm sorry, Sadie. I'm sorry for something I feel deeply, but don't quite have a handle on. But, you're different right now," his voice cracked. This was the second time in the past few days that he had felt her distance. He remembered the afternoon hiking trip on Labor Day. Sadie was having doubts again. "What's wrong?"

Her smile was weak, forced. "About half an hour ago, Brian Lofley was hauled out of class by DeJarlais and Begay. Kids said that he was read his rights—over there," she gestured toward a red-stoned building, "on those steps." Her eyes began to tear. "I know it has to do with the coat we found yesterday. And probably with my confession to DeJarlais about lying. Now the guy I went to the prom with is down at the police station with a murder rap hanging over his head. Then you tell me about your fight with Troy. Amos...all this stuff is blowing my little mind."

He offered his handkerchief to Sadie, "It's clean. Probably the only clean thing I have left right now." Sadie wasn't humored. Her pain and confusion of the moment ran much too deep. He held her delicate hand in his, and let her cry. Whatever suffering she needed to purge, Amos felt anguish of his own in near equal measure. He wanted to draw her near and kiss her—but he couldn't do that right now. He withdrew his hand, allowed Sadie the disconnection he thought she needed. He would apologize for anything and everything that was tormenting her. But she had to let him in first. As much as it hurt him to ask, Amos risked a question: "Do you want me to go? Let you be alone for a while?"

It broke her fractured heart to say what she did, "I think so, Amos. Yes. I've got a lot of sorting out to do. And, I need to do it by my self. I'm sorry..."

Amos knew the need for space better than most. Space had defined his life for the past several months—until just one week ago. Somewhere he had read that loving someone was like holding a bird. If you closed your hand the bird could not hope to fly. The only way to hold a bird was with an open hand. If his lovely bird needed to fly away from him right now, he had to let her fly. And pray that she might return to his hand.

He could reiterate his sorrow about all the lies he had told her. He could say that he was even sorry about Brian's dilemma. He could say he was sorry about the mess with the police that he—more than anyone else—had caused. He could say that he was sorry for a lot of things...but, he could not say any more 'sorry's' right now: His well of apologies had run dry.

Amos stood, offered a hand if Sadie wanted to do the same. "I'm going to sit here in the shade for a while, Amos." Her voice was sad and distant and even contrite. "Collect my thoughts, I guess."

"I understand," Amos said with as much empathy as he could muster. "See you later." As he walked away he said, "I love you, Sadie." But the breeze swept his words away unheard.

Amos was confused and frustrated. If Sadie wanted space...he might have to give her two thousand miles of it. He had a one o'clock class but lacked the volition to sit for an hour trying to comprehend a lecture that was going to sail over his head. And he was not going back to his dreary apartment until he had to. What were his parents up to this morning, he wondered? Pack was probably at the police station...Maddie had said she wanted to take advantage of the motel's swimming pool. Whatever, he would see them both later.

He thought of Brian Lofley, too. The coat was going to be a shocker for him. Would he break down? Would he implicate Troy, and probably Marty James, too? As he had often done, he tried to picture Sadie and Brian as a couple: all dressed up for the prom, or having drinks and dancing at the Quarter. Somehow, he could not fit them together.

Sadie. What was he going to do? Part of Amos wanted to go back and talk some more. He would be even more 'sorry' for everything and anything he had done to hurt her. "God, please don't let it be over between us. Please!"

Amos considered walking up to the Nativity church. An hour of refuge from everything. No. His car was parked in the north student lot off Butler. In the distance he spotted Bozo's Bus Stop, one of several popular

NAU student watering holes. Amos felt like getting drunk. No. He slid behind the wheel, pulled out into the traffic, and turned south toward I-17. He needed to drive somewhere. The late morning was a spectacular blue and Greene washed in a yellow glow.

The spirit of flight was back in his veins, almost pulsating. Phoenix wasn't much more than a two-hour drive and Amos had thirty dollars in his wallet. And, it was Friday...the weekend...he could spend some time with his old Chisholm friend, Mike Rapovich. Another no! His parents were in town and he couldn't abandon them again.

Instead of continuing south, he took the 89-A exit to Sedona. A few miles down the highway, he turned off into the Oak Creek Canyon overlook. Leaving his car in the lot, Amos wandered past a string of vendor tables to a shaded bench away from the milling tourists.

He sat and he cried.

44/ *EIGHT PER CENT*

From behind the viewing glass, Pack sat next to Roland Loshe and watched the interrogation. "Here it comes," Loshe whispered in Pack's ear. The young officer had only read about interrogations in textbooks and this experience had him leaning forward in his chair. Begay was spreading the trench coat over the conference tabletop.

Begay leaned toward the tape-recorder. "Yesterday afternoon, around three-thirty, Mr. Lofley brought this coat to the Quick and Clean Dry Cleaners on Beaver Street. He had been visiting with Miss Sadie Kearney and Mrs. Patrick Moran—the mother of Amos Moran who Officer DeJarlais mentioned in his earlier report."

Brian Lofley squirmed in his chair. "Moran's mother...that's bull— I mean, that lady was some aunt of Sadie's," he blurted his first full sentence of the proceeding.

"I object, Begay," Hendricks stood without really knowing what he was objecting to. "Where are you going with this?" his voice had a whiny shrill. From the expression on his client's face, however, he knew where Begay was going.

"Do you recognize the coat, Mr. Lofley?" Begay ignored the lawyer's objection. He held the yellow Quick and Clean receipt in his hand.

"Just a minute," Hendricks raised his hand in a 'stop traffic' gesture, got up from where he was sitting, and leaned over Brian Lofley's ear. Lofley nodded at the attorney's instructions. "Mr. Lofley will not answer that question," he spoke to Chief Roth.

Undeterred, Chief Roth instructed Begay, "Continue with what you were saying, Officer."

Begay explained what Mrs. Moran had done. "Any questions?" he asked when he was done.

DeJarlais stood, picked up the coat, "These stains..." he pointed to several obvious discolorations, "have not gone to the state lab yet. But they appear to be blood droplets."

Everybody in the room—and Brian Lofley in particular— knew an analysis could be performed quickly since the Arizona Crime Lab had a substation on the NAU campus a few blocks away.

Hendricks walked over to get a closer look at the coat, said nothing, and returned to his chair with a "humph".

DeJarlais continued, "According to the coroner's report," he picked up the manila folder, "Mister Axel Evering had a rare blood type: B-Positive. Statistically, that type is found in about eight percent of the male population. So, when we get the lab results..."

From behind the glass, Pack said "Bingo!" Loshe smiled, "DeJarlais is really good at this, isn't he? So is Begay. And the Chief is no slouch either." The young cop was obviously impressed with his superiors. "Look at the expression on Lofley's face."

Brian Lofley looked as if he were about to cry. Pack had been watching Lofley intently all through the session. His gut feeling was that the young man would ultimately break down.

~

Marty James was having lunch with his sister Sally in the campus cafeteria. "God, I'm scared, Sis."

Sally gave her brother a puzzled look, "What's the matter?"

"You can't say anything, okay? I'm in deep shit. Really deep shit! The kind of deep shit that's gonna put me in prison...for a damn long time, Sal."

Sally James connected her brother's plight to the alleged Tomlinson party last Friday night and the police questioning on Tuesday. The trumped-up alibi was probably falling apart. "So, what did you guys really do? Get high and bust up someone's property?"

"Yeah, I fuckin' wish that was all we did. You heard about what happened to Brian? This morning?"

Sally had—everybody had! She nodded. "That and the big fight in Liberal Arts. What's with Troy anyhow? Everyone says he went after Sadie's friend. And ended up on his ass," she laughed.

"My whole life's goin' down the tubes, Sis." In subdued voice, Marty told his sister what the three of them had done last Friday night. He concluded with venom, "That goddamned Tomlinson! He's crazy, Sal. He stuck the fucker right in the guts. Bry and me just ran like hell. All of us did."

Furrows etched deeply across Sally James' forehead as she listened. "This is a horror story, Marty. I can't believe..."

"I would'a swore nobody saw nothin', Sis. The drunks were passed out and the streets were empty. Then that fuckin' Moran kid that Sadie's been with lately. Saw it all from an apartment across the street from the Orpheum. And Fish callin' Tomlinson to tell him that Moran went to DeJarlais." Furtively, he glanced around the room, lowering his voice another octave.

"Troy and Bry beat the livin' shit outta Moran the other night. We thought he was outta town the next day. But, he comes back . . and takes Sadie to see the cops. Damn! Now Brian's been hauled in...like I said, it's all goin' down the tubes."

Sally hadn't known that her friend had gone to the cops. "Sadie went back to see DeJarlais? When?"

"Wednesday, I think. Why?"

Sally shook her head, "Me and Sadie were at the 'L.Q.' Friday night. That's where she met this Jerry kid. So, if she spilled to DeJarlais, that makes my story bogus. And lots of kids saw all of us there. Shit!"

"You think you got problems, Sis...what about me?"

Sally's appetite was gone. Pushing the paper plate and half-eaten taco aside, she asked, "So, what are you going to do?"

Marty knew exactly what he had to do. "Get my sweet ass outta here, Sis. Borrow me some money, I'm heading to Pasadena."

Their Uncle John lived in Pasadena.

Sally nodded, "I've got about seventy dollars of babysitting money at home."

Eight per cent! Brian Lofley had never been so scared in his life. The nightmare of that Friday night pounded in his memory. They were cruising in Troy's GTO drinking McDonald's coffee and whiskey. Tomlinson had spilled coffee on his Polo shirt, leaving a brown stain down the front. Troy, so fuckin' full of his vanity shit, couldn't be seen wearing a stained shirt. So, rather than go home and change, he grabbed Brian's trench coat from the back seat. Later, Tomlinson spotted Evering in the alley and said something like 'Payback time'. After parking on '66 across from Joe's Place, Troy went into the trunk of his car for the Rappala filet knife in his tackle box. The three of them walked to the Orpheum to *talk* with Donuts. After robbing Evering's stuff they planned to hang out at Bozos. But, when Troy lost his temper, the night took an ugly turn.

Lofley listened to DeJarlais. The Captain was showing the trench coat to Hendricks and Roth from across the table. "The Coroner's report has identified Evering's blood type..."

Brian turned away from the cop, scratched at the back of head. His fingers were as cold as the twinge in his spine. Lines of fear were etched across his drained features as his thoughts raced in anticipation of an impending doom. Questions without answers: Who was behind the glass, he wondered? Was it that woman he thought was Sadie's aunt from Denver? Or, Sadie? Perhaps, that Moran asshole? But, what if it was Troy Tomlinson? What if Troy had framed him? Were they all in some kind of 'Get Brian' conspiracy? What was he going to do now?

A sudden grip of paranoia caused Brian Lofley to suck deeply into his lungs for breath. That *was* his coat and that *was* Evering's blood spotting the front of it. A positive match was inevitable!

Hendricks seemed to have lost some of his earlier starch. The lawyer was slinking in his chair, wearing an almost humbled expression. Eight per cent had laid him low, too. An interrogation that seemed no more than a drizzle at first had become an ominous black cloud. Under his breath, Barry Hendricks prayed that the Lofley's had an attorney of their own.

Brian Lofley had a sinking feeling in his gut. He needed to talk with this lawyer in private. What was this 'plea bargaining' business all about? Turning 'state's evidence'? He'd heard the legal terms before—in the movies and on TV. Of one thing he was certain: he was not going to take a rap for Troy Tomlinson. "I wanna talk with Hendricks. Private, okay? No goddamn tape recorder."

Roth nodded, "Absolutely. You can use my office."

45/ TROY TOMLINSON

If Troy Tomlinson had experienced a worse day in his nineteen years, he couldn't remember when that might have been. The ego-sting of his encounter with Moran that morning lingered into the afternoon. Then, word of Brian's arrest. Lofley was a weak link. What would he do now? Should he talk to his mom? Tell her that his friend Brian was trying to frame him for something bad—something very bad! Mom had always been an easy mark for him. She believed everything he told her. His stepfather, on the other hand, was an absolute jerk. But, Harold was a faint-hearted man when it came to his mother. She had a way of getting him to do whatever she wanted. It had always been that way.

Troy Tomlinson found his stash of marijuana in a plastic baggy under the garden shed at the far back of the family house. He was toking a joint when his mother called from the door of the deck gazebo, "Troy, can you come in the house for a minute?" He could tell that she was stressed. He didn't answer. Instead he crept around the edge of the property to see who might be at the house.

"Shit!" As he expected, a squad car was parked in the front driveway. "DeJarlais." He mumbled to himself. Brian must have caved! That worthless son-of-a-bitch! His mind raced.

Troy was not going to deal with the scene that was awaiting inside. But the garage and his GTO were blocked by the squad car. Marty James. That was it. If he ran to Marty's house, he could loop around behind his property through Switzer Canyon and make it to the James place on Verde in about ten minutes.

DeJarlais joined Mildred Tomlinson on the deck. "Maybe he didn't hear you. Are you sure he's fixing the lawnmower? How about if I go back there and see what he's up to."

DeJarlais smelled the heavy scent of marijuana hanging in the still air. It took him about ten minutes to find footprints in the disturbed pine needles and gravel about thirty feet from the garden shed. They seemed to be headed east toward Switzer Canyon Road. DeJarlais tried to get into Troy Tomlinson's head. The boy must have seen his squad car and panicked. Heading into the barren environs toward the mountains was an act of desperation: How frightened was the young man?

Troy was out of breath and soaked with sweat when he knocked on the James' front door.

Sally's jaw dropped when she saw a red-faced and disheveled, Troy Tomlinson leaning against the doorjamb. "What—?"

"Marty," he gasped. "I've got to talk to Marty. Right now, Sal."

Sally could read fear in Troy's usually arrogant demeanor. "He's not home." She had promised to tell no one where Marty had gone. "I thought he was with you, Troy."

"Fuck!" Troy spit out the expletive. "I've got to find him."

Troy Tomlinson's bad day got suddenly worse. He turned at the sound of a horn behind him. Chief Roth and Officer Begay were getting out of the squad car and beginning to approach the front steps. Troy froze.

"Tomlinson?" Roth called, surprise in his voice. DeJarlais and Loshe were supposed to have picked up the young man at his house minutes before. "We need to talk for a minute," Roth said without trace of emotion.

Begay tucked his clipboard with the printed Miranda rights under his arm, reached for the handcuffs on his belt. He was expecting to read the guarantees to Marty James. Encountering Tomlinson was totally unexpected. "Sally, we need to talk to your brother, too."

~

Pack left the police station after the Brian Lofley breakdown. His confession detailed the Evering episode much as Amos had conjectured. Roth and company were armed with subpoenas and headed off to make two more arrests.

It was nearly two when he burst into the motel room. Maddie was sitting on the bed with her Bible opened on her lap. "I've got so much to tell you, Maddie. Brian Lofley cracked." Pack's fervor, however, brought little more than a weak smile on his wife's face.

Maddie had been on edge all afternoon. "Have you seen our son today? He promised to call around noon..." Her restless maternal instincts suggested something wasn't right. "I haven't heard from him all day."

Pack brushed her concern to the side, he was nearly bursting with excitement over the news. "Tomlinson did it," he blurted. "Lofley and James were with him."

"Oh my God," Maddie exclaimed as the news finally registered. "Does Amos know?"

"I doubt it. Let's find him. And Sadie," Pack said. He was as excited as he was starved "We can all go out and celebrate the news." He sat down beside Maddie and gave her a huge hug. "What a relief this will be for all of us. I can't wait to see Amos' face when we tell him."

"Do you have the address of Amos apartment? Sadie's house?" Maddie stood, found her purse on the bedside table, "I can't believe it all happened so fast, Pack. Tell me all about it on the way to Amos' place."

The apartment door was locked and Amos' car nowhere in sight of the McMahan building. "Do we dare drop in at the Kearney's house, Pack?" Maddie asked. "They are probably together."

"Wait a minute in the car. I'll call Sadie first. There must be a pay phone in the hotel across the street."

Five minutes later, Pack returned. "Her father said she's not home."

"Did you tell Mr. Kearney who you were?"

"No, Maddie...it didn't feel right. You must be as hungry as I am. Let's find a restaurant and try to find them later."

46/ *AMOS AND EDWARD*

Sadie walked aimlessly for nearly two hours. Her thoughts in turmoil, she recalled a verse she had memorized from lit class—something by Yeats. The last two lines played in her mind much like the lyrics of a favorite song. '*I have spread my dreams under your feet; Tread softly because you tread on my dreams'*. The profound prose made her realize the depth of her feelings for Amos. He had walked softly into her life and had, with his unassuming and tender manner, become the essence of her dreams,

Tears welled in Sadie's eyes. She had hurt Amos deeply and she was sorry. When he most needed a friend she needed space. Remembering their conversation, she cursed herself "...Sadie you really botched it." Where might Amos have gone? Before it was too late, she needed to find him and apologize. Sitting on a bench in Wheeler Park, she heard the chimes from the bell tower of St. Mary's on Beaver Street. It had been a long time since she'd been inside the impressive Gothic church. If Amos could figure out the right thing to do by praying, so could she. Maybe, she thought...maybe that's where Amos would be right now.

The church was empty but the colors from huge stained glass windows washed the long nave with a soft warmth. Sadie lit a vigil candle at the side altar below the Sacred Heart statue. Closing her eyes she said her prayers.

It was after three in the afternoon when Amos turned left off Butler onto Verde Street and pulled up to the curb at Sadie's house. He had to see Sadie and make whatever apologies it took to make her feel better. Their earlier conversation had torn him apart. Maybe he shouldn't have been so willing to give her space. She needed to know that. After hours of meditation and soul-searching in the quiet shadows of Oak Canyon, Amos was determined to make things right between them. Whatever that might take—he was determined to do it!

He took a deep breath, and knocked on the door. "Mr. Kearney, my name is Amos Moran...I'm a friend of Sadie's."

Sadie's father did not match the preconceptions Amos had imagined. Several inches shorter than Amos, Edward Kearney had a full head of dark hair, a square jaw with stubbled growth, and sparkling blue eyes. He reminded Amos of James Cagney from the old black and whites. He wore a cardigan sweater and wrinkled khakis. His handshake was firm. Sadie had told him that her father had been a pharmacist before retiring at fifty-two.

"It's a pleasure to meet you, son." He voice was clear and slightly tinged of liquor. "Sadie's told us a lot about you these past few days. Please come in and make yourself at home," he gestured toward a tidy living room nearby. "I expect she'll be home any time now."

Amos smiled obligingly, "Thank you, sir. If it's not an inconvenience, I'd like to wait for her."

"Can I get you something, Amos? Coffee, a soda...or a drink if you'd like?"

Amos opted for coffee, "Only if you have some made, black is fine."

"Dot!" Mr. Kearney called toward the kitchen, "We have company." He smiled with an unmistakable sense of pride, "Dorothy went grocery shopping this afternoon."

Dorothy Kearney was Sadie with a few years and a few pounds. Her brunette hair was shoulder length and her smile revealed perfect teeth. Her yellow dress was a simple yet stylish A-line. "Let me guess...you're the young man Sadie has been talking about. Amos?"

Amos stood, "Yes ma'am, Amos Moran. From Minnesota, ma'am."

"Would you kindly get us all some coffee, love? Then join us until Sadie gets home?" Edward leaned toward his wife, gave her a soft kiss on the forehead, winked: "And...add just a small *touch* to mine."

"Ahh yes, Minnesota." Edward sat deeply into the sofa with an engaging smile. "I'm a big Rod Carew fan, Amos. And I follow your Twins in the *Sun's* sports page every day. They're having a tough time again this year, aren't they?" Edward Kearney was in his element when talking about sports. He was a Cubs fan, but knew the rosters of most teams. He laughed at a memory and continued: "Back in '65 I lost fifty bucks on the Series. Won't ever forgive the Twins for that. They were a better team than the Dodgers, I thought—just not better than Sandy Koufax."

Amos smiled widely. A Twins fan. Here in Flagstaff. And, a knowledgeable one at that. Sadie had never mentioned her father's interest in baseball. There were so many things that she hadn't yet told him about her family—or, herself. "You'll have to meet my dad, Mr. Kearney. He rarely misses a Twins game on the radio."

"Well, I'd very much enjoy doing that someday, Amos."

Dorothy returned, set a tray with three cups, a decanter, and chocolate chip cookies on the coffee table. "Sadie made the cookies just last night, Amos. You must try some." She sat next to her husband, "Did I overhear you men talking about Minnesota?"

"Yes, ma'am. Twins baseball," Amos said. "I've just learned that we are both fans."

"You are only the second young man I've ever met from Minnesota,' she said. A sadness formed about her large eyes. "Our son, Mikey, had a friend from out there." Dorothy went on to tell the story about the soldier from Carlton. While she was talking about Mikey and Maggie, Edward went to the bookcase and retrieved some framed photographs of their two children, and passed them to Amos. "This is Mikey...he was only nineteen...and Maggie..." Although Dorothy remained dry-eyed while relating the tragedies, Edward's eyes were moist.

"After Maggie...well, we both...let me say, we both slipped pretty bad. Dot with her bouts of depression and me with the drink." With a candor that stupefied Amos, Edward Kearney explained their 'troubles'. "Our

Sadie's the one who holds everything together for us, Amos. She's our angel."

~

After coffee and pie, Pack and Maddie swung by Amos' apartment a second time. Again, their son was not there. "I remember Sadie mentioning Elden Street," Maddie said. "That should be just down the street from where we are." She gestured down Leroux toward the east. Pack found Elden easily and spotted Amos' car parked in the street out front. "Well, no surprise." Pack smiled. "Do you think we dare to intrude?"

Maddie frowned, "What do you think, Pack? It's kinda rude."

"Not at all. Amos has told us that they are going to be his in-laws one of these days. Let's introduce ourselves."

~

Sadie had lost all track of time. Looking up she realized that the tiny candle had almost expired. Her wristwatch read 4:45. "Excuse me, Jesus," she smiled at the benevolent face, "I've got to run. But, I promise to come back really soon. You've been very helpful. Thanks." She blessed herself and headed down the aisle. Her parents would be worried sick. And she had promised her mother to make supper.

"Oh, oh!" Sadie's jaw dropped when she saw Amos' car, and the Morans Oldsmobile, both parked at the front of her house. Her first thought was that something was wrong—seriously wrong! "My God...I'm not ready for this," she said out loud.

She raced to the front door, flung it open. Inside, she was struck with the smells of food. "Mom," she called ahead without looking into the living room as she rushed toward the kitchen. She froze in her footsteps. Her mother and Maddie Moran were shoulder-to-shoulder at the stove. "We just had to get started without you, Sadie," her mother said. "Maddie had this wonderful recipe for Swiss steak—it's Amos' favorite you know."

Dumbfounded, Sadie was speechless. Under an apron, her mother was wearing her favorite yellow dress. Her hair was neatly combed. And she and Maddie were preparing supper together. "Can I help?" she blurted.

"No, we've got everything under control," Dorothy Kearney assured. "In a few minutes you can set the dining room table. Why don't you find a Coke in the fridge and join the men in the living room?"

"Sounds like they are having a good time," Maddie added.

For the first time in a long time, a very long time... Sadie heard the laughter from her living room. Amos, and Pack, and her Dad.

Their laughter was music and her heart sang along with it. Everything was going to be wonderful from here on.

EPILOGUE

Amos mused while peering out the window. An easy smile creased his face. By now, his life had settled into a pleasantly satisfying routine. The disillusionment that had brought him to Flagstaff only weeks ago had settled, too. In many ways, he had never been more content with his life than he was now. His parents were back together and called weekly. After a shaky beginning, classes were going well, and all that had once been so unfamiliar was becoming agreeably comfortable to him. But, more than all of that— put together and multiplied by a hundred— Amos was falling more deeply in love with every passing day. Now, at the end of each day, he looked forward to coming *home* to his apartment.

It was Friday night. Autumn had settled another cool evening upon this Flagstaff October. In another hour, he and Sadie were going to watch some TV and maybe play some cards. Amos would pop some corn and open a bottle of red wine.

Sadie had told her parents that she was going to 'sleep over' at her friend Sally's house. But, in truth, for the first time she would be staying overnight with Amos.

Amos could only imagine waking up on Saturday morning and finding her nestled beside him. The window's reflection of his smile gave him pause to realize how truly happy he was. Turning away from the Orpheum's neon pulse outside, he regarded his once dreary living space. Sadie's creative touches were everywhere: black and white framed posters of old movies and rock groups on the walls; a purple and Greene sofa that virtually leaped to one's eyes; a multi-colored area rug that accented a softly golden love seat; and an oak cabinet with a color television set and high-amp stereo system. Comfortable. Pack and Maddie had been generous in financing their redecorating project.

Grand Jury indictments in the Evering murder had been delivered and the 'so-called' Cherry Hill trio were awaiting their separate trials. Brian Lofley and Marty James would be the leading witnesses when Troy Tomlinson's case ultimately went to court. According to newspaper accounts, the process would take several months. Amos and Sadie had both given testimony. On another page of events, Sam Yazzie was doing six months in the Coconino County work farm for assault and robbery.

~

True to his word, Pack met with a marriage counselor named Jack Hebert after returning to Hibbing. Maddie joined her husband for the second and third therapy sessions. The two of them were living together again and more in love than ever before. At the conclusion of their third meeting, Psychologist Hebert acknowledged: "My friends, this is a waste of my time and your money." Of course, both Pack and Maddie knew that from the start.

Pack continued to make periodic visits to his Bunker Road cottage south of town, but no longer to get himself away from 'the stresses of life'. With two acres of land, there was plenty of room for Maddie to start a vegetable garden of her own. The two of them enjoyed the rural experiences *together*. In the spring of '76, they began an extensive remodeling project. In addition to modernizing almost everything—plumbing and wiring included—they added a recreation room and another small bedroom. If Amos returned to Hibbing after graduating from NAU in four years, the cottage would be an ideal place for him to live. Both hoped that Sadie would be with their son and that the new bedroom might become a nursery.

By December, the San Francisco Peaks rising above Flagstaff wore their winter coats of white.

Sadie was even more excited than Amos. Holding up a pair of long underwear, she pronounced: "These might look hideous, but I'm going to be prepared!"

Amos chuckled as he watched her pack her suitcase. "You'll be just fine. It's not like we're going to the North Pole."

Sadie did a mock shiver, "But close enough."

The two of them had scheduled a morning flight from Phoenix to Minneapolis, then on to Hibbing the next day. "I can't wait to see your parents again—it's been months." Yet, Sadie and Maddie talked regularly by phone. "Your mom told me that Angela is my size and not to worry about warm clothes." By now she could make references to Amos' family members by their first names. " Oh, Amos, give me a pinch— I can't believe that I'm finally going to meet them all!"

Continuing a time-honored Moran family tradition, everybody was together at Grampa Kevin and Gramma Angie's huge home on Maple Hill south of Hibbing for Christmas festivities. As expected, the weather was colder than Sadie had ever experienced but the warmth of everybody's welcome more than compensated for the sub-zero wind chills.

Amos had given Sadie biographic sketches of his relatives and Maddie had mailed her photographs. But actually meeting them all in the flesh was far more fulfilling than all the stories and pictures. Sadie was fascinated by Amos' Aunt Mary's (everybody called her Maribec) photography collections. His Uncle Steven, an acclaimed musician, had insider stories that were almost beyond belief. Steven was a close friend of

Bob Dylan and other big name artists. He'd traveled to New York and LA often, booking major rock and folk concerts for venues in the Twin Cities. And, there was Marco—Angela's younger brother—a cellist with the St. Paul symphony orchestra—so big and so lovable and so musically gifted, as well.

It was early afternoon on Christmas Eve day. All of the Morans would be going to Mass at Blessed Sacrament later that evening. In the morning they would open presents and enjoy Angie's annual feast in mid-afternoon.

"They are all so wonderful," Sadie confided to Amos as they glided down the slope of the Maple Hill property on cross-country skis. Coming to a stop at the bottom of the hill, she added: "But there is something awfully strange about your family."

Amos slid up beside her. Sadie had used the word *strange*? He would probe," Let me have three guesses,"

"Okay. Give it a try."

Amos guessed: "Everybody is an artist of one sort or another?"

"Unusual, I'll agree about that...but that's not it. Try again."

Amos laughed, "Uncle Marco? Well, I've already told you about his peculiar *situation*."

"You have. But he's such a sweetheart." Sadie frowned, "I wonder if he misses being with his *partner* in the Cities for Christmas. Anyhow, I don't find Marco's situation, as you called it, to be strange at all. You're getting closer, though."

Amos mused. The Morans were all successful, wealthy, and outgoing. He laughed, "I've got it. Our incredible good looks."

Sadie gave him a wrap on the shins with her ski pole. "That's not the least bit strange, Amos. But it is true. I think your Gramma Angie is simply beautiful. I can't believe she's in her sixties. And what a life she has had. I could listen to her stories for hours on end." Amos had told her of countless episodes in his Gramma's life along with other colorful sketches of all the Morans. "That's three wrong guesses," Sadie announced her mild triumph.

"Okay, I give up. Tell me." A light snow had begun to fall and they were paused on the slope near the mansion, looking down at the barn and corral below. Tomorrow, Amos, Sadie, Pack and Maddie would go horseback riding on the trails to the south and west. The winter landscape was postcard splendid on this shadowed afternoon.

Without telling him right away, Sadie leaned over and gave him a kiss on the cheek. "There is something we—you and me, Amos—are going to have to change around here." Her voice held a familiar tease.

Amos puzzled without reply.

Sadie met his deep Greene eyes and smiled. "Children!"

Amos realized as if for the first time, Sadie was right. He had no cousins—the two of them were a generation or two removed from everybody else. The Morans were slowly becoming an endangered species! Maribec and Steven had never married, and Marco— He put his arm around Sadie's shoulder, "Are you really serious, Sadie? I mean about *'something we are going to have to change'?"*

"Absolutely and positively, Amos Moran. I consider it my duty."

Amos beamed. This was going to be his greatest Christmas ever. He wished that he had Sadie's gift in his coat pocket right now. If he had the small package, he would kick off his skis and get down on his knees in the snow right now and propose. But...that would have to wait until tomorrow morning. He was at a loss for words.

Sadie beamed, too. She would *secretly* be telling Amos on Christmas morning that her Moran *family project* was already a work in progress!

'FLAG'

~

The following June, Pack and Maddie took a two-week vacation and drove from Minnesota to Flagstaff, with an overnight in their *special* motel outside of Denver. Amos and Sadie were having their marriage anointed at the Nativity Catholic Church. Their son had called them back in February from Las Vegas: "We want your blessing before we get married," Amos had said. "We'll see a priest in Flagstaff later and try to get a church blessing sometime this summer."

At the time, Maddie had to remind Pack that Kevin and Angela had run off to get married themselves. "They were young and spirited back then—and still are. Amos and Sadie will be just fine." Pack could not argue the matter.

The marriage blessing ceremony took place on a Friday afternoon. It was an informal affair in the living room at the Kearney's home. Only the families and a few friends of the bride and groom attended. Sadie wore a simple maternity dress and Amos a white shirt and tie: Her due date was June 24— only three weeks away. Following Father Connely's anointing of the vows was a small reception.

"Another dismal season," Edward commented to Pack on the woeful Twins as the two men sat in the ponderosa shaded back yard.

"Well, we've got the Viking's season coming up, Ed. Don't be surprised if they get to another Super Bowl." Pack clinked his bottle of Coors with Ed's bottle of Pepsi in a toast to the Vikes.

Edward smiled, "Sorry I can't join you on that, Pack. I've been a Rams fan for years...and I always pull for the Packers to beat your team."

The women joined them with trays of hors d'ouvres and sweets.

Dorothy Kearney had lost twelve pounds. "You look wonderful, Dot," Maddie observed as she took a lawn chair next to Sadie's mother.

"Those darn pills were the problem," Dorothy admitted. "I feel so much more energetic without them."

Later that evening, Rudy and Theresa DeJarlais joined the small reception. Pack and Rudy had kept in touch over the past several months. Pack offered his colleague the best of luck on his recent promotion: "Congratulations...or condolences—I'm not sure which. Anyhow, I hope you enjoy the job a lot more than I did," he said.

"Funny thing, Pack...Roth offered me condolences as well," Rudy said. "But I'm planning to put away some of the extra salary for a fishing trip up to Northern Minnesota next summer."

There would be another marriage ceremony the following day. The new Flagstaff Police Chief was going to be the best man at Sergeant Arlen Begay's wedding. Arlen and Marva Solderholm were to be married at the Flagstaff Indian Bible Church downtown. A pony-tailed, clean-shaven, and sober, Samuel Yazzie would be a groomsman. Sam had turned the corner on his alcoholism and held a full-time job as a custodian at Flagstaff City Hall. Every morning he mopped the floor of the downstairs jail cell where his conversion began.

~

The machinery of judicial process moves with tedious deliberation. Such is especially so when a Grand Jury indictment precipitates the trial for a homicide case. When capital punishment is the ultimate sentence, as it is in the state of Arizona, the process becomes even more ponderous. To further complicate matters such as the *State of Arizona v. Troy Tomlinson*, the United States Supreme Court in *Furman v. Georgia* (1972) effectively declared death penalty laws in 32 states to be unconstitutional. The following year, the Arizona legislature enacted A.R.S. 13-454. The new statutory code set forth an elaborate procedure where "aggravated circumstances" in capital cases were more clearly enumerated.

On August 25, 1976, a jury in the trial court of Flagstaff, found Troy Tomlinson guilty of murder in the first degree for the brutal death of Alex Evering. During the proceedings, the defendant's frequent outbursts undermined the efforts of his legal team. The issue of mental competence was raised by lead attorney James J. Morrow, but to no avail. On one occasion, an enraged Tomlinson spoke with provocative eloquence while making a fatal admission. Referring to the victim of his crime, Tomlinson said: "I've done Flagstaff a damn big service by wiping out the likes of that dope-pushing asshole. Evering was no more than shit in clothes." Throughout the trial, Tomlinson ranted about being 'framed' by the Flagstaff police (namely Rudy DeJarlais) and the State's principal witness, Brian Lofley. The jury did not see it that way.

The *Arizona Daily Sun* had covered the often-stormy seven-week trial with careful journalistic restraint and without editorial commentary. The *Sun's* headline on 8/26 /'76 simply stated: *Conviction!* The reporter who wrote the culminating story for the Sun was a woman named Alice Nevins. Nevins was struck by something so unusual, that her last paragraph observed: *After Judge Stimson read the foreman's verdict, Tomlinson broke down for the first time in seven weeks. Sobbing profusely, the boy turned to his mother, Mildred Tomlinson "...I'm so very sorry, Mom" he cried over the din of the courtroom. Dry-eyed, Mrs. Tomlinson, turned away from her son without saying a word.*

In a capital case with possible execution, Arizona statutes mandate a separate sentencing hearing by a trial court rather than a jury. In an unprecedented defense strategy, not a single character witness was called before the court. Tomlinson's lawyers, however, argued two points with particular fervor and effectiveness:

> - *the defendant's capacity to appreciate the wrongfulness of his conduct had been impaired by alcohol at the time, and:*
>
> - *the defendant could not reasonably foresee that his conduct would cause the death of another person.*

On October 9, the court dispensed its final ruling. Pending an appeal, Troy Tomlinson is now serving a life sentence at the Arizona Correctional Facility in Florence, Arizona.

In separate trials, Brian John Lofley and Martin Albert James were found guilty of lesser crimes and given sentences of five years of probation.

~

At ten- twelve on Saturday, June twenty-sixth, a new generation of Morans entered the world. The first sharp cries of Meghan Michelle Moran were heard by all within earshot at the Flagstaff Hospital.

Minnesota author Pat McGauley is a former Hibbing High School teacher. Born in Duluth, McGauley grew up in Hoyt Lakes. He graduated from Winona State University (BS) and the University of Minnesota (MA). Former mineworker and historian, McGauley has lived in Hibbing for the past forty years.

Other novels and stories by Pat McGauley:

'Mesabi Series' Trilogy

To Bless or To Blame	*(2002)*
A Blessing or A Curse	*(2003)*
Blest Those Who Sorrow	*(2004)*

The Hibbing Hurt   *(2005)*

Children's Stories

Mazral and Derisa: An Easter Story	*(2004)*
Santa the King	*(2004)*

the HIBBING HURT
a novel

pat mcgauley

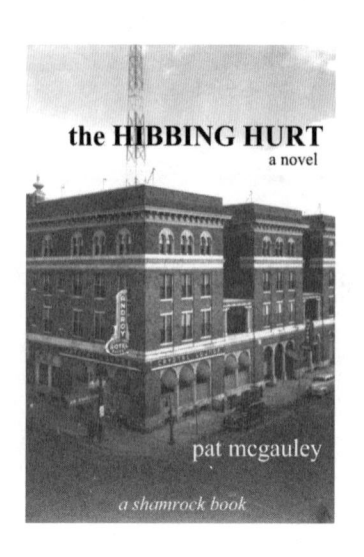

a shamrock book

In 1956, the ominous storm clouds of racial integration in the South seem far removed from the quiet streets of Hibbing, a remote mining community in northeastern Minnesota. Yet despite its relative isolation, an unimaginable tragedy happens here. A young black man disappears!

Hate should have been a conspicuous stranger in ethnically diverse Hibbing, but it was deep in the marrow of a local cop and his hooligan associates. Pack Moran must sort through clever deceptions and devious schemes in search of his missing boyhood friend.

the HIBBING HURT, Pat McGauley's fourth novel, builds toward the inevitable confrontation between the forces of good and evil. Blending tragedy and treachery with romance and reconciliation, **the HIBBING HURT** evokes painful memories of a dark chapter in American history.

NORMANDALE COMMUNITY COLLEGE
LIBRARY
9700 FRANCE AVENUE SOUTH
BLOOMINGTON, MN 55431-4399